THE
FALLEN
DEMON

R.L. PEREZ

THE FALLEN DEMON

WILLOW
HAVEN
PRESS

For Kaitlin, a force of strength during a tumultuous storm.

1

BRIELLE

I DREW THE HOOD OF MY CLOAK OVER MY HEAD, eager to avoid being recognized. My boots clacked against the cobblestone street. The city was lit only by moonlight and a few lanterns.

In the daytime, the village of Coca, Spain was vibrant and full of life—merchants selling spices and trinkets, children laughing and playing, villagers bustling about. The village was small, but the Castillo de Coca made it seem so much bigger—even though the castle was completely vacant now that Count Antonio de Silva and his mages were dead.

It wasn't necessarily a tragedy. The Count had been a monster who had tortured me, among many others. But it saddened me to know this giant castle, which could house hundreds, was just gathering dust. I'd been told the castle was now in the hands of the Duke—the Count's brother. So it was off-limits.

But just because one monster was dead didn't mean the city was safe. I drew my athame from my belt and kept it hidden in the folds of my dark cloak as I crept farther down the street. After several villagers had gone missing and rumors spread of vicious creatures skulking in the night, I'd taken it upon myself to go Demonhunting again.

Just like old times.

Or rather, *new* times? It made my head spin to think about it. I'd come from Miami in the year 2020 and had fallen through a time portal, winding up in 1735 Spain. Though I had been here for a year, it still felt foreign to me.

Especially since I was a light witch living among a coven of dark vampires.

Leo, the coven leader, had assured me he had the demon attacks under control. But I didn't believe him. And I wasn't about to let more innocent people die.

A sharp smell tickled the air, and I stiffened. My cloak swished as I hurried to the other side of the street. I melted into the shadows and gripped my athame tightly. Then, I waited.

The smell swirled, filling my nostrils. I closed my eyes, focusing on the subtle tinge of the demon lurking nearby.

It wasn't a vampire. I'd lived among them long enough to know what they smelled like.

I inhaled deeply. The scent vaguely reminded me of . . . fish.

My blood chilled. A shapeshifter. I hadn't come across one in years. Though Leo's coven technically descended from shapeshifters, they couldn't change forms as easily as a normal shapeshifter could.

In my time, shapeshifters could turn invisible. Which meant I had to be careful.

I kept my eyes closed, focusing instead on the smell as it drew nearer and nearer. When it was so close it nearly suffocated me, I lunged and sliced my blade.

A deep hiss filled the air, and blood coated my knife. But I couldn't see the creature. Raising my free hand, I muttered a spell,

"Magic above and powers that be,
Reveal this enemy in front of me."

A blue glow surrounded my hands and then burst forward. In a flash, a tall, lanky creature appeared before me, surrounded by my magic. Its skin was slimy and moist as if it belonged in the water.

It glanced down at its glowing body. Its all-black eyes narrowed when they rested on me.

I knew what it was thinking. It was the same thing every demon thought when they came across me.

I was a witch. But I didn't smell like one because I didn't have powers like a normal witch.

Taking advantage of the demon's surprise, I lunged

again, aiming a high kick at its chest. It staggered backward. I swiped my athame again, but the demon ducked to avoid getting cut. Its slimy hand snatched my throat and squeezed. Spots appeared in my eyes, and slices of pain tore through my throat. I hooked my foot under the shapeshifter's leg and tugged, bringing us both to the ground. Gasping for breath, I crawled forward and shoved my blade into the shapeshifter's stomach. The creature howled in pain. Blood blossomed from the wound.

I raised my bloody hands, prepared to cast the banishing spell, when a familiar spicy scent filled my nose. Shadows swirled around me, and I groaned.

A hand gripped my wrist, tugging me away from the demon. I whirled and faced Leo. His long dark hair was pulled back, and his silver-rimmed eyes went from me to the demon writhing on the ground.

"Brielle," Leo said. "What do you think you're doing?"

"Hunting," I snapped, rising to my feet. I peered over my shoulder to ensure the demon didn't escape.

Leo rubbed his forehead. "You can't hunt demons when you *live* with them."

"Haven't you heard the villagers? Demons are attacking them. I can't just sit around and do nothing."

"Yes, you can. I'm the leader of the demons in this city. The attacks are my responsibility."

"And yet they keep happening," I spat. "I'm not just

going to let more innocent people die while they wait for you to fix the problem."

Leo's eyes flashed, but that infuriating smirk rose to his face. "My dear Little Nightmare," he said in a soft voice, drawing closer to me. "If you wanted to be part of the investigation, all you had to do was ask."

I clenched my teeth. "I *don't* want to be part of it."

"But you're taking it upon yourself to execute men under my jurisdiction," Leo said, waving a hand toward the shapeshifter. "And you said so yourself, you cannot sit and do nothing. So make yourself useful and work *with* me. Help me track down these demons and find out where they're coming from."

"That's exactly what I'm *doing*."

"No," Leo said, his voice sharpening. "You're going rogue just like them. Your motives might be valiant, but you are undermining me." He drew even closer, his face only a breath away. My blood thrummed in response, and an undeniable yearning swept over me. "My men have noticed, Brielle."

I swallowed. I hadn't considered that. "What exactly do you want me to do?" I couldn't meet his gaze—not with the hunger roaring inside me, begging for him to come even closer. Ever since he'd forced me to exchange blood with him, we'd shared a connection. I was now technically his Donor. Ordinarily, we would feed off each other at regular intervals, but I'd been fighting it.

"Track down demons, just like you did tonight. But do it with my men. And don't banish or kill. We want to give these demons a fair trial and figure out what's caused them to stray from their own covens."

I rolled my eyes. "Leo—"

"You were about to banish this demon, weren't you?"

"It was self-defense!"

Leo raised an eyebrow and glanced at the shapeshifter on the ground. "You don't seem that defenseless to me."

I sighed. As much as I hated to admit it, Leo was right. When the attacks first started and Leo assured me he had it under control, I'd wanted to believe him. But then people kept disappearing and dying.

I was so used to Demonhunting on my own. Back in Miami, I'd been forbidden from attending coven meetings because I wasn't technically a "witch." At least, not in their eyes. So I had to Demonhunt on my own terms because I was a fighter and a skilled Demonhunter. I couldn't let those talents go to waste. Not when I could save people's lives.

Leo had been kind enough to offer his home to me when I'd fled from the Count's dungeon. And even after the Count was killed, Leo still hadn't thrown me out, though he had every right to. By the laws of magic, I was a light witch and could only belong to a coven that practiced light magic. But still Leo let me and my family stay.

I had to let him take care of this, though my chest tightened at the thought. "Fine," I muttered, wiping my athame on my cloak before sheathing the blade.

When I straightened, Leo smirked again and offered me his arm. I responded with a stony stare, my gaze flicking back to the shapeshifter on the ground. The creature was now gurgling on his own blood.

"What about the shapeshifter?" I asked.

"Jorge will take care of him." Leo steered me away from the demon struggling on the ground. After looping his arm through mine, Leo strode casually down the street as if we were on a romantic, moonlit stroll. As if I weren't covered in the shapeshifter's blood.

I swallowed down the warmth in my throat from being so close to him. "So Jorge's with you?"

"He isn't far."

I clenched my teeth. I didn't like Jorge. He'd hated me from the moment we met, and his opinion had never changed.

Leo laughed as if sensing my thoughts. "He's my most loyal comrade, Brielle."

"Every time I look at him, I think he wants to kill me."

"He probably does. He thinks you're a threat."

I scoffed. "I'm surrounded by vampires, and I have no magic."

Leo arched an eyebrow. "No magic? Hardly."

I had nothing to say to that. He was referring to Nix, the phoenix living inside me. She came to life when I slept and had the power to destroy an entire village. I'd seen it happen.

"Besides, you and I have more important things to worry about than Jorge," Leo said quietly.

"You mean this demon problem you have?"

"No. I mean Lilith."

My blood chilled at his words, and fire stirred in my chest. I sensed Nix awakening within me, jolted from hearing Lilith's name. The queen of demons who possessed witches throughout time.

But she only targeted Nightcasters—witches with phoenixes. Like me.

I shook my head. "She's gone." *For now.*

I felt Leo's eyes on me, but I couldn't meet his gaze. "You know she'll return. And you told me you'd be ready for her. So, Little Nightmare, how exactly are you preparing?"

I bristled at his nickname and the accusation that I wasn't doing anything about the situation. Truth be told, anytime I even *thought* about Lilith, the fire within me roared to life, and Nix's power surged. I was afraid. If something triggered Nix's power and she burst free on her own, I had no idea what destruction she would cause.

I knew Leo was waiting for an answer. And he had a point. Lilith *would* try again. She would try to claim another witch for her own, and I had to stop her before she took more lives.

I sighed. "I have to research first. If we want to stop her before she curses another witch, we'll have to find a way to summon her." *Which will be dangerous as hell.*

Leo nodded. "You're right."

I looked at him. "Any chance we could steal into the Count's library?"

Leo looked at me, his eyes glinting with mischief. "Why Brielle, you surprise me."

I rolled my eyes. "Will you help me or not?"

Leo grinned widely, exposing his fangs. Just the sight of them made my head spin. "Breaking into my old foe's castle? I'd be happy to help."

2

LEO

"YOU'LL GET YOURSELF KILLED," JORGE SAID, leaning against the wall as I strapped my swords to my back. The faint glow from the fireplace illuminated the ostentatious bedroom I rarely used. With the Count and his men gone, we no longer had to hide in the dank caves. Though strangely I often found myself missing them. The homes on this side of the neighborhood were far too grand for my taste.

I raised an eyebrow at Jorge. "Yes, the noble coven leader is killed while breaking into an abandoned castle."

Jorge pointed to me. "You're the one taking your weapons of war with you."

"For Brielle's sake. She thinks there might be someone lurking inside."

Jorge blew air through his lips but said nothing. I easily read the displeasure in his eyes, and I smiled.

"I know you don't care for her," I said as I donned my large black cloak, hiding my swords from view.

Jorge scoffed. "It isn't just that."

I waited for him to continue, but he remained silent. I turned to face him. "Go on."

"And risk incurring your wrath? I think not."

Irritation prickled through me. "Jorge, speak your mind."

Jorge sighed and leveled a gaze at me. "Your feelings for her are compromising your judgment."

I barked out a laugh. "Feelings?" He spoke as if I were a lovestruck youth sneaking away to meet my beloved in some forbidden rendezvous. I composed my face into a serious expression and said quietly, "I don't care what you say, Father. I'm running away with her, and you can't stop me."

The severity of Jorge's face never changed. "I simply mean that ordinarily you make extensive plans before breaching enemy territory. And yet here you are, about to go in unaided simply because Brielle suggested it. Does that not seem odd to you?"

"I won't be unaided. Brielle has her phoenix. Miguel will also be stationed outside should trouble arise. This isn't war, Jorge. This is an abandoned castle. Besides, Brielle is a skilled huntress."

Jorge stepped closer to me. "That she is." His eyes widened with significance.

I sighed and dropped my hands. "She hasn't made a move against me since she joined our coven."

"At least feed before you go. It will strengthen you."

I thought of Estrella, my human Donor, and the bond we shared. The idea of falling into her embrace and drinking her blood felt both enticing and repulsive all at once. My body ached for her as it normally did, but the feeling mingled with the conflict of yearning for Brielle's blood as well.

I didn't like the war of emotions battling in my mind. Estrella's company once served as a comfort to me. Now, it only made me more confused.

I shoved thoughts of Estrella out of my mind. "I'll be fine."

Jorge rubbed his forehead, once again reminding me of a frustrated parent. "Exercise caution, Leo. Sneaking into the castle spontaneously—and without your army to protect you—reminds me of your brother."

I stiffened. My brother, Ronaldo, had rebelliously abandoned his coven to sneak into the castle and rescue our sister, Lucia. It resulted in his capture, and he and Lucia had both been killed. "I am not Ronaldo," I said.

"Ronaldo acted with his heart," Jorge said. "You are different in that you act with your mind. Don't make the same mistakes he did, Leo. Don't let this girl be the death of you."

Rage roared within me, and I surged forward until my

fingers gripped the collar of Jorge's shirt. He sucked in a gasp but watched me with calm eyes. My blood boiled, rising to Brielle's defense. It wasn't until Jorge lifted his eyebrows pointedly that I dropped my hand, finally recognizing the reaction within me.

She's my Donor. I'd felt something similar when I'd first bonded with Estrella, my human Donor.

But the yearning inside me was so much more painful this time because Brielle and I had only exchanged blood once. And my body was desperate for more.

I smoothed my cloak. "I apologize. That was . . . dreadfully inappropriate of me."

Jorge said nothing, but his eyes were steely. I held his gaze unwaveringly, lifting my chin slightly.

At long last, he dropped his gaze. I had admitted my wrongdoing, but I was still his leader. And he needed to remember that.

"I appreciate your concern, Jorge," I said. "And I will take care."

Without another glance at him, I gathered my shadows around me and shifted to my bat form. I sensed Jorge watching me as I flitted around the room before exiting through the open door.

Brielle was waiting for me outside, her back to the front door and her body shrouded in her dark cloak, which billowed with the midnight air. There was something about her posture and stance that seemed regal.

As soon as I stepped forward, she turned, no doubt smelling me. Her eyes were impassive as she looked me over. Her pulse thrummed when our eyes locked, and a semblance of satisfaction surged through me.

"Ready?" she asked in a tight voice.

I inclined my head. "Of course, my lady."

Brielle snorted and took off down the street without bothering to glance and see if I followed. I matched her stride, and we silently crept down the street, pausing occasionally with the whisper of the wind or the faint smell of various demons.

We followed the winding road to the Castillo de Coca. The home of so many of my nightmares. Judging by the look of unease on Brielle's face, she felt the same. I didn't know the extent of her experience there, but I knew she'd been tortured and held captive for months.

As we climbed the steps, I could hear distant echoes of Lucia's screams. Ronaldo's sobs. The smell of their blood. The Count's cruel laughter.

I paused before the last step, my body overcome with tremors as I was suffocated by memories. I closed my eyes, my nostrils flaring as I focused on breathing. Though my body didn't need to breathe, it still brought me clarity.

Emotions were a human weakness that even vampires had to suffer through. Sometimes to overcome them, I needed to act human again—like by breathing.

"I know," Brielle said quietly from next to me.

I opened my eyes and looked at her. She gazed up at the turrets of the castle, her face paler than normal. Slowly, her gaze shifted to me. There was no scorn or anger in her eyes, which I'd grown so accustomed to. Instead, there was sympathy and grim understanding.

This place haunted her too.

But she hadn't lost anyone like I had.

I closed off the emotions, shutting the door before it was too late—before I dragged Brielle down with me.

My lips curled into a smirk, and I leaned closer to her. "Afraid of ghosts, are you?"

Brielle watched me for a long moment before irritation sparked in her eyes. She gritted her teeth and turned away from me, saying nothing as we approached the huge oak doors.

"Do you think—?" Brielle started.

I interrupted by pushing on the door. It opened easily with a loud creak.

Brielle's mouth clamped shut, her eyes widening. "No one locked it?"

"The staff has to maintain the castle, even when the Duke is gone." I offered a shrug and held the door open for her. "After you, my lady."

Brielle lowered her hood and slowly stepped inside. Her blond hair cascaded behind her in soft waves that I longed to run my fingers through.

Instead, I clenched my hands into fists. *Control yourself, Leo.* But my blood ached with longing. Her pulse quickened as she strode farther into the castle, and my blood sang in response.

I am the master of this beast within me, I reminded myself. *I'm in control.*

I thought of Ronaldo. He always believed the man was stronger than the monster. The day I'd ended the Count's life, I'd proven that. I'd resisted the temptation of his blood even as I opened his throat in front of me. I'd mastered the beast.

I needed to be in control again.

Brielle stared up at the dimly lit lanterns along the walls. She froze and looked at me with wide eyes. "Is someone here?"

I shook my head. "It's customary for the halls to be lit, even when the lord of the castle is absent."

Brielle's lips thinned into a flat line, and I grinned wolfishly at her. I had extensive experience sneaking around the castle at night, and she knew this too.

Our footsteps echoed in the empty castle. Though I was used to the darkness, it was strange not to see people roaming about or to hear their distant chatter. The same decorative vases and paintings lined the walls in all their glory, marking this as a place of wealth. Even in the wake of the Count's death, the castle still mocked those who were less fortunate.

"The library is this way," Brielle muttered, gesturing down the hall.

"I'm well aware," I said. "I caught you off guard while you were rearranging books in the middle of the night. Don't you recall?"

Brielle huffed a sigh. "Of course I remember."

I cocked my head at her. "Why were you doing that? Moving the books around? I'm sure the Count would've been appalled to find you doing the servants' work."

Brielle's gaze shifted to me before she responded. "I couldn't sleep."

I laughed. "So you took to rearranging the Count's library?" I paused, my smile fading. "Actually, that *does* sound like an amusing activity. I always envisioned myself hiding his traveling cloaks or setting the horses free. Anything to disrupt his life."

Brielle turned to me with a raised eyebrow. "That's all? That's pretty mild for someone who sought revenge."

"Well, naturally, I wanted to bleed him dry," I said. "But thinking of my revenge always brought on my rage. Imagining these minor inconveniences, however, often made me laugh and forget my troubles. Did you know we once snuck in here and looted all the silverware in the castle? The Count and his guests had to eat with their bare hands until replacements could be sent for."

Brielle laughed, and the sound echoed in the vast hallway like the peals of a bell. "The most I did was give him a sour attitude. But it was always satisfying to see the way his face scrunched up with displeasure."

I laughed too. "What a truly unpleasant man. I wonder if he ever experienced joy."

Brielle suddenly went very still, and I sensed her blood boiling. I knew I'd said the wrong thing.

Count Antonio de Silva *had* experienced joy—when he'd tortured his enemies.

We entered the library as a stony silence filled the space between us.

"Just so you know," Brielle said, striding toward the nearest bookshelf, which stretched higher than a cathedral. "I've scoured this entire place for information on Lilith's curse, and I didn't find anything."

"Ah, but you forget that self-righteous men like the Count often have other names for these things. 'Lilith's curse' can be seen as vulgar. A more appropriate name for Lilith herself is 'Mistress of Darkness,' 'Dark Lady,' or, my personal favorite, 'Lucifer's Whore.'"

Brielle wrinkled her nose and looked at me like I was insane.

I shrugged. "Given all the Count has done, does this surprise you?"

"No, I guess not." She frowned and tapped her chin. "I *do* remember coming across something like that, though. Here—" She bustled from shelf to shelf, fingering through various texts and muttering to herself. For a moment, I was content just watching her work—the way her eyes sharpened with concentration, the determined clench of her jaw, the fire in her eyes that made my blood yearn for her.

I stiffened, my skin prickling. Then, I sniffed the air, searching for what had set me on edge.

The scent of blood. Fresh blood.

In a flash, I was by Brielle's side. I grasped her elbow, and she jumped away from me with a yelp. "Leo, what—"

"Shh." I covered her mouth with my hand. When my skin touched hers, it felt like hot coals. A painful fire erupted inside me so severely that it scorched my hand. I jerked away from her, my eyes wide. Her face flushed, and she gasped for breath. A line of red surrounded her mouth —as if she *had* indeed been burned by my touch.

"What is it?" she said breathlessly, avoiding my gaze and searching the room instead. She closed the book she was perusing and slid it in the pocket of her cloak. "Did you find something?"

"Be still," I hissed, casting my gaze toward the open doors. "Someone is here."

Brielle froze. Though her body was completely motionless, her blood throbbed with anxiety. It made my head spin.

I scanned the room but found no disturbances. Then, I

gathered my shadows and shifted to my bat form, relying on the vibrations around me. I stretched my senses, searching for the source of the blood.

There. Somewhere in the hallway, an injured creature skulked toward us. It was slow and bleeding freely. The monster within me rejoiced, but I shoved it down. *I'm not here to feed.*

I shifted back to my vampire form and rejoined Brielle, who had drawn her athame. Wordlessly, I pointed toward the hallway where I'd sensed the intruder. Slowly, we crept toward the doors. As we drew nearer, a light scuffling echoed as the creature inched closer.

I stopped at the sound, but Brielle surged forward, wielding her dagger fearlessly. I almost called out to her, but I didn't want to scare off whoever was coming.

Besides, Brielle could handle herself.

Fear permeated the air, but it wasn't Brielle's. A shuffling sound met my ears, followed by a man's shout and a loud *thump.*

Then, Brielle gasped, "Ignacio?"

I stiffened, finally placing where I'd smelled the man's blood before. In the forest, the day I thought I'd ended his life.

It was one of the Count's mages.

"Impossible," I whispered, hurrying forward. Sure enough, the bald man was lying under Brielle's foot, clutching at her cloak as he tried to remove the weight from his chest. His face was covered in blood, and his once magnificent cloak was torn and stained.

"I thought you said you killed them all," Brielle snapped at me. As if this was *my* fault.

"We had," I said. "We cut their throats. He shouldn't have survived."

Ignacio moaned weakly, his arms seizing.

"Brielle," I said sharply.

Brielle eased her weight off Ignacio but kept her foot pressed lightly against him. "What're you doing here?" she growled at him.

Ignacio inhaled a rattling breath, and I stared at him. My skin prickled again, and suspicion crawled up my spine like a creature of darkness. Something wasn't right about him.

Then, his wide, fearful eyes turned all black, cloaking his face in shadows. He grinned widely at Brielle, and his teeth were stained with blood. He leaned forward eagerly. "I . . . am coming for you . . . dear one." His voice echoed with the chorus of a thousand voices that pierced right through me. I suppressed a shudder.

Suddenly, Ignacio slumped over with a groan, his body limp and unmoving.

Brielle's mouth fell open. "I—what?"

"He's dead," I said quietly. I felt his pulse dwindle and then disappear. His blood no longer coursed freely. He was nothing more than a corpse now.

Brielle's breaths were sharp wheezes, and she backed away from Ignacio's body. Her head was shaking back and forth in denial.

"What is it?" I asked, stepping toward her.

"That voice," Brielle rasped. "It—it was *her.*" She looked at me, her face stricken with terror. "It was Lilith."

3
LEO

I STARED AT BRIELLE FOR A MOMENT BEFORE looking at Ignacio again. He was slumped over, his eyes still open and a trickle of blood oozing from his open mouth. I inhaled deeply, detecting the faintest sliver of dark magic still lingering in the air with Ignacio's blood.

But it didn't smell familiar. I remembered what Brielle's blood tasted like. I craved it every day. Ignacio's blood didn't smell similar at all.

I frowned, my eyes shifting back to Brielle. "Are you certain?"

"I know what her voice sounds like, Leo," she snapped. "It was her."

I rubbed the back of my neck while Brielle watched me, her eyes blazing. "But how?" I asked. "Lilith only possesses witches."

"As far as we know. But I'm from the future, remember? Maybe I—maybe I changed something by coming here." Her brows furrowed, and uncertainty filled her eyes.

"Even if that were true, Ignacio isn't a Nightcaster," I said.

"How do you know?"

I raised an eyebrow. "Have you seen another firebird terrorizing the city?"

Brielle said nothing.

I shifted my weight and asked, "Can you . . . communicate with your firebird? Can it sense Lilith's presence? Does it know if there's another firebird out there?"

Brielle leveled a hard look at me. "Her name is Nix. And I haven't been able to reach her in a while. I think she's gone dormant again."

Nix. Right. I still found it odd that Brielle had named the firebird, let alone spoke of it like it was a person. But as an undead creature of darkness, I certainly had no room to criticize. "Again?" I asked.

"She was awakened by Lilith," Brielle said. "Now that Lilith is gone, Nix can rest without interference. Sometimes she rests for a week or more. It's like . . . hibernation. With the battle and her rebirth, she needs to recuperate. She was dormant almost my entire life, so I'm not too worried about it."

The small wrinkle between her brows suggested otherwise, but I didn't press her. Brielle was more stubborn than

I was at times. If she didn't want to discuss something with me, there was no way to persuade her.

I stepped closer, and Brielle's eyes flashed to me, her breath catching. Her heart rate quickened. I couldn't tell if it was fear or desire that made her eyes widen at my close proximity. But she didn't draw away from me, so I approached until I was close enough to smell the vanilla scent wafting from her hair.

"Have you heard Lilith's voice before now?" I asked in a low voice. "Since she vanished?"

Brielle shook her head. "No. Not once."

"How can you be certain it was her?"

Brielle rubbed her arm and dropped her gaze. "I *felt* it. My body responded to her. A chill raced through me, and Nix's fire came to life."

"But Nix is still dormant?"

"Yes."

I rubbed my chin. "Doesn't that seem strange? If Lilith is back, wouldn't your firebird be alarmed?"

Brielle's eyes narrowed. "You don't believe me."

"I didn't say that," I said softly. "I'm simply trying to learn more information. You said Lilith awakened your firebird before. So if she *has* returned, then where is your firebird, and why isn't she responding?"

Brielle swallowed, her brows knitting together.

I raised my hand and brushed my thumb along her jaw. Brielle's eyes closed, and her breath hitched. "You seem afraid, Brielle," I whispered. "Before this happened, you and I were searching for a way to summon Lilith. To bring her back. Are you sure that's what you want?"

Brielle's eyes opened, and her lips parted as she looked at me. She took a breath to respond, but then she stiffened. Suddenly, a white-hot pain exploded under my finger where our skin touched. The heat scorched and seared my thumb until I jerked it away, hissing in pain. Brielle clutched at her face, breathing heavily. Her cheeks were red, and she looked around as if to search for the source of the fire that had burned us both.

Our eyes locked, and we shared a look of confusion and horror. Then, she slowly backed away from me. Like it had been *my* fault.

"I want to bring her back," Brielle said at last. "But on *my* terms. If she comes back on her own, it means she's in control. I can't have that."

Before I could speak, she drew her hood over her face and strode away from me and Ignacio's body, her cloak billowing in the dimly lit hallway.

With a sigh, I stepped over Ignacio and followed her out of the castle.

Neither of us said a word as we met up with Miguel, who

was stationed outside. He reported that all was quiet—he hadn't seen anyone on the grounds.

Which meant Ignacio had been inside the entire time.

But how? I myself remembered draining his blood. He wouldn't have been able to heal himself.

But he *had* died. I was certain of it. I'd felt the life leave him. I'd felt his heart stop.

So the only two possibilities were: Ignacio *was* a Nightcaster and his firebird had revived him, or a powerful necromancer had reanimated his corpse.

My blood chilled as I considered this alternative. I'd met a few necromancers in a former coven I'd been in with Lucia and Ronaldo. The demons of death were disturbing creatures who communed with the spirits of the next life. Even I, who practiced dark magic, would never consider sinking to those depths. The idea of confronting the darkness beyond the veil made my very bones tremble.

My men, particularly Jorge, knew of my distaste for necromancers. But no one knew how truly afraid I was. Afraid of confronting my past and all the lives I'd taken. Or all the lives I'd been unable to save. My parents. Ronaldo. Lucia.

The thought of those spirits out there, waiting to snare me, made me want to gather my shadows around me and disappear altogether.

But it was a fear I could never share with others. I was Leonardo Serrano, the fearless coven leader. I had to be strong. For the sake of my coven and my people, I had to face this fear to uncover the mystery.

Because if Brielle *was* correct and Lilith had returned, then we were all in grave peril. But if she was wrong and a necromancer was reanimating corpses, then whoever was out there posed a threat to my coven and my city.

"Leo?"

I blinked and realized Miguel had asked a question. Brielle had returned to her home, and we stood at the end of the street where my coven lived.

"Forgive me," I said, shaking my head. "What did you say?"

Miguel leaned closer to me, his eyes shifting around the area. "We aren't alone."

I went still, sniffing the air. Then, I sensed it. The shifting in the shadows in front of us. The smell of canine fur and fresh blood.

"Werewolf," I hissed, clenching my teeth.

Damn you, Leo, I cursed myself. I'd been so lost in my thoughts and fears that my instincts had slipped. Miguel had noticed the wolf first.

I should've been more attentive.

"Do we attack?" Miguel whispered.

I shook my head slightly. "We don't draw first blood. Let's see what he wants. But ready your weapons."

Miguel nodded and drew a dagger in each hand. All I had were my swords, and I didn't want to wield them if I wanted to approach the visitor in peace. So instead I nodded to Miguel, who drew closer to me as we stepped forward.

The shadows between the buildings leapt for us, and Miguel and I shifted. He morphed into his raven form, and I changed into a bat. We flitted in the air, hovering over the attacker, and found a wolf the size of a carriage looming toward us. His white fur stood on end, and his bloody teeth were bared. Miguel and I hovered just out of reach.

Suddenly, black magic exploded from the wolf's body, consuming him until he shifted to his human form. Miguel and I followed suit, shifting in front of the man. This time, I drew my swords, since the wolf had challenged us.

When I approached the figure, my eyes widened. His damp brown hair fell over his face, and he shook it out of his eyes. His black eyes were rimmed in yellow—the mark of a werewolf.

For a long moment, I held my ground uncertainly. The face before me was one I hadn't seen in decades. Did he mean me harm?

When the werewolf relaxed and offered a crooked smile, I sheathed my swords with a sigh. Miguel glanced at me in confusion. "Relax, Miguel," I said. "Benito and I are old friends."

Benito de Vargas grinned wider, exposing his sharp fangs. He bowed deeply. "A pleasure to see you again, Leonardo."

I doubt that, I thought. "Did you come alone?" I asked,

glancing behind him. Remembering the blood on his teeth, I added coldly, "And I see you've taken the liberty of feeding on the people of my city."

Benito scoffed. "I would never." He wiped his chin, and his sleeve came back bloody. "I bit a rabbit in the forest. Couldn't resist the fresh meat."

I raised an eyebrow. A rabbit? A quick glance skyward told me it wasn't a full moon, so at least he hadn't created some demon were-rabbit.

"And no, I'm not alone." Benito straightened. "My pack is with me."

My eyes widened. "Your entire pack? Why?"

"There is something I must discuss with you in private." Benito's gaze shifted to Miguel.

"Miguel is my guard," I said sharply. "He stays."

Benito's jaw tightened. As the alpha of his pack, I doubted he was accustomed to taking orders from others. We stared each other down until he relented with a sigh. "Very well."

I forced a smile and beckoned toward the front door of my home. "Please come in."

Miguel stepped forward dutifully and held open the door for me. I strode into my house, and a servant by the door lit lanterns in the sitting room. I waved a hand toward the sofa, and Benito strolled inside, glancing around with an impressed frown on his face.

"How luxurious." He arched an eyebrow at me before striding into the sitting room.

I grabbed Miguel's arm before he followed Benito. "He's the alpha of the pack in Madrid," I whispered quickly. "Do not trust him. He has crossed me before."

Miguel nodded, his eyes darkening before he entered the room. I lingered in the doorway and took a long, slow breath.

Benito hadn't just crossed me. He'd assaulted my sister and tried to usurp my brother as coven leader. When he'd failed, he'd taken his fellow werewolves and abandoned our coven to start a pack in Madrid.

He was hardly an ally. But I needed to be civil if I wanted him to leave before he caused trouble.

I thought of Brielle tucked away in her home with her family. The last thing I wanted Benito to do was find out about her and her phoenix.

I straightened and arranged a carefully apathetic expression on my face before striding confidently into the sitting room. Miguel and Benito were sitting on opposite sofas. Miguel's black eyes were pinned on Benito, who watched with an amused expression on his face.

I sat next to Benito, draping my arm across the back of the sofa as if we were the closest of friends. "So, Benito, what brings you here?"

Benito shifted to face me, his eyes guarded. "How is

your coven, Leo? I heard you endured a nasty skirmish a few months ago."

Nasty skirmish. What an understatement. We'd faced a full-fledged battle, and many of my men had died. I smirked. "We did, but we emerged victorious. My coven is well, thank you for asking. And your pack? How do they fare?"

Benito shrugged. "We were concerned when we didn't hear from you for several years. Segovia has been untouched. Cloaked by dark magic. I feared for you, Leo."

I resisted the urge to snort. I had no doubt he was more curious about the power behind the Count's time curse and how he could wield it. When the curse had been broken, we discovered Segovia had been frozen in time for five years, though it had only felt like months to some of us.

I imagined Benito made plans to pay me a visit as soon as he discovered Segovia had been freed from the curse.

"Rest assured I am in excellent health," I said with a grin. "As is my coven. Now tell me, what can I do for you?"

Benito leaned forward, his eyes glinting. "I have a proposition for you."

I raised my eyebrows. "Oh? This should be good."

"I come here to offer an alliance between our people. A merger between my pack and your coven. A union of demons with our strength and numbers will be unstoppable." Benito's eyes darkened with hunger. "I propose we join forces, Leo."

4

BRIELLE

As soon as I opened the door to the tiny house where my family lived, I heard low murmurs from the living room. I was instantly reminded of my home back in Miami and how my parents would stay up late, speaking in hushed voices about me and Angel and our magical ailments.

The notion that only a year ago I was hunting demons on Calle Ocho in Miami made my head spin. I shook my head, lowering my hood before stepping into the living room.

The voices abruptly stopped, and I froze.

My older sister, Angel, sat on the sofa with her inky black hair tied up in a neat bun. Her arm was draped around the back of the sofa, and her legs were propped up on the table. She looked like the epitome of "chill."

But next to her on the sofa was Riker Wilkinson.

I crossed my arms, my nostrils flaring. "What the hell's going on?"

"Brie." Angel stood and strode over to me, taking my hands in hers. She stilled and looked up at me with worried eyes. "You're burning up. Come sit down."

I jerked my hands free, my eyes never leaving Riker. "What's he doing here, Angel? In our *house*?"

Riker was a British Seer I'd known during my stay at the Castillo de Coca. Well, more than just a Seer. We'd kissed a few times too. We'd almost become a "thing," until he'd allowed the Count to drag me to the dungeons and torture me. Riker had come to visit me but hadn't bothered to help free me. He'd just left me there to rot.

Riker's red hair had grown longer since I'd last seen him, and his blue eyes widened when they met mine. Slowly, he stood with his hands raised in surrender. "Easy, Brielle. We were just talking. I don't mean any harm."

I took a threatening step toward him. "Get out."

"Brie," Angel hissed.

"Are you defending him?" I whirled on her. "He left me in that dungeon to *die*!"

Riker flinched, his eyes tortured. *Good,* I thought savagely. *He deserves to feel guilty.*

"I thought you would slaughter the entire city!" Riker said. "Even if it had been my own mother, I would've made the same choice. One life compared to thousands."

Something within me resonated with his words. I'd

thought the same thing myself. In fact, I'd practically begged Leo to kill me last year because I thought it might spare my family.

But a lump rose in my throat, and I couldn't deny the pain coursing through me. Riker and Angel had been sitting next to each other like they were best friends. Perhaps even *more* than friends. Like it was the easiest thing in the world.

Like what he'd done to me hadn't mattered at all.

I swallowed, and my throat burned. "I'd like you to leave. Please."

Angel touched my arm, and I resisted the urge to shake her off again.

"Brielle, I'm so sorry," Riker whispered, stepping toward me.

I closed my eyes and raised a hand to stop him. "Please. I just—I need to speak with my sister alone."

I didn't open my eyes until I heard him step toward the door. I stared hard at Angel, who watched Riker leave over my shoulder.

When the door slammed shut, I pulled off my cloak and threw it violently to the floor. "Seriously, Angel? Riker? Of all people?"

Angel crossed her arms. "What, like there's a variety of guys I can choose to hang out with in this city? Would you prefer I meet up with Harrison?"

I winced. Harrison Porter was another resident of the

castle who had survived the battle last year. Along with Chris, Wes, and Samson, I referred to them as the "Four Douchebags" because, well, that was exactly what they were. Wes, Chris, and Samson had died in the battle. I'd wanted to feel relieved they were gone. But a part of me was filled with regret that they'd died serving the Count's purposes. That they'd been nothing more than pawns in his game.

When they'd fallen through the time portal, they'd been innocent. Just like me.

I sighed and rubbed my forehead. "Angel, he abandoned me when I needed him the most. The only person who was there for me when I was *dying* was Izzy." Well, and Ronaldo, Leo's brother. His distraction had provided me a means to escape. And he'd paid for it with his life.

I turned my thoughts to Izzy. I hadn't seen her in ages. She lived in the city too, but she chose to live in another neighborhood, separate from Leo's coven. Her goal was to find other light casters to start a light coven, but her efforts were pretty futile given that the Count had owned every light caster in the city—and they were all dead now.

Angel's face softened. "I understand that, Brie. But it's been almost a year since then. He regrets it every day. He says he has nightmares about you being tortured down there."

My mouth twisted in a sour grimace. "How sad for him."

Angel rolled her eyes. "Are you saying you've never made a mistake? That you've never unfairly judged someone's character?"

My lips pressed into a thin line, and I knew she had a point. When I'd first met Leo, I'd only seen him as my enemy. I'd captured and questioned him under duress, and even after that, he'd still welcomed me into his home without hostility.

I huffed a sigh and sank onto the sofa. "I don't know, I guess I just . . . don't want him to hurt you too."

Angel sat next to me, her prim posture making her look positively regal. She smiled and pressed her hand against mine. "You really don't have to mother me, Brie. *I'm* the older sister, remember?"

I shrugged. "I'm used to it. It's still weird for me to see you so strong." She was so different from the sister I'd had in Miami. In our time, she'd suffered from crippling seizures from her visions and was on constant medication. But here in this time, for some reason, she was perfectly healthy. A fighter, even. She'd fought in the battle with us.

"That's not the only reason you're upset, though, is it?" Angel asked, reading me like she always did. "Did something happen at the castle?"

I nodded and told her about Ignacio and the voice that had possessed him. I didn't think it was a coincidence that my fire burned up inside me when Leo touched me, either. Perhaps the power had been awakened by Lilith's voice.

Angel's face had gone pale when I finished. "If she *is* back," she said in a hushed voice, "how do we stop her?"

"I don't know." A Nightcaster's only hope to resist Lilith's influence was by bonding with the phoenix inside them. Sometimes it wasn't enough, though. Leo's sister, Lucia, had tried bonding with her phoenix, but the power had killed her.

But . . . what about those who *weren't* Nightcasters? If there was no phoenix to bond with, then how could someone resist Lilith's influence?

"The only thing I can think of is to find a way to summon her," I said, echoing the conversation I'd had with Leo. "If we can bring her here on *our* terms and catch her off guard, we might have an advantage."

"But you can't summon her if you don't know how to defeat her," Angel said. "You can't banish someone who's already dead."

I frowned, thinking hard. "I'll have to get back into the castle and look through the library again. Leo mentioned something about Lilith going by different names. If I go through the books more thoroughly, maybe I can find a way to banish her. If anyone knew how to destroy Lilith, it would've been the Count. He devoted his life to it."

"Almost makes you wish you'd kept him alive, huh."

My blood turned to ice at her words, and I glared at her.

Angel flinched. "Sorry. I didn't mean that. I just mean, he tortured you and countless others to achieve his goal.

Maybe it would've been better to play his game and torture *him* to find out how to defeat Lilith."

I released a breath, suddenly feeling exhausted. "Yeah. But at the time of his death, I was the only one in danger of being possessed by Lilith. But now? If she can possess Ignacio, then who else can she possess? Who else is in danger?"

Angel and I looked at each other with equally frightened gazes. She squeezed my hand, and we remained silent for a long moment as we sat in the comfort of each other's company.

The door opened, and my parents entered. Rain poured from outside, and Mom shook out of her wet cloak. Dad followed behind her with an umbrella, but even with the cover, they were still drenched.

"I really miss cars," Dad grumbled when he closed the door.

Mom scoffed. "You didn't even know what they *were* when we were dating."

I ground my teeth together, shoving down my bitterness at yet another reminder that my parents had lied to me my whole life. When they were teenagers, they'd both time traveled. And I'd never known until they time traveled to find me last year.

"Where were you guys?" Angel asked, slouching back against the sofa.

"Meeting with an acquaintance." Dad slid out of his

boots before he plopped on the sofa across from us with a sigh.

I raised an eyebrow. "What acquaintance?" He hadn't even been here a year. Who could he possibly know?

Dad's eyes lit up as he exchanged an eager glance with Mom. "He's actually one of my ancestors. His name is Ricardo Querida. I believe he's my mother's . . ." He trailed off, staring at the ceiling with a furrowed brow as he thought. "Great-great-great grandfather? I think." He ran a hand through his short blond hair, and flecks of rain spattered on the floor. "Anyway. He told me how to get passage to Cuba. Apparently, there's a group of Spaniards who just set sail recently."

My eyes widened. "Cuba?" My gaze shifted to Mom.

Mom bit her lip, slowly joining Dad on the sofa. She clasped her hands on her lap. "We, uh, we were thinking about going to live there."

I went very still, my heart racing. "Why?"

"We don't belong here, Brie. We can't live with a vampire coven. You, Angel, and I need our own coven, and there aren't enough light casters here for you to be protected. If we have to leave, we might as well go somewhere we know. You've been to Cuba before. Your father and I lived there for a while."

I swallowed down my retort, knowing my family had sacrificed everything to be here. To find me. They'd broken laws and tortured officials for information on my whereabouts. Aside from Angel's condition, they couldn't return to our time because they would be arrested on the spot.

So how could I blame them for wanting to go somewhere that resembled home for them? We'd visited Cuba several times in my time, but Mom and Dad had lamented that it wasn't the same. It wasn't the Cuba they remembered.

The Cuba they knew from 1898.

I hadn't realized at the time how strange their response had been. But now that I thought of it, how would Cuba be that different from what they remembered? In my mind, they'd lived in Cuba in the present, maybe twenty years before I was born. How could things have been so different back then?

But now that I knew about their time travel, it made more sense. They'd lived in Cuba before the Cold War. Before communism and Castro.

"We can't leave," I said at last. "I have work to do here." I thought of my decision to help Leo with the rogue demons in the city. And our efforts to summon and defeat Lilith.

"Brie, it isn't your responsibility to clean up the city," Mom said. "Let Leo and his coven handle that."

I resisted the urge to roll my eyes. "It isn't just that." I cut my gaze to Angel, but her eyes widened in warning. I knew what she was conveying. If I told Mom and Dad that I thought Lilith might be back, they'd ship us off to Cuba in an instant.

But if Lilith *was* back, then I was partially to blame. No doubt she was seeking retribution for the firebird she'd lost.

I had to fix this. I had to protect this city from my mistakes. If I hadn't time traveled here to begin with, no one would be in danger in Segovia.

I shook my head. "Mom, my place is *here*. I'm working with Leo. I have friends here. It's my duty to protect them."

Dad sighed. "What about *our* duty, Brie? Mom, Angel, and I have no place living among a coven of vampires. We came here for *you*, and now we're together. You expect us to just live among vampires like everything's fine?"

"No," I said sourly, crossing my arms. "I just—can you give me more time? I'm not ready to leave yet."

Dad nodded. "Sure. It'll take us a while to pack up and secure passage anyway. How about . . . a month?"

A hollow knot formed in my chest. *A month.*

Panic flared within me, and my very bones seemed to cry out, *I can't leave! I can't leave!*

Though I really couldn't pinpoint *why*. Hunting demons, yes. Fighting Lilith, sure. But . . . why? Did I really feel like I belonged here? Among demon vampires, half of whom hated my guts?

Leo's face swam in my mind, but I shoved the thought away. This wasn't some girlish crush. My doubts couldn't possibly stem from the stupid butterflies I got around him.

And I certainly wouldn't force my family to stay here just because I was attracted to him.

No, there was something bigger swelling within me. Something I couldn't identify.

But I had no logical excuse for my parents. So before I realized what I was saying, I whispered, "All right. One month."

5

LEO

I KEPT MY FACE CAREFULLY STOIC, TRYING TO HIDE the panic warring in my head. I exchanged the briefest glance with Miguel, whose whole expression had darkened. Then, my face split into a wide smile, and I laughed.

"Join forces with a pack of werewolves? Surely you didn't come all this way just to tease me, Benito."

Benito grinned, his eyes glinting. "I assure you I'm in earnest."

We held each other's gazes for a long, tense minute. I sensed Miguel shifting slightly as if preparing for Benito to attack.

I chuckled and rubbed my chin. "Ah, Benito, I hate to disappoint you. But I couldn't possibly accept your offer."

Benito sat back against the sofa and crossed his beefy arms over his chest. "Why not? From what my sources tell me, you could use the extra power on your side. I hear you have a problem with rogue demons in the city."

Suspicion prickled through me. *How does he know that? Either he's behind the attacks, or he's stationed spies in* my *city.* Rage pulsed through me, but I held it at bay and kept the same easy smirk on my face. "Have you ever met a demon of werewolf and vampire descent, Benito?"

The amusement faded from Benito's face. "I can't say that I have."

I leaned forward intently. "That's because the vampire venom wars with the werewolf venom and the call of the moon. The thirst for both drives him to madness until it takes him over completely. I've seen it for myself, Benito. I will not endanger my coven like that."

Benito's eyes hardened. "Are you suggesting I can't keep my pack under control?"

"Of course not. But accidents happen, and I'm sure there are men on both sides who wouldn't think so highly of our merger. All it would take is one meaningless fight between our men. One slip-up. One bite." I stared hard at him. "It would be catastrophic, Benito."

A heavy silence suspended in the air between us. Tension swirled, filling the room until I could barely breathe.

Benito sat forward, his yellow eyes gleaming and his jaw rigid. For a moment, he looked like the fierce wolf I'd seen earlier, and I resisted the urge to reach for my swords again.

"Something is coming, Leo. Something you and I are power-less to control on our own. And it will wipe out *everything*. Yes, you may lose one or two men to venom sickness. But it's a preferable sacrifice to losing everyone you hold dear."

The way his eyes narrowed and filled with darkness made me wonder if his words were a threat—if he and his pack would attack my coven if we refused his offer. I clenched my teeth, matching his fierce gaze.

Benito cocked his head and smiled like a predator. With a lithe movement, he rose from the sofa and bowed deeply to me. Miguel and I stood as well.

"I will be in Segovia for a fortnight," Benito said. "You have until then to give me your final answer."

He strode out of the sitting room with strong, confident steps that echoed in the huge house. The front door creaked when it shut with his departure.

Miguel and I didn't move. I stared at the open window as the white curtains rustled with the wind. Benito's foul wet-dog stench lingered on my nostrils. It wasn't until the scent vanished completely that I finally turned to Miguel.

"Gather the others and bring them here. Tell them it's urgent."

"Do you think he means to attack us?" Miguel asked. Though the question should've instilled fear, his eyes blazed with a hungry fire that told me he longed to drink Benito dry.

"Whatever he's here for, it isn't for an alliance. Benito de

51

Vargas doesn't share power. He's here for another reason." I suddenly went very still, thinking of how Brielle had insisted she'd heard Lilith's voice.

Did Benito know? *Something is coming. Something you and I are powerless to control on our own.*

Perhaps he was here to take advantage of the chaos of Lilith's return. If she truly had returned, then it would be the perfect opportunity for another demon to swoop in and take control of my coven. After all, Benito had tried doing it before. My brother had almost been killed because of the mutiny Benito had stirred up.

I strode to the desk in the corner, opened a drawer, and withdrew my daggers. After sliding the weapons into the sheaths on my belt, I turned to Miguel. "I'll be back shortly. Make sure the others are here, and tell them to keep quiet. We don't want Benito's pack to be alarmed."

Miguel nodded dutifully and left. Once he was gone, I raced into my room and reached under the bed to pull out several dusty boxes. My eyes narrowed as I searched through each one until I found what I was looking for—a pistol loaded with silver bullets. I ensured it was properly loaded before I slid it into my holster as well. After tightening my belt, I drew my cloak closer around me to conceal the weapons and left the house.

The street was eerily silent, and I had no doubt Benito's pack was lingering nearby, watching my every move.

I resisted the urge to smirk. Sadly for them, they would be disappointed.

My cloak swished with my quick movements, and shadows behind me made the back of my neck prickle. But I didn't dare turn around. Instead, I darted down an alleyway and gathered my shadows around me before shifting to my bat form. I flitted high above the houses next to me, leaping from rooftop to rooftop until I was several streets over. After circling the neighborhood and hovering in the shadows of the vacant fruit market, I stilled, waiting. Listening.

Crickets chirped. The wind rustled the leaves of nearby trees. The air smelled fresh and crisp.

But just in case, I stayed in my bat form, relying on the vibrations of my surroundings to lead me to Brielle's house. Instead of knocking on the door, I flew around the porch to the servants' entrance in the back. Then, I shifted to my vampire form and slid inside as easily as if I belonged there.

A woman scrubbing clothes in the back yelped, but I put a finger to my lips and smiled at her. Her face drained of color, and she seemed too terrified to say anything.

I slipped past her and entered the dining room where I found Brielle poring over a book. Of course. She still wore her black cloak, and I frowned.

"What're you doing here?" she asked in a bored voice without looking up.

I stifled the mild disappointment at the realization that I

hadn't sneaked up on her. Of course, the maid had shrieked, and Brielle could probably smell me. But still, catching Brielle off guard was always so amusing.

I leaned against the wall and watched her until she looked up at me with a raised eyebrow. Her brown eyes were rimmed in red, and her hair fell around her face in disheveled clumps. Though she looked sleep-deprived, the effect on her appearance made her look wild and untamed. My blood pounded with desire, and I dropped my gaze.

"I need to discuss something with you," I said, moving closer to the table.

Brielle sighed and shut her book, clasping her hands in front of her. "All right. What is it?"

I glanced around. "Where is your family?"

"Sleeping."

I smirked. "And yet you're not?"

Brielle rolled her eyes. "What do you want, Leo?"

My smile faded, and I crossed my arms. "I want you and your family to leave the city."

Brielle's face slowly slackened in shock, her eyes widening. Something like hurt flashed in her eyes, but she masked it quickly. Her voice was tight as she asked, "Why?"

For a moment, I considered lying to her. Or telling her it was private information I couldn't disclose. But knowing Brielle, that would be insulting, and she would take it upon herself to find out anyway. Exhaling slowly, I slid into the chair next to her and told her of Benito's visit and his offer.

When I finished, Brielle sat back in her chair and scoffed. "That's it? Leo, I can handle a werewolf."

"It isn't just a werewolf. It's his entire pack. And don't underestimate him, Brielle. He almost killed my brother, and Ronaldo was always a stronger fighter than I was."

"I can take care of myself," she said in a hard voice. "Besides, I have Nix."

"Do you?" I challenged. "Last I heard, she'd gone dormant. What if your life is on the line and she's nowhere to be found?"

Brielle's nostrils flared as she held my gaze.

I shook my head. "Besides, it's your firebird I'm concerned about. If Benito finds out you're a Nightcaster . . ." I trailed off, unwilling to finish the sentence. I swallowed and tried again. "He is attracted to power, and he will do whatever it takes to obtain it. I fear that what he'll do to you will be far worse than what the Count did."

Brielle's eyes darkened. "How can anything be worse?"

"Because the Count, at least, was trying to eradicate your powers. Benito will try to harness them for his own means."

Brielle went very still, her mouth twisting slightly as if she were ill. And I knew what she was thinking. When the Count had held her captive, he had managed to unleash the phoenix's power and give Lilith brief control of Brielle's magic. An entire village had been destroyed as a result.

I had no doubt she was now imagining all the horrors

Benito would have access to if he had control of the phoenix.

I almost brought up my suspicions about Lilith, but the terror and anger warring in Brielle's eyes made me hesitate. No one in Benito's pack could be a Nightcaster—nighttime was when they shifted to their wolf form, and they couldn't do that without magic. Brielle surrendered her magic to her phoenix at night. At least, she did when the creature was present.

Could Benito have a dormant phoenix living within him?

No. Impossible. Brielle had had *no* magic her entire life. Benito wouldn't be able to shift at all.

This logic satisfied me, and I looked back at Brielle expectantly.

At long last, she sighed and deflated slightly. "My parents spoke to me of leaving soon."

My chest swelled with relief. "Good. The sooner the better."

Brielle winced. "Leo, they want to go back to Cuba."

My brow furrowed as I tried to remember where Cuba was. Vaguely, I remembered Brielle mentioning a small island in the Caribbean where her family was from. My blood chilled in my veins as I considered how far she would be—how unreachable.

Panic boiled in my blood. *I can't lose her.*

I couldn't tell if that was my hunger speaking, or some other part of me desperate to keep Brielle close.

"Oh," I finally managed to say. "I see."

Brielle and I gazed at each other from across the table, both of us remaining silent. I sensed a battle of emotions waging within her too, but it was impossible to tell how she felt. I sensed her blood pulsing and her heart racing, but was it out of fear? Excitement to be free of my coven? Or desire to remain here with me?

I tried telling myself it made no difference to me how she felt. But my heart and my body knew it was a lie.

If she stays and Benito kills her or tortures her, I will never forgive myself. I cannot survive the loss of someone I care about. Not again.

I'd lost too much already.

So I swallowed down my regret and said in a casual voice, "That's good then. You already have a way out. Perhaps you should take it."

Brielle looked at me, her eyes curious. Could she sense the lie in my words? The way my blood yearned for me to take her in my arms, touch her soft skin, and run my hand through her hair?

"It isn't safe for you or your family," I said quietly. "Can you imagine what Benito would think if he found out a family of light casters lived among us? Your family's presence here is curious. He'll want to know more. That is, if he doesn't decide your family is fresh prey for his pack. He may assume you are enemies to my coven and think he has the freedom to do with you what he wishes."

Brielle's face turned ashen. I knew her well enough to know she didn't fear for herself—but she *did* fear for her sister. And her parents.

Brielle would never tell me so, but I knew she felt guilty for bringing her family here to this time—to live with a coven of vampires. She hated subjecting them to that, even if her father had personally admitted to me that he knew his family was safe here.

"Benito says he'll remain for a fortnight," I said, rising from the table. "I suggest you and your family make a decision by then. I fear he will wage a war against my coven when he learns I've refused."

"What if you don't?" Brielle said, jumping to her feet. "What if you decide to join him?"

I watched her, waiting for some sign that she was teasing. "I can't do that, Brielle."

"You and I both know we have a problem with rogue demons. Maybe Benito can help. Maybe having the pack on our side can help us against Lilith."

There it was. I knew I couldn't avoid discussing the subject of Lilith. I sighed. "I will not ally myself with someone I don't trust. I can't trust Benito, and I can't risk you or the members of my coven to be unprotected under his watch."

Brielle raised an eyebrow, and I suddenly realized I'd listed her separately from my coven. "Me? Surely you're not worried about *me*."

The smirk on her face almost made me laugh. It challenged even my own charm, and the way her eyes glinted made my stomach churn.

I took a step toward her and felt a thrill at the way her blood pulsed with urgency. I considered taunting her, but something within me yearned to be forward. To see how her body reacted.

To see if she possibly felt the same way.

I took another step toward her until I was close enough for our chests to brush. I felt her breath hitch, and I smiled.

"I wouldn't be here if I weren't worried about you, Brielle," I said in a soft voice.

A blush bloomed across her face, and her eyes shone as she gazed up at me. Her lips parted, and I lifted a hand to rub the pad of my thumb along her lower lip. A low, soft gasp escaped her mouth, igniting a fire within me. Her lips felt hot under my touch, and I removed my hand, afraid that same fire would consume both of us and break this perfect moment. Heat swirled in her eyes. I lowered my hand to the tousled hair hanging over her shoulder, running my fingers through it so it fanned out over her cloak.

I smiled again, and the hunger within me roared with desperation. "I like your hair like this. Wild and free."

Brielle exhaled, and her breath tickled my nose. "I—I can help you, Leo." She swallowed and wet her lips, and I instinctively leaned in, desperate for a taste. "If—if Benito attacks, I can help you."

"Brielle," I breathed her name like a secret, and her eyes closed as if relishing the sound. "You are fierce and formidable. But you're far too precious for me to risk." My fingers twirled the ends of her hair. "Please take care. And advise your family to do the same."

Before she could respond, I took her hand and lifted it to my lips. My mouth opened as I pressed a long and tantalizingly slow kiss against her skin. Flames erupted from beneath her skin, scorching my mouth, but I lingered until I heard her breath catch in her throat. Then, I dropped her hand and vanished out the servants' door, my head reeling and my blood thrumming.

6

BRIELLE

I HADN'T REALIZED HOW LONG I'D BEEN HOLED UP IN the dining room until Angel came downstairs dressed in her nightgown. She frowned when she saw me poring over my book.

"Shouldn't you be sleeping?" I asked.

"Bad vision," Angel mumbled with a yawn. "Can't get back to sleep. Besides, I could ask you the same question."

"Can't sleep either." I returned my gaze to the book in front of me, unwilling to reveal *why* I couldn't sleep. Yes, I was obsessed with finding Lilith, but after Leo's visit, my heart wouldn't stop skittering. Sleep was far from me. "How are your visions, by the way?"

Angel shrugged one shoulder and drew closer to the table. "Better. I don't get seizures or migraines anymore. But the nightmares still haunt me." She shuddered and shook her head.

"I'm sorry," I said, looking at her with a grimace. "But I'm glad you aren't sick anymore."

"What're you doing?" Angel sat down next to me and propped her head on her hands.

I raised an eyebrow. "Reading."

She snorted and rolled her eyes. "I got that. But *what* are you reading?"

I briefly flipped back to the title page and read, "*Magical Portals and How to Open Them.*"

Angel's eyes widened, and she lifted her head. "Why in Lilith's name are you reading that?"

"It was the only book I could grab from the castle. I figured I might as well make use of what I've got."

"Find anything interesting yet?"

I shook my head. "I've read this book before, though. Back when I lived at the castle and was trying to find a way past the time loop. I thought this might tell me how to access the portal and get back home." I rubbed my eyes, which strained under the dim candlelight.

Angel remained very still. "You went through hell last year, didn't you?"

I looked at her. Her dark blue eyes were tormented and full of regret. I offered a soft smile and placed my hand on hers. "I have my family here now, Angel. Everything's fine. I have everything I want and need."

Angel nodded, but her lips turned downward. "Brie, I—I never apologized for not being there for you."

I stared hard at the polished mahogany table, gritting my teeth as memories of last year flooded my mind. The smell of blood and rust in the Count's dungeon. The screams and sobs of the demons imprisoned along with me. The betrayal of those in the castle I'd thought were my friends.

I thought of Riker and Angel, sitting together in my house like it was the most normal thing in the world. I slammed the book shut, and Angel flinched.

"Sorry," I muttered. "I'm just tired."

"Maybe you should—"

"Can't sleep." I smiled wryly.

Angel chuckled. "Wonder what that's like." She sighed, stretching her arms along the table. "We need to talk about what happened earlier."

I suppressed a groan. *Dammit. I really don't want to talk about this with her.* "All right," I said, exhaling.

"What do you want to do about it?"

About her and Riker? I wrinkled my nose. "What am I *supposed* to do about it?"

Angel frowned. "So you want to do nothing? Just stay here in a coven you don't belong to?"

I blinked, momentarily bewildered. Then, I realized she was talking about our conversation with Mom and Dad— the possibility of leaving Spain. "Right. Well—I, uh, I'd like to stay." It wasn't entirely untrue.

"Why?" Angel's eyes sparked as if she already knew the answer.

"I . . . I feel like I belong here. There are . . . people I care about. Things I feel responsible for." The words sounded lame when I spoke them.

"Uh-huh." Angel raised her eyebrows, her expression smug.

My face felt hot. "Stop that."

Angel groaned. "Oh, come on, Brie! What did you think would happen in the long run? You'd just be adopted into this coven as a light witch and live happily ever after with Leo?"

My blush deepened, and I gaped at her. "What? No, I—"

"Or maybe you're considering becoming a demon so you can join them officially?" Her brows pinched as she looked at me in genuine curiosity. "Is that it?"

"*No*," I said quickly. "Well—I don't know." I hadn't officially ruled that out yet. After all, Dad was a demon and he turned out all right. "Look, I'm still worried about Lilith. There's a mess in this city I want to help clean up. It's why I asked Dad for more time before I decide." Slowly, my eyes met hers. "But . . . *you* want to leave, don't you?"

Angel remained silent for a moment, and her lips pressed together. "I don't know," she said quietly, turning her head to stare at the floor. "Like you, I feel tied to this place, but . . ." She shook her head, running a hand down her face. "I don't belong here. Neither does Mom. Dad could probably fit in fine, but you know how he butts heads with Leo and Jorge."

I swallowed and nodded. It wasn't fair to expect my family to live here among demons. They came here for me, and I was the reason they stayed. It was my choice to stay here, but it wasn't theirs.

I rubbed the back of my neck, remembering Leo's words about keeping my family safe. If Leo was seriously worried, perhaps I should be too.

But he isn't worried for himself, a small voice said in my head. *He's worried about* you. *If the threat were that dangerous, wouldn't he fear for himself and his coven too?*

Leo had been overprotective of me before. Perhaps he was doing it again now.

Angel took my hand. "I'm with you, Brie."

I looked at her. Her eyes shone with tears. A lump formed in my throat. "I know."

"No, I mean, I am *with* you." She leaned forward, her eyes intent on mine. "If you decide to stay here, I will happily make a life here in Segovia. Even if Mom and Dad long to return to Cuba, I *will* be happy here." Her eyes grew distant, and I uncomfortably wondered if she was thinking of Riker. Would she make a life with *him*? The thought made me sick.

"Thanks," I muttered. "But if anything happens to you guys while you're here, I'll never forgive myself."

Angel's brow furrowed. "But it isn't—"

"Even if it's not my fault," I said, my voice sharpening. "I'm the reason you're here to begin with. Even if Mom and Dad *wanted* to stay here, I would still feel responsible." I took a deep breath. "It might be safer if we left the city."

Angel's mouth fell open. "Why? Because you're worried Lilith will come back? Brie—"

"I don't know," I said, rubbing my forehead. "I just feel like something is . . . off. It's why I'm researching so much. I'm trying to be prepared." I sighed and looked at her. "I just want to keep you safe."

Angel offered a sad smile. "It's not your job to protect everyone, Brie. We're all adults."

I almost laughed at that. Angel, Mom, and Dad were adults, but I technically wasn't eighteen yet. And sometimes I still felt like the protective older sister to Angel.

Angel yawned again and stood up, stretching. "I'm going to read upstairs. Don't stay up too late, okay?"

"Sure." I dropped my gaze to my book, knowing I wouldn't be heading to bed anytime soon. Angel's soft footsteps echoed on the stairs as I reopened the book to where I'd left off.

My vision blurred, my eyelids drooping as I kept reading. But I didn't want to give in to sleep, not when I'd wasted so much time reading this damn book. I wanted to emerge with *some* kind of helpful information.

Just give me something. Anything.

I reread the same page again and again, my muddled

brain making no sense of the words. Then, suddenly, I went still as I came across the words *Dark Lady*.

I straightened in my chair and leaned forward, reading the passage more carefully.

The gate to the Underworld can only be opened when a mortal is sacrificed. When innocent blood is offered, the Dark Lady will be summoned and abide in the mortal realm.

My blood chilled as I read the words again and again.

If *Dark Lady* referred to Lilith—and I was pretty sure it did—then Nightcasters weren't her only access to the mortal world. If someone opened the gate to the Underworld, she could be summoned.

A thought sprang to my mind, but I squashed it before it fully formed. I would *not* consider opening the gate just to banish Lilith. I couldn't kill an innocent person. Ever.

I slammed the book shut and groaned, running my hands through my messy hair.

So, my two options were to wait around for Lilith to return on her own or keep researching and hope to find a way to defeat her.

My eyes stung with exhaustion as I pried open the book and kept reading, prepared to stay up all night if I had to.

But in the back of my mind, the thought lingered: could I kill an innocent person if it meant I could banish Lilith?

The longer I stayed up, the less insane the idea sounded.

7
LEO

MY BLOOD STILL BURNED WITH URGENCY, AND MY mind was a torrent of images and emotions. I wanted Brielle. I *needed* her.

But I couldn't tell if it was the hunger talking or my own desire.

So, for the time being, I had to keep her at arm's length.

I pushed her from my thoughts as I hurried back to my home, ducking in alleys and shifting to my bat form to avoid anyone who might be following.

When I arrived, a familiar array of smells filled my nose: woodsmoke and cinnamon, a sharp spicy scent, and several others I identified as those of my coven. I strode inside, handing my cloak to a servant before joining my friends in the sitting room.

My cousin, Guadalupe, was speaking with Jorge and Miguel in low voices. Eduardo was standing off to the side, his arms crossed and an almost bored expression on his face. But his brows were furrowed slightly, and his body was angled toward the conversation. I knew he was listening carefully.

Guadalupe approached me first when I entered, her silver-rimmed eyes wide. "Is it true? Is de Vargas's pack here in the city?"

I nodded and raised a hand before she responded. My eyes flicked to the open window, and I jerked my chin toward Jorge. He strode over and slid it shut. Then, I ticked my head toward the kitchen, and my comrades followed.

A few servants gasped when we entered. They bowed and curtsied before scurrying out of the room like mice.

When I was sure we were alone, I said quietly, "It's true. I sensed the wolves lurking in the streets. They're watching us. I think they're searching for a weakness they can exploit."

Guadalupe's brows knitted together. "Miguel mentioned an alliance."

I shook my head. "It must be a ruse. Something to rattle us."

Jorge scoffed and crossed his arms. "Well, it's working."

"Benito never shares power," I said. "If he's here, then he's interested in taking our coven for his own." I leveled a look at Guadalupe, and her eyes darkened. She remembered what had happened between Benito and Ronaldo years ago.

"What can we do?" Miguel asked.

"Keep a close eye on the pack. If you notice one of them following you, try to lose him. Keep your movements undetected, and don't have any private conversations out in the open." I looked at Jorge. "I'll need you to track down each werewolf. Do it discreetly. Make a note of everything you can—physical descriptions, weaknesses, patterns of behavior, and what they look like in their human forms. Try to find out the rankings and who Benito trusts the most—and who he doesn't trust. Perhaps we can use the lesser wolves as allies."

Jorge nodded, his jaw rigid.

I looked at Miguel. "I need you to stay with Brielle."

If Miguel was surprised by this order, he didn't show it. I heard Guadalupe's sharp intake of breath next to me, but I ignored her.

"Watch over her family," I continued. "If they're being followed, report it to me immediately. Make sure a guard is always stationed outside their house."

"And if the lady asks why I'm there?" Miguel asked.

I smirked, knowing Brielle would detect his presence in an instant. "Tell her the truth. If need be, remind her of her sister and her parents. They will be targets for Benito. He'll be instantly suspicious of what a trio of light witches are doing in a neighborhood full of vampires. See that he never finds out."

Miguel nodded tersely.

I turned to Eduardo, who had a sour grimace on his

face. "I need you to train the men. Make sure the coven is fully prepared to use firearms if needed. You have my permission to take a few men into the woods for target practice."

Eduardo nodded.

Guadalupe looked at me expectantly, and I said, "I need you to care for the Donors. Make sure each Donor is in a protective hideout secured by their vampire. Bring Estrella to stay with me, and quietly discuss the matter with the other members of our coven."

"What will you do?" she asked.

"I will carry on as if everything is normal. I am the most likely of all of us to be followed." I paused and leaned closer to my comrades. "Do you all still have the silver bullets?"

The four of them nodded grimly. When Benito attacked my brother all those years ago, Ronaldo had ensured each of us had access to silver bullets to kill a werewolf if needed. I'd carried on the routine, making sure every new addition to our coven had the weapon securely hidden but still easily accessible. Now I was glad I did.

"Brielle," Guadalupe said in a whisper.

For one wild moment, I thought Brielle was in the room and Guadalupe was alerting me to her presence. My blood boiled in response.

Calm yourself, Leo. Don't be so ridiculous.

When I met Guadalupe's concerned gaze, I realized her meaning. Brielle and her family didn't have a silver bullet.

At the time of Brielle's arrival to my coven, it had been the last thing on my mind, and I hadn't known she'd be staying so long.

I swallowed and nodded. "Right." I hesitated as I considered this. We didn't have any spares—each vampire in the coven had enough rounds to fill their pistol, and I didn't want any of my men to be short a bullet. "Guadalupe, you visit the silversmith tomorrow. See if he can fashion you a weapon of some kind. A silver stake perhaps."

I was unpleasantly reminded of the wooden bullets the Count had made last year that he'd tried to shoot at me. How odd to be shifting weaponry around like this—wooden bullets and silver stakes.

But it had to be done.

"Of course," Guadalupe said, inclining her head.

"Report to me tomorrow night with your progress," I said. "We'll rendezvous nightly and alternate between each other's homes. Try to use the servants' entrance if you can."

My friends all nodded, exchanged fierce glances that reminded me why I trusted them. The five of us were the only demons in the coven who were Second Tier, which gave us an extra burst of power due to the blood rituals we'd performed. Normal banishing spells and forms of torture didn't weaken us as they would First Tier demons, but they were still harmful.

"Thank you all," I whispered. "And please be safe."

I clasped hands with each of them before they left.

Guadalupe, Miguel, and Eduardo all departed, but Jorge lingered, his arms still crossed.

I raised my eyebrows. "What is it?"

"If Benito does intend to challenge you—"

"Then it will mean another battle for our people. I know." I sighed and rubbed the back of my neck.

Jorge's lips pressed together in a thin line. "I don't think we will win a battle against Benito's pack. Not so soon after the losses we suffered at the Count's hand."

"I know."

Jorge's eyes were guarded as he watched me. "But . . ." He trailed off, dropping his gaze.

"Speak your mind," I said impatiently.

"But with the firebird," Jorge said, "we will have an advantage."

I looked at him sharply. "No."

"Leo—"

"I am *not* endangering her. And you know what Benito will do if he finds out what she's capable of."

"She's a part of this coven, Leo!" Jorge said, his voice rising. "You fought for that, and now she's here. You've ordered us to protect her as one of our own. She should fight as one of us too."

I shook my head. "Her connection to the firebird is unstable. I fear releasing the creature in battle might do us more harm than good."

"If Benito wipes all of us out, it won't matter what harm the creature causes."

I flashed him a dark look as rage stirred within me. "Don't challenge me on this, Jorge. We still have a fortnight. For now, let us wait and observe. If the situation proves dire, then . . ." I paused, unwilling to make a promise I wouldn't keep. "Then, I'll consider it."

Jorge raised an eyebrow, his eyes filled with doubt. "Thank you. And in the meantime, I implore you to consider our previous conversation."

I stiffened and clenched my teeth, recalling how he'd accused me of making poor decisions because of my feelings for Brielle. "Jorge," I growled.

Something in my voice must have struck him, because his mouth snapped shut as if he reconsidered arguing with me. Instead, he inclined his head politely before departing.

I ran a hand down my face, feeling as exhausted as a mortal. My hands shook as I left the kitchen.

I couldn't bear this hunger, this crippling ache in my bones. I had to do something, especially if I needed to keep my wits about me with Benito's pack lurking nearby.

Without bothering to wait for Guadalupe, I sought out Estrella myself. Like with Brielle, I entered through the back and found Estrella lounging on a chaise sofa and reading a book. Her robe fell off her legs, revealing a smooth stretch of tan skin that made my stomach clench.

She looked up at my presence, not at all surprised to see me. No doubt she sensed my presence through the bond we shared. My own blood hummed with satisfaction upon seeing her.

"Leo," she purred, dropping her book to the table and sitting up. "It's been so long, dear."

Yes, it has. Because my blood yearned for another.

But I shoved the thought from my mind and strode toward her. She made to rise, but I growled, "Don't."

I discarded my cloak and slid onto the sofa next to her, cupping her face in my hands and kissing her fervently. She gripped my collar, pulling me closer until I was reclined on top of her. My skin burned and fire coiled in my chest. My blood cried out with urgency, and I lowered my lips to her neck. She moaned in my ear as my fangs pierced the skin of her throat. Her blood flooded my mouth, filling me with the sweet, tangy nectar I longed for.

But even as we fed on each other, even as we succumbed to the urges spurred on by the feeding, as we drowned ourselves in pleasure and pure ecstasy, I couldn't deny the growing regret inside me.

The desperate desire to share this with someone else. Someone who wasn't Estrella.

8

BRIELLE

FIRE CONSUMED MY DREAMS. A PIERCING SCREAM cut through the haze of my subconscious. I tried to hide from it, but it grew louder and shriller.

No, I tried to shout. *No, please don't make her do it. Please don't make Nix kill innocent people again!*

But as the scream drew closer to me, I realized it wasn't a person.

It was Nix.

I jerked awake covered in sweat. My chest rose and fell with rapid breaths, and I sat up quickly. Moonlight streamed in through the window, illuminating the sleeping form of my sister next to me. Wiping sweat from my brow, I slowly climbed out of bed and crept out of the room. In the privacy of the hallway, I sucked in several deep breaths, trying to clear my head and calm my racing heart.

I closed my eyes once my breathing had slowed. "Nix?" I whispered. "Are you there?"

I waited, trying to wipe my mind clean and allow her access. I thought of her flames and the heat that often boiled within me.

But I heard nothing. She wasn't there.

Unease spread through me. I'd been so certain she was dormant and there was nothing to worry about. But with Lilith returning, and now this nightmare, I feared something was terribly wrong with my phoenix.

My fingers itched to move, to find a task to keep me busy. Unfortunately, our tiny house didn't have much of a library. Just a few dusty tomes I'd already organized last week in my desperate need to feel useful.

It almost made me miss the days in the Castillo de Coca when I would creep downstairs to the massive library and organize shelves of books in rainbow order.

My breath caught in my throat. *The Count's library.* Leo and I hadn't finished searching because Ignacio had interrupted us. Now that I'd finished reading the book about portals, I'd reached a dead end. I needed something else.

If I could steal into the castle and find more books about Lilith, maybe it would tell me how to defeat her once and for all. Then, I could get Nix back.

Resolve pulsed through me, and I slipped back into my room to change into my shirt and trousers. After arming myself with my athame and stake, I drew my cloak around me and crept out the back door.

The night was eerily still. Even the crickets were quiet, which made my skin prickle with suspicion. I pulled my hood up to cover my face in case anyone lurked nearby. My fingers brushed against the hilt of my athame, and its weight was a comfort as I walked between alleys to get onto the main road.

A sharp, vinegar stench filled my nose, and I stopped in my tracks. The scent lingered for a moment before it vanished. Still, I waited. My limbs were tense, and my body straightened, ready for a fight.

I knew a demon lurked nearby. But he obviously wasn't going to show himself.

At least not yet.

Let him think I haven't smelled him. I strode forward purposefully, quickening my pace. The smell returned, and I had to squash my instinct to whirl around and draw my weapon.

I turned a corner, then rushed down a side road before pivoting back down a different road.

Heavy footsteps sounded behind me. *I knew it.*

Under my breath, I whispered a spell.

"*Magic above and powers that be,*

Conceal me from he who follows me."

My hands glowed blue. Magic burned along my entire body, filling me with warmth.

I pushed faster and farther until I reached a towering cathedral with massive turrets that cast shadows on the concrete. I melted into the shadows and held perfectly still, trying to calm my thundering heart so it wouldn't give me away. Hopefully, the cloaking spell would conceal my scent from whatever predator was chasing me.

A figure emerged at the end of the street and faltered, looking around. When he stepped into the glow of the moonlight, my mouth fell open.

It was one of Leo's men—Miguel.

Why the hell is he following me?

As soon as I thought it, the answer was obvious. Leo ordered him to. Whether to protect me or to keep me from hunting demons myself, I didn't know. I gritted my teeth in anger. Leo didn't have the gall to tail me himself? Or even warn me? I might've attacked Miguel if I'd acted on instinct.

I almost stepped forward to reveal my hiding place when Miguel suddenly whirled around, drawing his dagger. Then, he relaxed. "What is it?" he hissed.

A second figure emerged from behind Miguel. "Leo needs you. Now."

I recognized that voice. It was Jorge. I resisted the urge to back farther into the shadows. Jorge hated me. It wouldn't be pretty if he found me sneaking around the neighborhood like some hoodlum.

"He told me this takes top priority," Miguel said, gesturing around vaguely with his dagger.

My heart lurched at his words. *Top priority?* Why was Leo so concerned about having me followed?

Something heavy settled in my stomach. Perhaps he didn't trust me. It shouldn't have been surprising. I was unpredictable and stubborn. I didn't follow the rules. And most importantly, I was a light witch who didn't technically belong to his coven.

Despite all this, I couldn't deny the disappointment that filled me.

"He said your assignment can wait," Jorge said in a low voice. "This is urgent."

Miguel nodded once and followed Jorge back down the street. I waited until their figures vanished before I emerged and hurried after them.

I wasn't sure why I followed. It obviously wasn't my business. But if it was urgent, maybe I could help.

I also suspected this might be another rogue demon. Lately, Leo seemed more concerned with apprehending the demons peacefully than with saving innocent mortals. I couldn't let someone else get hurt. Not if I could help.

Grateful I cast the cloaking spell, I edged closer to Jorge and Miguel until suddenly, they shifted. Black smoke unfurled from their hands, enveloping them like an embrace. Then, they both reappeared as ravens, soaring high into the sky.

"Damn it," I muttered, gazing upward to where the two ravens circled each other in the sky. Squinting, I struggled to keep up with them, but they blended into the midnight sky perfectly.

I was about to give up and head toward the castle like I'd planned when a bloodcurdling scream pierced the air, chilling me to my bones. Goosebumps rose on my skin, and I sprinted toward the screams, clutching my athame tightly as I ran.

I paused to sniff the air, and a familiar fishy smell filled my nose. *Shapeshifter.* Could it be the same one I'd encountered before?

Damn Leo. I would've banished the demon if Leo hadn't interrupted.

Following the scent, I rounded another corner and then froze.

Jorge, Miguel, and Leo surrounded a motionless figure on the ground. The same fishy smell mingled with something charred like smoked meat. The mixture was so foul I almost plugged my nose.

Behind Leo and his men was another man I didn't recognize, but his yellow rimmed eyes marked him as a werewolf. He struggled with a woman whose face was taut, her eyes wide with horror. Her robe hung loosely over her shoulders as if she'd rushed out of her house, and her hair was a dark, tangled mass.

When I drew closer, Leo's eyes locked onto mine. Something churned within me, and my blood burned as if sensing his nearness. Suddenly, my mouth felt dry, and I yearned for the sweet, empowering taste of his blood. The thrilling sensation of his fangs cutting into me, and the delicious feel of his lips as he gulped down my blood . . .

Get a grip, Brie! I suppressed a shudder of revulsion and squashed the feeling down.

"Who's this?" the unfamiliar man said sharply.

"A friend," Leo said shortly, his eyes never leaving mine. His jaw was tight, and his eyes blazed with a warning.

Was he warning me? Or this stranger?

"Don't hurt her!" I shouted, hurrying toward the woman as she thrashed against the new guy's grip. I touched the woman's shoulder, drawing her eyes to me. "Are you all right?"

The woman's lower lip trembled, and she pointed a shaky finger at the lifeless creature on the ground. She crossed herself and whispered, "*Monstruo.*"

Monster.

I followed her gaze and realized it was the shapeshifter. Half its body was a smoking husk that filled the air with ash. Red welts covered its arms and legs. I knew with certainty that it was dead.

But what had killed it?

My gaze slid to Leo, who was watching me, his brows knitted together. His eyes were guarded, and concern swam in his gaze.

Concern for *me*?

"What the hell's going on?" I demanded.

"Who are you?" the man in front of me barked, baring his teeth at me. Fangs extended from his front teeth, and his yellow eyes gleamed.

"I'm the only one here who gives a damn about the civilians, apparently," I snapped. I turned back to the woman and touched her cheek. She flinched before meeting my gaze.

"Are you hurt?" I asked in Spanish.

The woman shook her head.

I took a breath and leaned closer to her. "You're safe now. The monster is dead, and we're here to protect you. But you have to go back inside. Lock your door. Stay off the street until sunrise. Do you understand?"

The woman nodded so rapidly she looked like a bobblehead. I clasped her hand in both of mine and said, "It'll be all right."

The woman just kept nodding as she slowly backed up until she reached the door behind her. Her hands fumbled as she opened the door and disappeared inside. The fluttering of curtains at the window told me she was watching closely.

My sharp gaze cut to the new guy. "What's your problem?"

His nostrils flared as he crossed his arms, looking me over from head to toe. "What kind of lady addresses me like that?" He looked at Leo and I realized this man wasn't speaking to me.

Rage boiled in me, and I took a step toward him, raising my athame until the dagger's edge rested on his chin. The man didn't even flinch.

"I'm no lady," I growled. "And I can cut you to ribbons if I wanted to."

The man smirked as he gazed down at me. He towered over me by at least a foot, so I knew I wasn't very intimidating.

Perhaps he needed a demonstration.

With a swift movement, I sliced my athame against his cheek, creating a long line of blood that dripped onto his shirt.

He sucked in a breath and raised a hand to his injury. His fingers came back covered in blood. Suddenly, he rose several inches in height, and white fur sprang on his arms and face. In a beastly growl, he said, "You little—"

"Benito!" Leo roared.

Benito's yellow eyes fixed on Leo, and slowly he shrank back to his normal height. His fur receded, and he hissed, "Tell your whore to control herself."

Anger burned within me, but a flash of black shadows swept past me. In an instant, Leo had Benito by the throat. Both demons bared their fangs at each other, and their eyes glowed with intensity. Magic swirled in the air like a looming threat.

"How about I let her run you through instead?" Leo said, his voice dangerously soft. "I'd rip your throat out myself, but she's more than capable." He turned to me. "What do you say, Little Nightmare?"

An unfamiliar feeling swelled within me, and it wasn't until I lifted my chin that I realized it was *pride*. Leo was complimenting me.

I turned to face Benito. "You must be the new werewolf in town."

Benito jerked away from Leo, his nostrils flared and his brown hair mussed. After straightening his shirt, he looked at me and raised an eyebrow. "What are you?" He sniffed, and I knew he was trying to figure out if I was a demon or a witch.

His sense of smell wouldn't help him at all.

My eyes flicked to Leo, who went rigid as Benito scrutinized me. Remembering Leo's warning about Benito, I sheathed my dagger and crossed my arms. "I'm Leo's Donor."

Leo stiffened, and Jorge's eyes went wide.

I really had no idea why I said it. I just knew I couldn't tell him I was a witch, but I couldn't lie and say I was a demon. My best defense was something close to the truth— something that wouldn't make Benito dig further into my background. Or my family.

I couldn't summon any magic. So it was smartest to pretend I was a mortal.

Benito's eyes narrowed as he looked at Leo, whose face

had smoothed into a look of amused interest. "What's your Donor doing wandering the streets at night?"

"Leo taught me to fight," I said before Leo could respond. "And I don't follow orders very well. As you can see." I offered an embellished curtsy that made Leo smirk.

"Some demons in the city have been giving us trouble," Leo said smoothly. "It isn't anything we can't handle, but I tasked Brielle with helping us with the mortals while we take care of the rogue demons."

"Brielle?" Benito looked at me with a frown. "Are you—"

"I'm not French," I said loudly.

Leo snorted and quickly disguised it as a cough. I glared at him.

"And what happened to this one?" Benito gestured to the smoking husk that had once been the shapeshifter.

"Dark warlock, no doubt," Leo said, nudging the shapeshifter's leg with his boot. "We've been chasing an Elemental demon for a few days now. We found a few other bodies just like this. At least this time it seems he did us a favor by taking out one of his comrades."

I remained very still, knowing Leo was lying. I'd been hunting the streets for weeks. There hadn't been a single body like this before. And there certainly wasn't an elemental warlock running around.

Leo met my gaze, his eyes flashing with intensity. A sick

feeling of realization settled in my stomach as I remembered the nightmare I'd had. The screaming.

Had Nix done this?

The grimness in Leo's face told me he suspected the same. Which was why he had urgently sent for his men. And also why he hadn't wanted me there to begin with.

I swallowed, trying to hide the horror on my face.

"Thank you for intervening, Benito," Leo said, hitching a smile back on his face. "But we'll take it from here. Go and tend to your pack."

Benito's yellow eyes drifted over each of us. Jorge and Miguel looked him in the eye, their gazes hard and determined. When Benito looked at me, he eyed me up and down with such slowness that I wanted to punch him in the face. I balled my hands into fists as he smirked at me.

"A pleasure to meet your acquaintance, Miss Brielle." He bowed deeply. As if he weren't still bleeding from my attack.

The bastard.

I scowled at him and made no response. After a moment, he chuckled before turning on his heel and vanishing down the street.

I edged closer toward Leo. "What—"

He raised a hand to silence me, his gaze fixed on the end of the road. I looked around nervously, and then I sensed it. A faint dog smell whispered in the wind. Shadows shifted around us.

Benito's pack was watching.

"I think we're long past overdue for a feeding, my dear," Leo said, smiling at me with a startling amount of warmth. "Shall we?"

I glanced at Miguel, who shrugged, and Jorge, who eyed me with suspicion. Then, I cleared my throat. "Uh, yeah. Let's go."

Leo took my arm and guided me down the street. My arms and back felt stiff, but I couldn't relax knowing there were werewolves hiding and watching us. Leo, on the other hand, stepped with smoothness and grace, his face the picture of confidence.

Sometimes I hated how effortless he made everything look.

After a few minutes of silence, we reached the street we both lived on. My house was the third on the left, and Leo's was the huge mansion at the end of the road.

I relaxed my grip on his arm. "Thanks," I muttered. "I'll take it from here." My house was mere steps away.

But Leo gripped my elbow, his eyes flashing with warning. With the barest shake of his head, he said, "I need to feed, Brielle. I promise it won't take long." His voice was pitched a bit louder than normal, and my insides froze with realization.

The wolves were still watching.

I couldn't smell them. Which meant they were stealthier than I thought.

My skin crawled at the thought of the wolves watching *my* house. Were they spying on my family too?

Fear gripped my throat, threatening to suffocate me. I nodded slowly and followed Leo to the end of the road. The back of my neck prickled with the presence of unseen foes, but I resisted the urge to draw my weapon and turn to face them.

When Leo reached the huge oak doors of his home, a servant pushed them open for us to enter. The servant bowed low without glancing twice at me.

The doors shut behind us, and I exhaled with relief. Leo raised a finger and gestured toward the end of the hallway. Frowning, I followed him past an ornate spiral staircase and paintings that reminded me of the Castillo de Coca. We descended downstairs until we reached the servants' quarters. A few maids looked up at us with wide eyes before bustling out of our way.

"Is this really necessary?" I grumbled, crossing my arms.

"If we want privacy, yes," Leo said in a low voice.

I huffed a sigh. "So how long before I can go home? My parents are probably worried."

"I'll send word that you're safe."

I narrowed my eyes. "Are you saying I can't go home?"

Leo pressed his lips together and exhaled through his nose. "You shouldn't have told him you were my Donor."

I threw my hands in the air. "What else was I supposed

to say? He'd know I was lying if I said I was a dark witch! I couldn't exactly tell him the truth, could I?"

"You shouldn't have been there at all!" Leo snapped. "What were you even doing out in the middle of the night? I told you to take care while Benito's pack is here."

"You failed to mention I'd have to remain locked in my own house," I said coldly. "Must I ask your permission to go to the market? Or visit my friends? Or go for a stroll?"

Leo's eyes flashed. "Don't patronize me, Brielle. You know full well those tasks wouldn't arouse as much suspicion as you sneaking out to hunt demons."

"I wasn't Demonhunting!" I cried.

"Then what the hell were you doing?"

I bit my lip and hesitated. Anger blazed in his eyes, mingling with an earnest emotion I almost didn't recognize. Concern.

He was worried about me.

I swallowed, my throat suddenly dry. "I was trying to get back into the castle. To find books about Lilith."

Leo ran a hand along his face and turned away from me, swearing under his breath. "Brielle, tracking down Lilith *cannot* be your priority right now. If one of Benito's men found you with a book about summoning Lilith—"

"I didn't have a choice!" I said. "I think something might be wrong with Nix." I paused. "And judging by that shapeshifter, I think you do too."

Leo fell silent, his face slackening in surprise. "I—I can't be certain that's what happened."

I lifted my chin. "But you suspect it. Don't you?"

He read the implication in my eyes. The words I wouldn't say: that Lilith might be possessing my phoenix again and killing people.

Leo's eyes were grim as he nodded. "Did you . . . feel anything from her? Anything to indicate she might've attacked someone?"

Though my instincts screamed to keep it to myself, I knew I could trust Leo. Sooner or later, I had to face the fact that I wasn't alone. "Yes. But in my dream, she was screaming in agony. I thought *she* was hurt. It didn't sound like anyone else was there."

Leo rubbed his chin, his eyes distant.

"What happened when you found the shapeshifter?" I asked quietly.

"Jorge and I felt a burst of dark magic. I arrived first and found the shapeshifter already dead. Whoever killed him was long gone."

My stomach roiled, and my arms felt numb. I closed my eyes. "Last time . . . last time she attacked, I time traveled. That didn't happen this time. Maybe . . ." I trailed off, realizing how hopelessly optimistic I sounded.

What other explanation was there? Unless there *was* another Nightcaster somewhere out there.

It wasn't a great alternative.

Leo crossed his arms and drew closer to me. My blood thrummed at his nearness, and heat swelled inside me. "I am here for you, Brielle. I will help you locate your firebird and end this. I promise you."

I raised my eyes to meet his. His gaze burned with sincerity and desire. My lips parted, and my throat felt unbearably dry. I wanted to lean in, to press myself against him, to feel his skin against mine.

"I need to go," I said, my voice cracking. I dropped my gaze and turned away, but Leo gently grasped my wrist.

"I'm afraid you can't leave."

Unease spread through me. "Why not?"

Leo grimaced. "I'm sorry, Brielle. But if you're to keep up the ruse that you're my Donor, you need to stay here with me."

I stiffened. *Stay in Leo's house? No. Absolutely not.* "Leo—"

"Estrella is already here," Leo went on. "I've ordered everyone in the coven to gather their Donors to ensure they're safe while the wolves are here."

My head reared back, my blood boiling. "Estrella is living with you?"

Leo raised his eyebrows as if to say, *So what?*

Something in me deflated. Right. *So what, Brie? Why does that matter?* I shook my head. "Are you telling me I can't go home? I can't see my family again?"

"Of course you can see them. But it would be better for

you to pretend they are only acquaintances. If Benito knows your entire family is here, he's bound to find out they aren't all demons, and he'll want to know *why*." Leo paused. "It isn't just for your protection. It's for your family's. Don't you think it would be safer if you stayed with me while we try to locate your firebird? What if something happens while you sleep?"

A lump formed in my throat. I knew he was right. Leo never slept because he was a vampire. But if I caught fire or Nix exploded in the middle of the night, my family would be vulnerable. Unprotected.

I rubbed my forehead. "How long do I have to stay here?"

"No longer than a fortnight. By then Benito will be gone."

I swore and dropped my hand. *Merciful Lilith, how am I supposed to survive here for two whole weeks?* I pictured Leo and Estrella having intercourse in the room next to mine, and my blood throbbed with rage and longing.

There's no way. I can't do this.

But what choice did I have?

With a sigh, I said, "Fine. I'll stay here."

9
LEO

You must be insane, Leo Serrano.

Of course I was. I'd insisted Brielle stay with me even though I'd been trying to distance myself from her to keep the bloodlust at bay. I'd reignited the bond between myself and Estrella for that particular reason.

But then she had to lie and say she was my Donor.

In all honesty, the lie had been clever. Pretending to be a mortal was the safest thing for her. I couldn't deny her resourcefulness in coming up with the lie so quickly.

But damn it all, she'd be living in my house.

Though my muscles ached and my mind spun from the human blood living under my roof, I forced myself to stay indoors. If Brielle was having trouble with her firebird, I couldn't leave her unattended while she slept.

I tried to avoid imagining her sleeping blissfully, her beautiful golden hair strewn all over her face. Instead, I undressed and wrapped my satin robe around myself before disappearing into the library.

My sister, Lucia, had taken extensive notes during her time as a Nightcaster. Perhaps she had written something that could help Brielle.

As I read, I had to reconcile myself with the fact that Lucia envisioned her phoenix as a male while Brielle insisted hers was female. I wasn't sure how they knew, but each Nightcaster had a special bond with their own particular phoenix—who was I to question them?

After hours of searching, my throat felt dry and my body yearned for blood. I knew it was the bloodlust talking. Ordinarily I could go at least three days without feeding.

Having my Donors here in the house wasn't helping.

I was about to slam my sister's journal shut when I came across an interesting entry.

Today I fed from a light witch. I left her alive, of course. She attacked me and I had little choice. But the blood of a light caster within me makes me feel ill.

The firebird senses it. I can tell. He has distanced himself from me. I fear I have lost him. And if that's true, then he will be claimed by Lilith.

I must find a way to draw him back. But I don't know how. I will talk to Ronaldo to see what he thinks.

My body went rigid, and a gasp of surprise stuck in my throat. I feverishly turned the page, but the next entry was blank. I flipped over several pages until I found another entry.

The fevers continue. I know Ronaldo worries. He doesn't hide it well from me. Leo, however, could fool us all. But I can read the sorrow in his eyes. He knows I'm not well.

I've tried connecting to the firebird to no avail. I fear Lilith will take him and destroy those I love.

I will try one last time and pray to God I succeed.

My throat felt tight as I turned the page, knowing what I would find. I'd read this entry a thousand times.

I am too late. The fire consumes me. All is lost.

Pray for me, Ronaldo.

Pray for us all.

I closed my eyes and clenched the spine of the journal so tightly it started to bend. My hands shook, and my eyes warmed with tears that would never come.

I had no doubt Ronaldo had prayed for her. But his prayers hadn't saved her. Or himself.

I took a breath. *Focus, Leo.* My eyes opened, and I turned back to the entry about the light witch. With a frown, I read through it twice before something struck me.

Could the light magic in my sister have pushed away the firebird? Was that why Lucia had never been able to bond with her phoenix?

Had my sister died because she'd drunk from a light witch?

My blood pulsed with urgency as I looked up from the journal. My thoughts turned to Brielle.

Was she about to suffer the same fate?

I stayed in my study for hours, leafing through notes and research from Lucia and Ronaldo. I had a few texts about demon lore, dark spells, and exorcisms that I'd purchased long ago to try to help Lucia. Though I'd scoured them and knew they wouldn't be much help, I still thumbed through them again to see if I'd missed anything. The longer I worked, the more I convinced myself I had to find the answer to Lilith's return.

And I had to know if Benito was involved.

My original intent in researching was to help Brielle. But I was certain the recent events in the city were connected: Lilith's voice, the rogue demons, Benito's surprise arrival, and Brielle's difficulty communicating with her firebird.

The question was, how was Lilith able to influence all of this? How was she connected?

Jorge's familiar cinnamon and woodsmoke scent tickled my nose, and I felt his presence before he knocked on the open door.

"Enter," I said without looking up.

"Guadalupe needs help," Jorge said. "There's a situation with the silversmith."

I lifted my gaze from Ronaldo's notes about Lucia's curse. "What kind of situation?"

"He's been infected by a werewolf."

I lurched to my feet, dropping books and papers on the floor in my haste. I quickly dressed and grabbed my pistol and knives. Before I reached the door, a voice at the top of the stairs stopped me.

"Where are you going?"

I looked up to find Brielle wearing a robe, her arms crossed and her hair distractingly wild and free.

I swallowed and plastered an easy smile on my face. "Coven business. Don't trouble yourself."

Brielle took a step down the stairs and leveled a hard gaze at me. "If this is related to demons attacking villagers, I need to come with you."

I sighed. "Brielle—"

"You said we would do this together, Leo," she snapped. "Besides, it's the middle of the day. You need someone who can be in daylight. *Without* enduring pain," she added when I opened my mouth to tell her I was perfectly able to walk about in broad daylight.

"What I *need*," I said in an even tone, "is someone who understands the politics of having another demon clan in the city. A werewolf is involved, and the last thing I want is to inadvertently start a war with Benito's pack."

"I can be civil," Brielle said, lifting her chin.

I raised an eyebrow and exchanged a doubtful look with Jorge.

Brielle dropped her arms against her thighs, her robe falling open to reveal a tantalizing portion of her collarbone. "Look, I'll come with you only to handle the commoners. Crowd control. I won't interfere with any of Benito's wolves."

Crowd control. What the hell did that mean? I sighed and ticked my jaw back and forth. If I refused, she would just follow me. Of that I was certain. "Do you swear it?"

"Absolutely."

I exhaled, ignoring Jorge's warning look, and gestured for Brielle to join me.

"One second." Brielle turned and dashed back down the hallway to change. A minute later, she emerged in trousers and a tight tunic. Knives and stakes were holstered along her belt, and her hair was tied into a braid that fell over one shoulder. A fierce glint in her eye made her seem like a soldier ready for battle.

She was the most beautiful thing I'd ever seen.

Calm yourself, Leo. You've been holed up in your study for too long.

I shook my head and raised my eyebrows, trying to appear mildly interested. "Shall we?"

Brielle offered a stiff nod. I shot a wary glance at her stakes, and Brielle rolled her eyes. "Force of habit," she said.

"Who knows? Maybe a vampire from another coven will start attacking. Then, you'll wish someone had these."

Brielle strode out the door before I could respond. I moved to join her, but Jorge caught me by the arm.

"You're letting her carry stakes?" he said in a low murmur, his eyes flashing.

I stared at him. "I don't *let* her do anything, Jorge. She makes her own choices."

"If she's a member of this coven, she should abide by your rules."

"I trust her." I eyed the skepticism in Jorge's face and added, "It's your suspicion of her that convinces me she should be armed with stakes. If I trusted every vampire in my coven not to harm her, then I wouldn't be concerned."

Jorge's head reared back. "You think *I'll* harm her?"

"No. But you aren't the only one to have misgivings about her presence in the coven. I know she feels safer being armed. And so do I."

Jorge shook his head, his nostrils flaring. "You treat her as an equal, Leo. She is *not* your equal."

"She isn't my subordinate either. She's here temporarily, Jorge. As my guest."

"Are you certain of that?"

We stared at each other for a long moment. Jorge's eyes blazed with a challenge, and I clenched my teeth, refusing to answer.

We joined Brielle outside. Jorge and I both stiffened in

the blinding light of the sun. Together, we pulled our hoods over our faces, and the burn against my skin subsided slightly.

Jorge took the lead, guiding us through a throng of people gathered in the market exchanging coin for produce, clothing, and other goods. I sensed the steady pulse of Brielle behind me, and my blood knew she wasn't far behind. I tried to ignore how unsettling it was to be able to sense her so clearly among so many other mortals.

It's fine, I told myself. *I can control this.*

With each passing day, I questioned my decision to share blood with her. But every time I reconsidered, I knew it had been my only option. She'd been battling Lilith. If I hadn't jolted her from it, Lilith might have claimed her.

And if I hadn't fed her my blood, she might have died from the blood loss.

But with that simple exchange came an unbreakable bond. It wasn't enough for me to taste her blood—I'd done that before when we first met. No, once I tasted her and she had tasted me, our blood was linked.

And I wanted more.

She seemed to be handling it quite well. Perhaps the bloodlust didn't affect Nightcasters as much.

Or perhaps being a witch helped her control it.

I shook the thoughts from my head, focusing on the dark shape of Jorge in front of me. *Not now, Leo. There are more important things to think about.*

We entered the silversmith's forge and lowered our hoods. Brielle approached behind me and looked around, inhaling deeply. I smelled it too. Wet dog.

A werewolf had certainly been here.

I ensured my pistol was loaded properly before cocking it and nodding to Jorge.

He jerked his head toward the back. We weaved through tables stocked with tools and various hunks of metal.

The forge was quiet. *Too* quiet.

I sniffed the air again. A subtle smell tainted the scent of wet dog. I also sensed mortals—their blood and sweat—but something else whispered past me. Something dark and familiar.

I flung out an arm to stop Brielle. She froze, looking at me in alarm.

I'd smelled the same thing when we'd encountered Ignacio. I widened my eyes at Brielle, and she frowned, closing her eyes. I felt her inhale again, focusing. Then, her eyes snapped open, and I knew she sensed it too.

"Over here," came Jorge's faint voice.

We followed him around the corner to where a prone figure lay on the ground, his eyes wide open. Guadalupe was crouched at his side, staring grimly into his face.

He wasn't breathing.

"Paralysis from the infection," Guadalupe said quietly. "That has to be it. I've never seen a mortal die so suddenly from a werewolf bite."

I drew closer and lifted the man's arm where a large gash still dripped blood. The jagged teeth markings surrounded the angry, festering wound. I pressed a hand against the man's chest, searching for some sign of life.

Nothing. His blood was silent, and his heart was frozen. But energy still thrummed from him, tickling the hairs on my arms.

"This is no ordinary infection," I murmured, glancing back at Brielle. Her face had gone pale, and her wide eyes moved from the silversmith and back to me.

"It's Lilith," Brielle whispered.

Jorge stiffened and cast a bewildered look at me. "Lilith? You can't be serious."

"I smell her, Jorge," I said sharply. "This is more than just a werewolf attack. Something dark was here. Something bigger than one of Benito's dogs."

But that didn't mean Benito wasn't behind it. If anything, this confirmed my suspicion that Lilith was somehow involved with the werewolf pack.

"Miguel sent for Benito," Guadalupe said quietly. "He should be here soon to answer for this."

I looked at Brielle. "If you wish to do something here, make it quick."

Brielle's brow furrowed as she looked at me questioningly. I held her gaze for a moment, and slowly, she nodded. She took a deep breath and crouched down to the silversmith's body. Pressing a hand against his chest, she uttered a spell.

"*Surrounding magic, gather near.*

Reveal the presence of darkness here."

Her hands glowed blue, and she pressed her magic against the man's chest.

Suddenly, the man gasped—a sickening, rattling sound that made my bones quiver. The silversmith's eyes opened, and they were all black. He sucked in breaths as if his lungs were filled with ash.

"Who did this to you?" Brielle asked in a hushed voice. Her hands still glowed blue.

The man inhaled as if to speak and then choked, his body seizing.

"Hold him down," Brielle ordered.

Guadalupe pinned the man's arms to the ground to stop him from thrashing.

"Who did this to you?" Brielle shouted. She pressed her hands more firmly against the man's chest, and he cried out as if in pain.

"Wolf," the man croaked weakly. "Darkness. Her eyes. So—so much darkness." He coughed and wheezed. "She calls to me." Slowly, he turned his head to fix his black eyes on Brielle. "She calls to *you*." His head turned even more, and I felt him looking at me. As if he were looking into my soul. "She calls to you too."

A chill swept over me. *Impossible.* I was no Nightcaster.

But even as I thought it, I recalled Ignacio. I remembered how certain Brielle had been that Lilith had possessed him. Despite not being a witch *or* a Nightcaster.

I hadn't believed her. But looking at this man, this mortal who had no connection to Lilith, I couldn't deny the truth.

A grim realization set like ice on my bones. Slowly, I looked at Brielle, and her expression matched mine.

It was true. Lilith had returned. And no one was safe.

10

LEO

BENITO ARRIVED NOT LONG AFTER THE BLUE LIGHT
faded from Brielle's spell. The air was still thick with
tension and fear from what we'd witnessed. As soon as the
spell faded, the man slumped backward. The blackness
from his eyes vanished, and his face went still. Whatever
had possessed his body was now gone.

"What the hell happened here?" Benito demanded
when he appeared behind us.

I shot a glance at Jorge, who nodded slightly. We'd
agreed ahead of time to conceal the truth from Benito.

I turned and gestured angrily toward the dead man. "See
for yourself. One of yours attacked him."

Benito stiffened, his dark eyes narrowing. "Impossible."

Miguel scoffed and crossed his arms.

Benito's yellow eyes flashed to Miguel. "As the alpha,

my mind is linked to my subordinates," Benito said. "I would know if they'd committed this crime."

"And we're supposed to just take your word for it?" Brielle said.

I swore inwardly. Damn that girl and her sharp tongue.

Benito's head snapped toward Brielle, his nostrils flaring. Slowly, his gaze cut to me. "Do you normally bring your Donors to investigate crimes?"

"When it involves mortals, yes," I said in a cool tone, cocking my head at him. "I do find it odd that this city hasn't seen a werewolf in months and yet the day after your pack arrives, we see evidence of a werewolf attack."

A low growl rumbled from Benito's throat as he took a menacing step toward me. Jorge immediately tensed, and Miguel slid between Benito and me, his eyes flashing.

"Consider what you are accusing me of, Leonardo," Benito hissed. Long fangs protruded from his teeth, and gray and white hair sprouted along his arms and neck. "Why would I offer an alliance and then immediately attack your people?"

I waved a hand at the silversmith's body. "He's the only silversmith in the area, which leaves my coven with no means to defend ourselves against your pack." I raised my eyebrows. "Perhaps it isn't an alliance you seek after all, Benito."

Benito crossed his arms, his yellow eyes gleaming. "Then, arrest me. Challenge me to a duel. Take action, Leo."

I said nothing. Instead, I watched him carefully, searching his face and his body for any sign of a lie.

But his chin lifted in confidence, and his eyes revealed nothing but anger.

"I won't challenge you without proof," I said in a soft voice. "But if I find a witness who identifies one of yours as the culprit, I will not hesitate to wage war on your pack."

A tense silence filled the air between us. Brielle's shrewd eyes flicked from me to Benito. Jorge's hand hovered over his dagger belted at his waist. Guadalupe and Miguel stared at Benito with such intensity I was surprised he didn't flinch.

At long last, Benito's mouth stretched in a wide smile, revealing sharp fangs that gleamed with hunger. "As enjoyable as it would be to defeat your little coven, I assure you there isn't any proof to find." He offered a mocking bow and smirked at me before sweeping out of the forge without a second glance.

Brielle exhaled, her shoulders sagging as she stared hard at where Benito had disappeared.

"Do you believe him?" Guadalupe asked in a low voice.

"Of course not," I said with a dry chuckle. "But this means we must be vigilant of all our assets." I looked at Miguel. "Reach out to our blacksmith in Madrid and ensure he is looked after. If Benito cuts off access to our weapons, we won't have much hope of winning a fight against him."

Miguel nodded and left the forge. Guadalupe and Jorge

looked at me expectantly. Brielle, I noticed, kept her gaze fixed on the silversmith's body. Her jaw was taut and her eyes were hard, but I could still sense fear emanating from her.

"Brielle," I said softly, and she met my gaze. "I need to speak with your father. Perhaps, with his vast knowledge of demons, he can help with the situation. Can you arrange a meeting?"

She blinked at me. "I—of course."

I raised my eyebrows, and she looked around in surprise. "Oh, now?"

I laughed. "If you would be so kind."

"Right. Sorry." She shuffled around awkwardly for a moment before disappearing from the forge. I focused on the smell of her blood as she pushed past the throng of people waiting outside.

"Guadalupe," I said in a low voice. "I'll need you to speak with the local authorities. Invent any story you wish, but make sure it does not incriminate our coven."

Guadalupe nodded and left. Above the babble of the crowd, I heard her call for a constable.

I looked at Jorge. "Stay on Benito. I want to know who he corresponds with and where he goes. Intercept his letters if you can. But be discreet."

Jorge nodded but didn't move. He dropped his gaze.

"What is it?" I asked.

"Are we not going to discuss what really happened?" he murmured.

I sighed, rubbing my forehead. "What is there to discuss? We know a wolf was involved. Whatever transpired here is tied to Benito. If we uncover his plan, we'll know more about"—I gestured vaguely around the forge—"all of this."

Jorge raised an eyebrow, his eyes full of doubt. "While I don't doubt Benito is planning something nefarious, I fear you are too blind to see the true source of this."

When I stared blankly at him, he sighed and said, "Brielle."

I stiffened. "What about her?"

Jorge waved a hand at me. "This is what I mean. Your body instantly reacts like I've personally insulted your mother."

I crossed my arms and leveled a stare at him. "What about Brielle?" I growled.

"Lilith wants her firebird. And now Lilith is possessing innocent civilians—not just Nightcasters or even demons. But *mortals*. Her presence here is endangering our coven and this entire city, Leo."

"And if I send her away, then she will simply draw Lilith to a different city," I said through clenched teeth. "It doesn't solve the problem, Jorge."

"Leo—"

I raised a hand to silence him, my body prickling with

unease and alarm. The hairs on my arms stood on end, and I sniffed the air, searching for the danger.

There it was. Blood boiled with fear and anger, mingling with a familiar wet-dog smell.

I surged forward, ignoring Jorge's protests, and shoved through the crowd gathered around the constable and Guadalupe, who had a convincingly distressed look on her face.

A voice echoed in my head. *Stop it,* it said. *Get away from me, or I'll cut you open.*

A chuckle resonated, so close I could practically smell Benito's foul breath. *Oh, I do love your fire, my darling.*

Urgency pulsed through me. Villagers cried out in indignation as I violently pushed my way through them. *Faster. Faster.*

I rounded the corner and found a darkened alley between the church and the fruit market. Two figures huddled together against the wall, one towering over the other. I recognized paws and a long, white tail.

Benito. He'd half shifted.

And he had Brielle pinned against the wall.

A roar split through me, and I saw nothing but red. Nothing but Benito's blood as it cried out to me.

End him. Rip out his throat. Feast on his blood.

Benito suddenly reared back, howling in pain. Brielle's knife protruded from his gut, and he slumped over, his legs shifting back to his human form. Slowly, he staggered to his feet, but Brielle was ready for him. She aimed a kick in his face, and then another in his chest. He toppled over with a groan. Long claws sprang from his fingers, and he swiped them toward Brielle. She leapt out of the way, but one of them sliced through her shirt.

"Enough, Benito!" I bellowed, aiming my pistol at him.

Brielle and Benito looked up. Brielle's eyes were wild with fear and anger, and Benito's face was contorted with rage.

A crack split through the air, and Benito dived out of the way just before the bullet exploded against the concrete of the church. Screams echoed in the market next to us, and Brielle covered her ears, her face draining of color.

In a puff of black smoke, Benito vanished. His white wolf appeared and leapt for me. I ducked, but he soared over my body before vanishing into the crowd. I stared after him, waiting for him to return and finish me off. But the lingering dog scent disappeared entirely. Instead, a gaggle of people peered around the corner into the alley, looking at Brielle and me in panic and concern.

I took Brielle's elbow and looked into her face, searching for any signs of injury. "Did he hurt you?"

Brielle shook her head, her eyes wide and vacant. "N-no. No, I'm fine."

I nodded once, not trusting myself to speak. Instead, I looped her arm through mine and guided her out of the alley. We swiftly made our way through the merchants and villagers, keeping our heads down. I didn't even bother to draw my hood, though I barely felt the sting of the beating sun. All I felt was pure fury coursing through me, setting my blood on fire.

End him. Find him and bleed him dry.

"Leo," Brielle hissed.

I blinked and looked at her. Her eyes were on my lips, and for one wild moment, my stomach flipped with desire. Then, I realized my fangs were out and cutting into my lower lip. A bead of blood welled and dripped onto my shirt.

I took a breath and relaxed my body until my fangs receded. Luckily, the villagers were all too busy haggling to notice.

"Forgive me," I muttered hastily. I felt Brielle look away from me, but I couldn't look at her. To see the fear in her usually fierce expression would be too much for me.

Especially knowing that fear might be directed at me.

I hastily guided her back to our street and to my home. The doors opened at our entrance, and as soon as they shut, I turned to face Brielle. My hands gripped her shoulders, and I ducked my head to look into her eyes. "Tell me what happened."

"Shouldn't we—" Brielle's eyes flitted to the hallway that led to the servants' quarters.

"Let them hear," I growled. "What happened?"

Brielle swallowed and shook her head. "He lingered in the crowd. It was my fault. I wasn't paying attention. I was so focused on that silversmith that I didn't even smell Benito until he'd cornered me."

"What did he want?"

Brielle's mouth twisted in a grimace. "*Me.* He wanted to—" she broke off with a shudder, then shook her head. The fierceness returned to her eyes as she looked at me with a spark of irritation. "I could've handled it without you."

I suppressed a smile. *There's my Brielle.* "I know. You had the situation well in hand."

The corners of her mouth twitched as if she knew my thoughts. Her eyes searched mine, and her face sobered. She touched my arm. "Are *you* all right?"

I blinked. "Me?"

She nodded. "I've never seen you like that before."

I watched her for a long moment, waiting for the fear to return. The revulsion. The horror at what I was. What she undoubtedly knew I wanted to do to Benito.

But there was nothing there but concern. And an emotion swirling in her caramel-colored eyes that I couldn't identify. Something hot and wild that made my blood yearn for her.

"He touched you," I said in a low voice. The animal within me roared, longing to be unleashed. But I had to keep it contained. "He dared to—" I broke off with a choke as crimson anger took over my vision again.

"Hey." Brielle pressed her cool fingers against my cheek,

and I stilled. "Don't you know me? I wouldn't have let him. I can take care of myself."

I knew this. She was one of the most capable huntresses I knew.

And yet, seeing Benito touching her, his hand on her thigh, and his hips pinned against hers . . .

I pushed those thoughts from my mind, knowing they would only ignite the animal within me. Instead, I looked at Brielle, whose eyes blazed with a challenge.

I almost laughed. "I know you aren't weak, Brielle. You bested me in a fight, didn't you?"

Smugness took over the fire in her eyes. "So you admit it?"

I chuckled, but my smile quickly faded. "He had no right to touch you."

"I could smell the lust on him." Brielle swallowed. "If it wasn't me, it would've been someone else."

"But you aren't just anyone," I whispered.

Her fingertips trembled against my cheek, and she sucked in a breath. Her eyes met mine, and they scorched with a familiar heat—similar to the fire that swirled in my stomach. Her blood cried out for me, and I leaned in. She caught her bottom lip between her teeth, and a low growl rumbled in the back of my throat. Her cheeks flushed, but her eyes sparked with desire.

She wants this.

The thought practically jolted me from my haze. It

couldn't be possible. Perhaps I'd misread her. In truth, a woman like Brielle couldn't possibly yearn for a monster like me.

But then her fingers trailed down my jaw until they brushed against my neck. She lifted her other arm until both hands were tangled in my hair.

"Leo," she murmured, her voice a light caress against my face.

Brielle. Oh, my Brielle.

She smelled of the ocean after a storm. Her scent enveloped me in a passionate embrace until it was all I could smell. Slowly, I moved my arms so my hands pressed against her waist. She pushed up against me in response until her hips were touching mine. Her pulse raced, and her face was still red, but she raised an eyebrow at me, beckoning me closer.

Taunting me.

I surged forward until I had her pinned against the wall. The vase on the table next to us rattled, but we never broke eye contact. She grunted when her back met the wall, but her hands gripped my arms, pulling me closer. Beneath me, I felt her legs clench. I ground my hips against hers, and she gasped, closing her eyes. The rapture on her face was almost too much for me. I lifted my hands to her face and stroked my thumb along her lower lip.

"Leo," she rasped again. This time my name was a plea against her lips.

And I couldn't hold back anymore.

I leaned in, tasting her breath, relishing the smell of her sweat and the desire resonating from her. Her lips parted in an invitation. Heat burned where I touched her, rising within me and only adding to my passion.

My lips brushed hers.

Then, fire exploded around her.

At first, I thought I'd imagined it. The heat within me was so severe that it seemed to blend in with the flames burning before me.

But after a moment, I backed away from her, my eyes wide. Her body, her clothes—*everything* was on fire.

"Brielle!" I shouted over the roaring flames that stung my eyes. I resisted the urge to cover my face.

Brielle cried out something incoherent. I almost surged forward to reach her, but the fire then vanished as abruptly as it came. Small patches of ash were smeared along Brielle's cheeks, and my blood chilled at the sight.

Those were the spots I'd touched her.

A charred shadow was imprinted on the wall behind her, but luckily she appeared unharmed. Her blond hair had fallen loose from her braid, and her eyes were wild with panic. But she was fine.

I swallowed, shoving down the painful desire still throbbing within me. "What—what happened?"

Brielle panted, pressing a hand to her chest. "Nix. She's back."

11

BRIELLE

GET AWAY. MUST GET AWAY.

The voice roared in my head until I couldn't see straight. My body ached from the energy the flames had taken from me. My heart still skittered as I remembered what had almost happened between Leo and me.

Get away, Brielle! Now!

"Away from what?" I asked. I felt Leo's questioning eyes on me, but I couldn't meet his gaze.

Away from Lilith. Please, Brielle, get away from her.

Panic lodged in my throat, and I looked around. "She isn't here, Nix."

I felt her. She summoned me.

My blood chilled at her words.

Leo must've noticed the distress on my face. He stepped toward me. "Brielle—"

No! Nix roared. *Get away!*

Her voice was so shrill in my head that I stepped away from Leo, who blinked at me in surprise.

A cold realization settled in my chest. I swallowed and finally met Leo's gaze. "Nix," I whispered, slowly reaching for Leo's hand. I laced my fingers through his, trying to ignore the way my heart thrummed at his touch. His thumb brushed over my knuckles, sending a ripple of pleasure through me. I closed my eyes. "Do you feel her now?"

Leo stiffened and almost dropped my hand, but I squeezed his fingers in mine. Heat burned between our skin.

Yes, Nix said. *Yes, she's here. Please, Brielle, get away from her!*

I let go of Leo's hand and sucked in a breath. "Nix, it isn't her. It's just Leo."

I feel her in him, Brielle. The darkness closes in. She draws nearer. Please.

I blinked, my hands aching to do something productive. But how could I help Nix if I didn't know what was wrong?

She felt Lilith. But it was just me and Leo here, and I trusted him with my life.

Please, Brielle, Nix begged, her voice practically a sob.

I closed my eyes, my throat feeling tight with emotion. When I opened my eyes again, Leo was a few steps away from me, his expression guarded.

I swallowed. "I just need a minute," I told him.

He nodded stiffly, but the concern in his eyes mingled

with something vulnerable that made my stomach clench. Slowly, he turned and walked down the hallway and out of sight. My heart twisted at his departure, but I had to help Nix. If being around Leo caused her pain, I had to find out why.

I sat down on the sofa of the sitting room and smoothed my sweaty palms against my trousers. "He's gone, Nix. How do you feel now?"

A pause. Then, *It's hard to say. I've felt her everywhere, Brielle. It's why I've been so distant.*

I went still. "Where did you go?"

I'm not sure. I could still sense you, but it was a brief echo compared to the connection we once shared. All I knew was darkness. I couldn't fly. I couldn't breathe fire.

"What awakened you?"

Lilith did. When I felt her, I panicked, and suddenly my fire was back. And so were you.

I frowned, shaking my head. "I don't understand. You were disconnected from me, and then you felt Lilith, and now you're perfectly fine?"

That isn't it, Brielle. I'm not fine. I can't access your magic. I can't find it at all. When you were with Leo, I caught a glimpse of it, so I reached for it and—well, you saw what happened.

"But we bonded. I thought once we'd bonded, we shut Lilith out."

So did I. But it seems she's influencing me in other ways.

"How can I stop her? I thought the way for me to shut her out was by bonding with you, but we've already done that."

Yes, Nix said. *You shut her out, so she can't possess you anymore. But she can possess others.*

"Even if they aren't Nightcasters?" I suddenly remembered what Leo had asked me that night in the castle. "Nix, can you sense other phoenixes in the city? Are there any other Nightcasters?"

No. But that's not the only path to Lilith.

"What do you mean?"

Lilith is the only one with direct access to mortals. Specifically, female Nightcasters. But she can still be summoned just like any other demon from the Underworld.

My heart stopped for a full beat, and a shiver raced down my spine. "Are you saying . . . someone has *summoned* Lilith?"

It's the only explanation I can think of. Why else would I be able to sense her everywhere at once? As you said, there are no other Nightcasters. Which means she's here by another method. One we weren't expecting.

I rubbed my forehead. "Nix, what can we do? How can I help you? I can't lose you." Despite the fact that our souls were bonded, I felt a kinship with her that I couldn't understand. She'd saved my life multiple times. Last year she'd even sacrificed herself, reducing her body to ashes in the process. Though she had been reborn and had returned to me, it had still taken its toll on her abilities.

You have to find her and banish her. If she's been summoned, then she can be banished. This makes her more vulnerable than when she'd tried to possess your body.

I nodded. "I'll do what I can. But Nix . . . I can't do this alone. If I work with Leo, is that going to be a problem?"

Nix was silent for a long moment. *I know you trust him, Brielle. But when he touches you, I feel her.*

My whole body felt numb. I couldn't breathe. "No, it can't be true," I whispered.

I can't be certain, Nix said. *It's possible she only has a small hold on him. So small he doesn't even know it's there.*

I knew she was only trying to make me feel better.

But if Leo had been controlled by Lilith this entire time, would I have noticed? Or was I blinded by what I felt for him?

I hunched over and pressed my forehead against my knees, suddenly feeling sick.

"Is everyone a suspect now?" I moaned, my voice slightly muffled. "Should I be suspicious of my parents? My sister? Am I truly alone in this?"

No, Nix said. *It's impossible for her to possess everyone at once. And some people are not compatible hosts for her essence. What I know of the demons of the Underworld is they each have a unique ability, but it has its limitations. Find out what Lilith's limitations are.*

I swallowed and nodded. "Okay." An idea wormed its way into my head, and the tiniest ray of hope shone on the gloomy despair taking over my mind. Maybe there *was* a way to find out who was at risk.

But I had to talk to my parents first.

I grabbed my cloak and left without preamble. A slither of guilt nibbled at my stomach as I realized Leo would probably be worried. But he'd had a tail on me before. I had no doubt Miguel or someone else would be close by if I needed help.

Besides, Benito needed time to heal from my knife wound. I had at least a little time before he retaliated.

I hurried down the street and knocked on my parents' door. A servant opened it and showed me to the sitting room, where I sat awkwardly.

So weird, I thought. *Just a few days ago, I was living here.*

Hasty footsteps pulled me to my feet. Angel stood in the doorway, her eyes wide.

"Brie!" She swept me up in a tight embrace and buried her face in my shoulder. "We were so worried about you! When Leo sent that note, we thought maybe it was a trap—"

"Shh," I hissed urgently, glancing around. "Not here. Look, are Mom and Dad home?"

"Yeah."

"Okay, grab them and meet me downstairs. But don't say anything you don't want overheard."

Angel's brows furrowed in confusion, but she nodded before leaving the room. I hurried down to the servants' quarters, and a few maids immediately stood at my entrance.

"I'm sorry," I said with a grimace. "I need the room for just a moment. If that's okay. You two can go to the sitting room if you like."

The women exchanged appalled looks but hastily curtsied before bustling from the room. I exhaled and wiped sweat from my brow. I still wasn't used to living in the eighteenth century.

In a few moments, Mom, Dad, and Angel joined me at the small table, their expressions equally concerned.

I took a moment to explain the situation with Benito and his pack and the possibility of spies lurking nearby. I omitted my altercation with Benito and the heated moment between me and Leo—but I told them of my conversation with Nix, and her suspicion that someone had summoned Lilith.

After I finished, Mom exchanged a grim look with Dad. "Whoever summoned her was most likely promised something in exchange," Dad said slowly. "Your mom and I once fought an entire army of undead demons brought here by Asmodeus. The demon who summoned him wanted access to this army to make him unstoppable."

I curled my fingers into fists on the table. "Do you think Lilith has promised the same?"

"If every demon has a different specialty, as Nix says, then I'm sure it's something different," Mom said. "But Lilith has a lot of power. She has access to Nightcasters. And, if she succeeds, she'll have access to your phoenix, Brie. It wouldn't be hard to convince someone to join her side in exchange for that kind of power."

A tense silence passed between us as we looked at each other grimly.

"Mom, how much tech did you bring with you?" I asked.

Mom blinked. "Uh, only what I could fit in my bag. Why?"

"Is there a way for you to—I don't know, scan people to see if they're being possessed? To see if Lilith is influencing them?"

Mom's brows furrowed as she thought about this. "Maybe. I do have the aura scanner, but it doesn't work as well in this time period. I can try it. It worked on you when you were comatose for those few months. I was able to confirm Lilith was gone." She exchanged a look with Dad. "That knowledge made things a bit easier while we waited for you to wake up."

I suppressed a shudder. For me, it had been merely hours. But sometimes when Nix lost control, I traveled forward in time.

I remembered Leo's desperation and his overwhelming relief when he'd seen me wake up. My stomach twisted.

"We can't scan *everyone*," Angel said in a quiet voice. "Can we?"

"From what I understand of demon possession, each victim has a marker," Dad said. "Something that lures the demon to them. Like a magnet. Not everyone has this marker. If you can find out what it is, it might help narrow down your suspects."

A marker. My body went numb, and my mouth twisted in a horrified grimace. "A marker . . . like being a Timecaster?"

A stunned silence filled the air around us. Mom had told me she'd scanned the time portal I'd fallen through. Only those who were Timecasters could pass through.

Meaning only those Lilith could possess, since Lilith was reborn through time

Mom sucked in a sharp breath and straightened in her seat. "Of course," she breathed. "Nightcasters have the time travel marker in their blood. But they aren't the only casters who have it."

"How can we find out if someone has the marker?" I asked.

Mom stared hard at the wooden table, her gaze distant as she muttered something incoherent. "Okay, I think I've got it. I'll have to run a few tests on you, Brie. If that's okay. But I should be able to pinpoint the marker so I can identify it in other subjects."

"This is good, though, right?" Angel asked. "There can't be that many Timecasters here."

Mom's lips pressed together in a thin line. "You, me, and Brie," she said quietly, her gaze cutting to me. "Plus anyone who came through that portal. Anyone who lived in the castle with Brie last year."

"That's not all," I said as nausea filled my stomach. "Leo too. His sister was a Nightcaster. He has the marker in his blood."

Which meant Nix could be right.

Lilith could be influencing Leo.

12
LEO

THOUGH EVERY PART OF ME WANTED TO SEARCH FOR Brielle, I knew she needed time away from me. From what I could gather, her phoenix was convinced I was deadly.

Convinced I was *Lilith*.

The thought sent a bolt of unease slicing right through me.

In addition, Benito would be healing from his wounds soon, and I had no doubt he would seek retribution. Perhaps it wasn't the wisest decision to shoot a silver bullet at him. It was practically an act of war.

With a sigh, I changed my clothes and left the house again, saddling the mare from our coven's stables. We didn't often ride horses, as they were frequently spooked by the dark presence inside us. But since there were no Teleporters in the coven, it was our only means of transportation.

Rosita, the skittish mare, was tense during most of the

ride. I paused frequently to murmur soothing words in her ear, which calmed her after a while. We rode hard toward the outskirts of the city. Dark clouds lingered after yesterday's rain, and a thick wind tousled my hair around my face.

At long last, we reached a vast farm manned by slaves. The land stretched for miles, and the air smelled of wheat, sugar cane, and other fresh crops.

I slowed Rosita and dismounted, keeping the reins in my hands as I eased her toward the barn. After ensuring she was properly fed, I approached the farmhouse. It towered impressively over the fields like a grand castle. Which, I'm sure, was exactly what the owner preferred.

Discomfort swirled within me, but I shoved it down. This was my only option.

To a bystander, the farmhouse appeared charming. But dark magic swirled from within its depths, seeping into the air like an invisible fog that threatened to choke me.

I smelled death. I smelled my parents, Ronaldo, and Lucia.

A shudder swept through me, and I clenched my fingers into fists before climbing up the porch steps and knocking on the door. A servant showed me into the parlor and offered to take my cloak, which I refused. Then, I was left alone to breathe in the foul stench of decay and dark magic.

Could the mortals here not sense it? The presence of some otherworldly power that extended beyond the grave?

"My, my," said a calm, frail voice from the doorway. "I did not expect *you* to grace my doorstep, Leonardo Serrano."

My blood pounded in my veins, but I slowly and calmly turned to face the owner of the farmhouse. Forcing a smile, I bowed my head politely. "A pleasure to see you again, Alejandro."

Alejandro offered a cold smile. His wispy white hair was pulled back at the nape of his neck, and his icy gray eyes seemed to peer into my soul. Though he was an old man, he stood almost as tall as I did and strode toward me with elegance and grace. His long, narrow fingers clasped together in front of him.

"There is no need to lie to me, Leonardo," Alejandro said in a soft voice. "You know I can see beyond this facade."

I swallowed and lifted my chin. "I've come to inquire about certain . . . events that are transpiring in the city. Events that seem to be the work of a necromancer such as yourself." *Best not to give away everything and mention Lilith just yet.*

Alejandro's eyebrows lifted. "Indeed?" There was no surprise in his expression.

I stared at him, my mind spinning with possibilities. *Is he involved in this?* "What do you know of it?"

Alejandro chuckled darkly. "No, Leonardo, you cannot intrude on my property and ask me for information while offering nothing in exchange."

A chill of suspicion raised the hair on the back of my neck. *Don't do it, Leo.*

But he obviously knew something. How could I leave here with nothing?

"What is it you require of me?" I asked, struggling to keep my voice even.

"Allow me to read you." Alejandro's eyes glinted in a way that made nausea swirl in my stomach.

No! my mind screamed at me. *Do not go back to that darkness, Leo. Don't do it!*

But this was about more than my own fears. This was about protecting my city. My people.

"Very well," I said quickly before I could change my mind. Every instinct shouted for me to run, to flee this place and never return.

Which was why I hadn't seen Alejandro in so long. Not since my father was alive and had engaged his services.

Because of Alejandro, my father was dead—a memory I often pushed from my mind. Ronaldo and Lucia's deaths I bore with me like a heavy cloak because I was to blame.

But Father's death was different. He sank to the darkest depths of black magic and paid the price for it. Something I swore I would never do.

Which was why I never let the memory inhabit my mind. Until now.

Alejandro's face ignited with a sinister hunger that made my skin crawl. Slowly, he extended his hand for mine. I stiffly stretched my arm and placed my palm against his.

A jolt seared through my skin, creeping through my body like an intruder. I felt the presence probing, searching, invading every inch of me. A biting coldness gripped me, freezing my limbs in place and seeping through my bones until I felt nothing but the chill. Alejandro's presence was a winter storm smothering me in snow and ice until I couldn't see or breathe.

What do you fear? a curious voice murmured in my ear.

Though I was powerless against him, a feeble part of my mind tried to resist. *Keep the door closed, Leo,* I told myself. *Do not open it for him.*

But my own voice was faint compared to Alejandro's. His cold laugh whispered against me as his magic raked through my mind, peeling apart layer after layer.

You fear the dead, Alejandro said in my mind. *You fear the undead as well. The curse of your losses. Facing that pain again and again. You fear the judgment of those who have died because of you.*

A bitter agony hardened in my chest until I hunched over, groaning from the weight of my emotions.

You fear causing further death and pain, Alejandro went on, his voice laced with glee. *You fear darkness beyond your control. Darkness you do not understand. And above all, Leonardo Serrano, you fear me and what I can do. To you. To your family. To your loved ones. And to* her.

With a roar, I shoved against Alejandro's presence in my mind, blocking his access to Brielle. But even as I resisted him, her face swam in my head. Her smile. The fierceness in her brown eyes. The way her golden hair hung over her shoulders.

Alejandro laughed again, and a wild snarl built in my throat. Black magic swirled around me, and the smell of my own powers brought me back to my senses like a memory of home. My shadows gathered around me, and I shifted to my bat form.

Another powerful jolt quivered through me as I shifted and the link between Alejandro and me was broken. I flapped my wings, flitting about as the darkness seeped out of me like ink. I soared higher and higher until I reached the ceiling and could finally breathe again. Then, slowly, I circled back down and shifted back to my vampire form when I landed on the floor.

Panting, I straightened and faced Alejandro, who wore a smug expression on his face.

"When will you learn you cannot hide from me, Leonardo?" he said.

My nostrils flared. "I paid your price. Now answer my questions. What do you know of the events occurring in the city?"

Alejandro smirked and clasped his hands in front of him again. "It is *not* the work of a necromancer."

I already knew this. My eyebrows rose, and I waited for more.

"The gate to the Underworld has been opened," Alejandro said quietly. "Can you not feel it? The change in the air?"

I scowled at him, and he smiled as if I'd said something humorous. "How can it be stopped?" I demanded.

Alejandro shook his head. "You cannot stop it. The price of opening the gate has been paid. The gate cannot be closed without that same price."

"What price?"

"The death of a mortal. Once innocent blood has been shed, the gate is yours to control."

My blood chilled at his words. I didn't like the wicked grin that spread on his face as he talked of killing an innocent mortal.

"It's her, isn't it?" I whispered. "It's—"

"Do not speak her name!" Alejandro bellowed. Shadows crept in the corners of my vision, and an otherworldly power gripped my tongue, freezing it in place so I couldn't speak. Slowly, the shadows receded and the restraint on my tongue loosened. I gasped for breath, hunching over again as I tried to rid myself of Alejandro's power. But it was all around me. Suffocating me.

I have to leave this place.

"The Dark Lady is one of many to abide in the Underworld," Alejandro said. "I cannot tell who has joined us in this realm. I only know the gate is open. My spirits are restless from the energy they feel calling them to the gate."

"If it *is* her," I said slowly, massaging my throat. "How can I stop her?"

Alejandro's lips spread in a cruel smile. "You are powerless against her, Leonardo. There is no use in fighting."

I stepped toward him, rage pulsing within my blood. "Tell me what to do! There must be *something*!"

"The Dark Lady wants something. Something you can help her with. You cannot match her power, so the only way to escape her is to bargain with her."

I blinked. *Bargain with Lilith?* The idea sounded mad. And dangerous. "What—"

"The Seers can tell you more," Alejandro said. "I cannot see the future, Leo. But they can."

Seers? I shook my head, frowning. My mouth opened to ask another question, but Alejandro lifted his hand. My whole body tensed, preparing to fight off his magic again, but nothing happened.

"I have answered enough of your questions, Leonardo," Alejandro said, his voice suddenly cold. "Leave my presence before I demand another reading from you."

A small part of me wanted to argue, to fight for more answers. But I knew better than to challenge him. The image of my father's blank and lifeless face flashed in my eyes—a reminder. A warning.

Alejandro's grin widened, and I knew he could see into

my mind. He saw the fears and darkness there. Grief, regret, and anger flooded my chest like a dam had burst. I'd lost control of myself. My head, my emotions. I couldn't see straight anymore.

Without a word, I turned from Alejandro and strode toward the door. Before I stepped through, Alejandro called out from behind me.

"The girl will be your downfall, you know."

I went rigid, my blood burning within me, urging me onward. But Alejandro seemed spurred on by my stillness.

"You will fall," he said, "because of her."

Enough. I didn't glance over my shoulder. I didn't respond. Instead, I hurled the door open with far too much force and let it slam shut behind me. As I left the farmhouse, the darkness that had clouded my thoughts slowly drained from me, leaving my head clear. But I still felt him probing through me. His presence, like long, clawed fingers, peeling aside every barrier I'd built up over the years, exposing my greatest fears and horrors.

Though his power was gone, the damage had been done. The grief and fear swirled around me like a second cloak as I rode Rosita back to the city.

13

LEO

ONE MORE PLACE TO GO.

I pushed aside the lingering horrors of Alejandro's powers. *Focus, Leo. You have another task at hand. Find the Seers.*

I took a breath and strode down the main road until I reached an unfamiliar house. The dusty concrete was surrounded by a wild azalea bush. I wrinkled my nose as the flowery scent suffocated me, and I rapped briskly on the door.

I blinked when a redheaded fellow cracked open the door and peered curiously at me. Frowning, I glanced behind him. *Where are his servants?*

"Sorry," the man said, opening the door a bit wider. "I'm still not used to having servants in this bloody time." He rubbed the back of his neck and looked me over. Then, his eyes widened. "Leo Serrano? What are you doing here?"

I cleared my throat. "There is something I must discuss with you. May I enter?"

The man's face split into a smile, and he wagged a finger at me. "One of those myths about vampires not being able to enter without an invitation, right?"

I raised an eyebrow, and his smile vanished. He stepped back with a nod. "Of course. Sorry."

The man closed the door after I entered, and I turned to face him. "Riker Wilkinson, I presume?"

Riker nodded and extended his hand. I frowned, and Riker laughed nervously. "Where I'm from, you shake it. It's a greeting."

I stared at him, ignoring his hand. "Brielle says you're a Seer. Can I ask you about your visions?"

The color drained from Riker's face. He glanced over my shoulder as if expecting someone else to appear. "Brielle told you about me?"

Curiosity wriggled through me, but I didn't let it show. Instead, I smiled. "Yes. Would you be able to assist me?"

Riker shifted his weight from one foot to the other. "I, uh, don't normally remember my visions."

"Do not lie to me." I fixed a hard stare at him. "I know you've been discussing them with Angel Gerrick for months now."

Riker staggered back a step and gaped at me. "I—have you been bloody *spying* on me?"

"You live among my coven now," I said coldly. "I keep

my distance, but I have to stay aware of the goings on of my people."

Riker shook his head, his eyes dazed. "Right," he said in a clipped tone, his nostrils flaring. He ran a hand through his hair. "What do you want to know?"

"I need to know the precise wording of the first prophecy you remember."

"Well, I have it memorized. It's—"

I raised a hand to stop him. My gaze darted to the door and windows and back to Riker. "Could you perhaps write it down for me?"

Riker glanced over his shoulder nervously. "Uh, sure. Follow me."

He led me to the study where he scribbled several lines on a piece of parchment. When he handed it to me, I read two similar prophecies:

Three months hence, a choice will be made. A threat will emerge, powerful and afraid. Darkness will rise and cover us all. And then her magic will make us fall.

On this day, a choice will be made. A threat will emerge, powerful and afraid. Darkness will rise and cover us all. And then her magic will make us fall.

"The first is mine," Riker said. "I had the vision with Brielle—er—in the castle." A blush exploded across his face, and I raised an eyebrow at him. He cleared his throat. "And the second one is Angel's. She said it during the battle with the Count."

I studied the words, reading through them several times. Then, I glanced up at Riker. "Do you have any idea what this vision refers to?"

Riker blew air through his lips. "We suspect it's about Lilith. And Brielle. I'm not exactly sure of the timeline, but when I had the vision, it was a few months before Brielle was—" He stopped abruptly, and regret swelled in his eyes.

I stared hard at him. *He's responsible for her imprisonment.* The guilt written on his face was undeniable. Anger boiled through me, but I shoved it down. *You were her enemy too, Leo,* I reminded myself.

"Anyway," Riker went on, his voice cracking. "We think the threat refers to Lilith, but the 'powerful and afraid' refers to the phoenix."

I nodded. Judging by what I witnessed from Brielle, *powerful* and *afraid* were certainly two words that described her firebird.

"When Angel spoke the prophecy on the battlefield," Riker said, "it wasn't long after that Lilith's red magic filled the sky. We presumed the last line referenced that event."

Yes, I remembered. The event that almost destroyed the city.

And Brielle.

Soon afterward, Brielle had sunk into the recesses of her mind and battled Lilith alongside her phoenix. Then, she'd been unresponsive for months.

I suddenly straightened as I realized something. Brielle

had felt disconnected from the phoenix since she'd woken from her motionless state. She claimed Nix was recovering from the fight with Lilith.

But what if something else had happened to the phoenix during the battle?

"*On this day, a choice will be made,*" I murmured. "*A threat will emerge.*" I frowned at the wording. Emerge? By then, the threat had already been revealed—it was Lilith. This prophecy made it seem as if the battle marked the *beginning.* As if the threat hadn't yet been uncovered.

I looked at Riker. "What if those middle two lines haven't transpired yet? What if something occurred on that day that set other events into motion?"

Riker muttered the words under his breath. "*Darkness will rise . . . Her magic will make us fall.*" His eyes widened. "Are you saying those things haven't happened yet?"

"I'm not sure."

"But if Lilith—"

I shook my head violently and pressed a finger to my lips. "I would advise you to take care when discussing this with others," I said softly. "It's very possible we are being watched."

"By whom?" Riker whispered.

I leaned closer to him and hissed, "Be wary of the wolves."

Riker swallowed and nodded.

"And it would probably be better if you kept your distance from Angel Gerrick."

Riker stilled. "Is she in trouble?"

I studied him, reading the blatant fear and defensiveness shining in his eyes. *He cares for her. Probably more than he should.* "Not at the moment," I said. "But I'd like to keep it that way." I raised the parchment. "Have you or Angel had any more visions like this?"

"I've had three since then, and Angel has had two. We don't think they are related."

"Could you write those down for me as well?"

Riker nodded and jotted down several more lines. Instead of studying them, I folded the parchment and slid it into my pocket. With a smile, I nodded to Riker. "I'm obliged to you, Mr. Wilkinson."

I turned to leave, but Riker said, "Wait."

I raised my eyebrows expectantly.

Riker shifted his weight again. "Brielle—is she all right?"

I paused, scrutinizing him. *Why is he asking?* "As far as I know."

Riker nodded, his expression distant. "Good. That's good."

I sighed and stepped closer to him. "One thing I have learned about her is that she doesn't offer trust unless she wants to. Unless she has a reason to."

Something like hurt flickered in Riker's eyes. "She trusts you then?"

"I believe so. But only because she had no other choice. And no one else to turn to."

Agony swelled in his face, and I almost pitied him. But he'd abandoned Brielle when she needed him the most. To be frank, I was surprised she'd let him live after a betrayal like that.

I clapped Riker on the shoulder, and he flinched as if I'd struck him. "Good luck to you," I said before I left the house.

Drawing my hood over my face, I smelled the familiar wet-dog stench indicating Benito's wolves weren't far. But this time it was different. This time I smelled fury and blood. I fingered the pistol in my belt, my skin prickling with unease. My magic crackled within me, prepared to roar to life if needed.

Easy, Leo, I warned myself. *Stay calm.*

I strolled casually down the road, focusing on the scents around me with every breath I took. Bread and spices from the house next door. Ash and metal from the blacksmith forge. Dust and concrete. Azaleas and pine trees.

And wolves. At least three bloodthirsty and angry wolves.

Benito was seeking retribution indeed.

A quick glance up and down the road told me I was completely alone. Which was quite odd for midday.

Had Benito caused a distraction to clear the way? Or had he harmed innocent mortals in order to get me alone?

I sighed and dropped my hands, already tired of this foreplay. "You might as well come out!" I shouted, spreading my hands wide. The sun burned against my skin, but I pretended like I didn't notice. *Let them think I'm unstoppable.* "I know you're there. Come, let's settle this as gentlemen."

A figure emerged from the shadows, and I raised my eyebrows expectantly. He was a thick fellow—taller than me, and at least twice as wide. His yellow eyes flashed at me, and his graying hair was pulled back at the nape of his neck.

"Was it gentlemanly of you to shoot at my leader while he was wounded?" the man bellowed, his voice deep and booming.

"It certainly wasn't gentlemanly of him to assault a member of my coven," I said, my voice icy.

"Ah, Leo, since when do you care about the welfare of mortals?" hissed another voice from the left. I turned and found a face I recognized from years ago. Andre—a tall, wiry man with shrewd eyes. His bronze and bald head gleamed in the sunlight.

I barked out a laugh, though my insides quivered with anticipation. I knew there was at least one more wolf lurking nearby. I could take on two perhaps, but three would be a challenge. "Andre, if you think I care nothing for the mortals, then you don't know me at all." Which wasn't surprising. He'd weaseled into my coven under the pretense of friendship only to turn us over to Benito. "I protect all members of my coven, even Donors. If Benito thinks he can come into my city and take what he wants at the expense of my people, then our alliance will not last long."

The bulky gray-haired man sneered at me. "You had no intention of allying with us, Serrano. Benito knew that from the beginning." He stepped closer to me.

Shadows swirled around me, preparing to shift me to my bat form. Then, the gray-haired man lunged. My magic sprang to life, enveloping me. Black smoke surrounded me, but before I could shift, a slice of pain seared through my shoulder. The force knocked me off my feet. I collapsed to the ground. Fire pulsed through my wound, incessant and lethal. The pain festered, intensifying until I was certain it would swallow me whole. I gritted my teeth. Sweat formed on my brow, and my hood fell back. The sun scorched my skin, intensifying my injury.

I shifted on the dusty ground, trying to remove the knife from me. But when I glanced at my shoulder, I found it wasn't a blade.

It was a stake.

My eyes found Andre, who stood over me with a triumphant glint in his eye. The gray-haired man had been a distraction.

I wriggled, trying to free myself, but the stake pinned me in place, freezing my arm. Already, I felt my blood chill from the effect of the wood buried in my flesh. From the corner of my eye, I noticed another man emerge, though he was unfamiliar to me.

Andre crouched to my level and cocked his head at me. "We know she's more than just a Donor, Leo. Did you think you could hide that from us?"

Horror trickled into my stomach. I struggled again, swinging my uninjured arm uselessly, but Andre easily dodged my blow. "What—what have you done with her?" I rasped. "Where's Benito?"

Andre smiled widely. "That isn't your concern."

Even though it wasn't my dominant hand, I groped with my free hand to reach my pistol. But as I shifted, Andre lunged, shoving another stake in me.

I roared so violently it felt like my throat ripped in two. White-hot flames of agony throbbed in my other shoulder. Now both arms were numb, and darkness clouded my vision. I sucked in rattling breaths, but it wasn't enough. I'd never needed to breathe, but suddenly it felt like I was suffocating. My throat closed and my body twitched. My legs, the only parts of my body still intact, flailed uselessly. I couldn't even turn my head. My wide eyes remained on Andre as I fixed a loathsome stare at him. He straightened and chuckled darkly.

"Consider this a declaration of war, Leo Serrano. Our

pack is coming for you. Starting with that mortal you fancy so much."

14

BRIELLE

I left my parents' house with Mom's scanner tucked in my cloak. She'd walked me through how to use it three times. At first, I'd urged her to scan people *for* me, since she was the aurologist, but she claimed she had a spell she could use and would get to work testing the other half of the coven for signs of Lilith.

I took a breath and strode straight for Leo's house, my pulse thrumming with anticipation.

I need him to be on my side, I thought. *Even if Lilith has possessed the entire coven, I know I can handle it if Leo is in the clear.*

I was almost at Leo's house when a voice shouted, "Brielle!"

I froze and whirled around, frowning. Then, I noticed movement from a carriage bustling down the road. A white-haired figure waved eagerly at me from the carriage window.

A startled laugh burst from me. "Izzy? What're you doing here?"

The carriage pulled to a stop in front of me. Izzy slid out, wearing a deep purple dress and a bonnet that covered the top of her stark-white hair. She put her hands on her hips, fixing a stern look at me. "You forgot, didn't you?"

I blinked, racking my brain. Then, I smacked my forehead. "Dammit! Our weekly lunch. I'm so sorry, Izzy, it's been—" I exhaled through my lips. Remembering what Leo had said about spies lurking nearby, I straightened and gestured to the house. "Why don't you come inside?"

Izzy's brow furrowed as she looked up and down the magnificent home next to me. "Isn't that Leo's house?"

I chuckled. "Yeah, it's a long story. Come on in."

Izzy wiggled her eyebrows suggestively and bounded forward with a grin. I glanced at her footman, who closed the carriage door and hopped back on with the coachman before the carriage rattled away.

I raised an eyebrow at the coach as I knocked on Leo's door. "Fancy."

Izzy smirked at me. "I have connections."

A servant opened the door for us and took our cloaks. I showed Izzy to the sitting room, where we both sat grinning like the teenagers we were.

"So, you're *living* with Leo?" Izzy asked in a hushed voice.

My face burned, and I nodded, scooting closer to her. "Yeah. Uh, keep your voice down, though, will you?" In a whisper, I quickly filled her in, making sure to warn her about the wolves watching the coven.

When I was finished, Izzy's face had gone pale. "Crikey, Brielle," she said in a faint voice. "Do you really think she's back?" She mouthed "Lilith," but I understood who she meant.

I nodded. "I suspected before, but my conversation with Nix confirms it." I sat back against the sofa, and something poked me in the side. Frowning, I withdrew Mom's aura scanner. My gaze flicked to Izzy. "Hey," I said slowly. "Mind if I scan you real quick?"

Izzy stiffened, eyeing the device warily. "Uh, I guess? Will it hurt?"

"Not at all. I'll show you." Remembering Mom's instructions, I turned it on and then pointed it right at Izzy's heart. The device whirred and grew hot in my grip, but I held it tightly and focused on my magic. The scanner glowed blue, and a small white light appeared on Izzy's chest. She gasped and looked at me with wide eyes.

The device stopped whirring and beeped three times. I stared at the tiny screen that read: *two souls detected.*

My blood chilled, my eyes roving over those three words again and again. *It can't be.*

"What is it?" Izzy asked, peering at the screen.

I quickly turned it over. "Um, let me try again." Izzy's brows pinched, but she nodded. I scanned her again, but the same result bleeped on the screen.

Two souls detected.

Slowly, I raised my eyes to Izzy's face. Fear stirred in her dark eyes, mingling with the confusion that creased her brow. "Brielle," she said with a nervous chuckle. "What's it say?"

I pocketed the scanner and pressed my hand against hers. "It's going to be fine, Izzy." I held her hand for a long moment, waiting for the fire to overtake me.

But nothing happened. Her skin was cool against mine. Certainly not like the heat I felt when Leo touched me.

Although, I thought, *I feel an entirely different kind of heat around Leo.*

I blushed and released her hand. "Nix?" I asked quietly. "Are you there?"

Nothing.

"Damn," I muttered.

"It said she's possessed me?" Izzy whispered.

I swallowed. "It—it's probably broken. I'll talk to Mom about it. Maybe it got fried when they came here. Or maybe—"

Izzy raised a hand to stop my rambling. She exhaled a shaky breath. "What was it like? When she tried possessing you?"

"Izzy—"

"I need to know, Brielle," she said, her voice sharpening. "Your device thing might be wrong, but if it's not, I need to know what to look for."

I sighed, my mind returning to those dark moments I'd tried so hard to forget. "There was lots of heat. And fire. Though that might've been Nix and not Lilith. I felt . . . bloodthirsty. Like I was hungry for death and suffering. And when she took control of Nix, she was euphoric. Delighted with the bloodshed." I shuddered. "She wanted to be free. She wanted to become the fire and death that destroys everything."

An ominous silence pressed between us, and Izzy sucked in a sharp breath. Then, a loud laugh burst from her lips. "Yeah, I haven't bloody felt anything like that."

I was so startled by her reaction that I snorted and then dissolved into a fit of giggles with Izzy joining in. When our laughter faded, Izzy wiped a tear from her eye. "Don't worry, Brielle. I'll only be here for the day and then head back to my neck of the woods. If Lilith is trying to possess me, I'll show her the most boring life in the world. I don't even use my magic much anymore."

I crossed my arms and leaned against the sofa. "How are things going with you on that side of town?"

Izzy frowned and shook her head. "Not good. I've found a few light casters, but they aren't interested in joining a coven. Not after what happened with the Count and his mages."

Something in me deflated. I'd known Izzy was trying to start a light magic coven in the city, but I hadn't realized it would be this bad. Part of me hoped she'd been successful so my family would have a safe place to go. Especially now that Lilith was back.

"But Harrison and I are keeping at it. He's very optimistic." Izzy smiled, her expression warming.

My eyebrows lifted. "Harrison? Harrison *Porter*? The Douchebag?"

Izzy slapped my arm. "Stop it. He's not like that. The battle changed him. I think after losing Wes, Chris, and Samson, he kind of woke up a bit."

I eyed her—the way her cheeks went pink when she spoke of him, and the light shining in her eyes. "You *like* him!" I accused.

Izzy covered her mouth as she laughed again. "A—a bit. I think he likes me too. I mean, he's a great bloke, Brielle. We've been working together for months now." She shrugged, but she still had a goofy grin on her face. "I dunno, I suppose we'll just see what happens."

I laughed again, feeling lighter than I had in days. It was nice to just chat with her like we were in high school. I hadn't realized how heavy my brain felt, what with living among vampires and fighting off Lilith's influence . . . Sometimes I just wanted to be a teenager again.

A sickeningly fruity scent suddenly stung my nose. I straightened and glanced toward the open door. Estrella leaned against the door frame, her light brown hair in tangles around her face. She wore nothing but a loose, satin robe and raised one eyebrow at me.

"Forgive me," she said in a deep, throaty voice. "I didn't realize you were entertaining."

Izzy turned to look at the interruption. She snorted loudly and tried disguising it as a coughing fit. I elbowed her in the ribs and plastered a false smile on my face. "Hi, Estrella. Nice to see you too. Have you seen Leo?"

"He's upstairs where I left him." Estrella smiled widely.

A sickening coil of agony laced through my stomach, and my smile faltered.

Upstairs where I left him.

The words churned in my head again and again. How could I have been so stupid? Of course he was still intimate with Estrella. She was his Donor, after all.

Was that the only reason we'd had that moment earlier? Was he expecting the same relationship from me that he had with Estrella?

Idiot, idiot, idiot. I shoved the unpleasant thoughts from my mind and sat up a bit straighter, trying to arrange my face into something neutral. But the gleam in Estrella's eyes told me she hadn't missed my reaction.

"Great," I said, standing from the sofa. "I need to speak with him about something." I looked down at Izzy, who watched me with sympathy in her eyes. I smiled as naturally as I could. "It's been fun, Izzy. I'll see you next week?"

"Of course." She stood too and embraced me. "Hang in there," she whispered so Estrella couldn't hear.

I swallowed and nodded before seeing Izzy out the door. As I watched her hop into her carriage, I felt a swell of relief knowing she lived away from the coven. As long as Lilith was targeting us and Benito was skulking around, she was safer living on the other side of the city.

I waved as the carriage rattled away, and a pang of loneliness shot through me. With a sigh, I turned and found Estrella was gone.

Good. I didn't exactly want a witness when I went to find Leo. I thought of when I'd last seen them in bed together back in the caves—the way they'd laughed together when I'd stumbled in awkwardly. The way her body had been entwined with his . . .

Stop it, Brie, I told myself.

I took a deep breath and climbed up the staircase to Leo's room. His door was closed, and when I pressed my ear to it, I heard someone bustling around. Maybe he was getting dressed.

I cleared my throat and knocked loudly.

The shuffling stopped. Then, a muffled voice said, "Come in."

I frowned and pushed open the door. A figure stood on

the opposite side of the room, rifling through drawers. But it wasn't Leo.

I froze, my heart lurching in my throat. When the figure turned to face me, an icy slither of horror curled in my stomach.

It was Benito.

Like Estrella, he wore nothing but a robe, and his dark hair was disheveled. My gaze flitted to the bed and found a messy pile of sheets. Bile rose in my throat.

Oh, no . . .

"I'd offer to bed you, my dear, but I'm a bit winded from my latest dalliance," Benito said, straightening to grin wolfishly at me.

Oh, hell no. My mouth opened and closed, and I turned to leave. Estrella was suddenly behind me, blocking my exit. She cocked her head and smiled at me.

Anger swirled within me, thawing the fear in my chest. "What the hell's going on?" I glared at Estrella. "What have you done?"

Estrella just laughed, her dark eyes gleaming.

Benito swaggered toward me, and I shoved Estrella out of the way. She yelped, but I pushed past her—she was as fragile as a flower—and flew down the stairs. When I flung open the front door, a man stood on the porch and grinned at me. His yellow eyes marked him as a werewolf.

No, no, no.

I whirled and raced down the hallway, but someone

grabbed my arm. With a scream, I tried pushing him off, but he held fast. My free hand searched my trousers for the dagger I usually carried, but a sharp pain sliced into my shoulder before I could grab it.

"Sleep, little mortal," Benito's voice hissed in my ear.

Then, I blacked out.

15
LEO

"WELCOME, LITTLE DARKLING," CROONED AN amused voice.

I tried moving, but I was still frozen. The scorching sun seared through my closed eyelids. "Who's there?" My tongue felt like lead in my mouth.

"I've been waiting for you," the voice said. It was a deep female voice.

"Who are you?" I tried opening my eyes, but they were cemented shut. A prickle of dark magic swirled around me.

The voice brushed against my ear. I tried to pull away, but my body couldn't move. "I'm yours now, Leonardo Serrano."

I jerked awake. The sun was behind the cathedral now, casting a cool shadow on my body. The stakes still pinned me down, and the street was eerily quiet.

Where are the mortals?

I tried moving my arms, but the stakes held me down. When I searched inwardly for my magic, I felt hollow and empty.

I was too weak. My powers wouldn't work.

I thought of Benito's wolves and their threats. My blood raced with urgency.

Brielle.

With a groan, I strained against the weight of the stakes. Flames of anguish pulsed in both shoulders, but still I pushed. My groans turned to agonized shouts as I struggled. At long last, I managed to wiggle my fingers.

But my arms still wouldn't move.

I slumped backward against the dirt, exhaling. I felt so weak.

Something foreign curled within me—a wisp of magic. I stilled, my gaze shifting around as I searched for this new presence. But I was alone.

Then, crimson smoke pooled from my fingertips.

A jolt of alarm swept through me. My magic was normally black. I'd never seen a person use *red* magic before.

The magic surrounded me, stinging my nostrils with the scent of blood and death. I thrashed, trying to avoid it, but the magic grew thicker until it nearly suffocated me. I coughed and closed my eyes against the burn of it.

Sharp pain slammed into my shoulder. I roared in agony, and then, suddenly, my shoulder was free. My arm flew forward with ease. I snatched the stake in my other shoulder and yanked it out with another yell. Weakly, I staggered to my feet. Agony still throbbed in such nauseating waves I was sure I would retch.

Can't stop, I told myself. *I must find Brielle.*

I glanced around, but the red magic had vanished. A shiver of foreboding rippled through me, but I didn't have time to question it. I was free now. I could investigate the mysterious red magic later.

My legs felt numb as I broke into a weak jog, rounding two corners and cutting through an alley to return to my house. Suspicion prickled along my skin as I reached the house and pushed open the door.

It was completely silent. No servants. No movement.

Wrong, wrong, wrong, the silence shouted at me.

"Hello?" I shouted. My voice echoed in the vast, empty space. "Brielle? Estrella?"

No one answered.

I hurried upstairs and checked all the rooms, but they were empty. When I reached my own room, I stopped, my blood chilling. The bed was rumpled and messy, and the drawers of my desk were open with papers strewn about.

Someone had been snooping.

As I inhaled, I knew exactly who had been here. The air reeked of wet dog and rage.

Benito. He'd been in my house—in my *room.*

I stared hard at the messy bed, and blood-red fury clouded my vision.

He hadn't—he wouldn't dare—

With a swift movement, I overturned my desk and roared at the empty space. The desk crashed loudly on the floor, and a wooden leg snapped off. The image of Benito advancing on Brielle flashed in my mind again and again.

My head was spinning as I hurried downstairs, stumbling my way to the servants' quarters. A limp body lay on the floor. When I stepped closer, I found three more motionless forms on the other side of the room.

I crouched down and inspected the closest one—Francisco, my valet.

He was dead.

One other was also dead, but the last one was still breathing. A maid named Juanita. Her breaths came in sharp wheezes, and her wide eyes remained fixed on the ceiling.

I pressed a hand to her cheek. "It's all right. You'll be all right." With a grunt, I swept her in my arms and staggered to my feet. Agony sliced through every part of my body, but I pushed forward, clutching the girl against my chest and bringing her into the kitchen. I carefully laid her on the table and bustled through cabinets before I found my potion ingredients. My head throbbed as I tried to recall the healing potion Ronaldo had taught me to make all those years ago.

We vampires could heal on our own, but Juanita was a mortal. She wouldn't last long without a potion. And my powers were useless at the moment.

Muttering to myself, I threw several ingredients together into a pot. Angelica, osha root, caterpillar heads, and bitterling. The pungent smell stung my nose, making me dizzy again. I shook my head to clear it and mashed the ingredients together until it formed a thick, gray paste. Then, I grabbed a spoon and dipped it into the paste before bringing it to Juanita's mouth. Her breathing became slower and more ragged.

"Take this," I murmured. "Please, it'll help you."

I pressed the spoon against her mouth, and she slurped up the paste. She coughed and sputtered, but I urged her to take more. "I know it's unpleasant, but Juanita, you *must* eat it."

Somehow, I got through to her, and she gulped down a bit more of the potion. Then, I pressed my hands against her chest and breathed deeply.

I just need a bit more magic, I thought. *Just a bit to heal her.*

I took a breath and summoned my magic. Instead of the usual black, it was deep red again. I blinked in alarm but kept my hands on Juanita's chest. The red smoke billowed around her, surrounding her face. With a sharp gasp, Juanita's chest jerked upward, and she cried out.

I pulled away from her, and the red magic receded into

my hands. Panting, I stared at Juanita, who had slumped backward against the table. Her eyelids fluttered, and I resisted the urge to shake her.

Come on, I urged. *Wake up! Speak to me.*

Suddenly, Juanita coughed so violently I feared she might retch. I hastily searched for a bucket when she grabbed my sleeve.

"My lord," she wheezed, blinking incoherently.

"I'm here." I clasped her hand in both of mine. "You're all right, Juanita."

"Men . . . attacked the manor. Lady Estrella—" She broke off coughing.

"Where is Estrella?" I asked. "And Brielle? Are they hurt?"

Juanita shook her head and coughed again. "Lady Estrella . . . betrayed you."

My body went numb, and my blood chilled in my veins. *Estrella?*

No. We were bonded. She wouldn't—

I sucked in a breath, trying to clear my spinning head. "What—what has she done?"

"The wolf," Juanita panted. "The man. He seduced her. Took Lady Brielle."

He took Brielle. Fire blazed within me, and red clouded my vision. I gritted my teeth and growled, "Where? Where did he take her?"

Juanita took a shuddering breath before she whispered, "*El Castillo.*"

I stilled. *He took her to the castle? But why?* My aching head swirled with red magic and dizziness, and I struggled to think straight.

If Benito knew about Brielle's phoenix, he would try to extract it somehow. What better place to do it than the very prison Brielle had been trapped in? Back when the Count had tried to do the same thing.

"M-my lord," Juanita breathed.

I blinked. A red fog poured from my fingertips, clouding the air like a mist. It reeked of black magic, blood, and darkness. I'd smelled plenty of demons in my time, but this was much stronger and fouler.

It smelled of death itself.

I gasped, and the red magic receded into my hands. *What the hell is happening to me?*

"Juanita," I said quickly, remembering the task at hand. "Will you be all right?"

Juanita nodded. "Yes, my lord. Go to them. Bring your lady home."

Her words lanced through me like a blade. Despite what I felt for her, Brielle wasn't my lady. She wasn't mine at all. I hadn't protected her. Instead, I'd let her leave, despite knowing there were threats out there.

"My fault," I whispered.

Juanita clutched my sleeve again. "No, my lord. You

cannot protect everyone. There are always monsters in this world. It isn't your responsibility to stop them all."

"It is if they threaten my people," I said in a weak voice.

Juanita shook her head. "You are a leader, my lord. Not a god. All you can do is follow the light and teach your people to do the same."

The corners of my mouth twitched. "But I'm a vampire."

Juanita offered a hoarse chuckle. "Even vampires can walk in the light, my lord."

I pressed a kiss to her hand and thanked her before darting out the back door. Red magic swirled around me, and I shifted to a hawk. My wings stretched wide, and I took off into the sky, gliding effortlessly through the air. I landed on the ground in front of Jorge's house, then shifted before darting inside.

The door banged open loudly with my entrance. "Jorge?" I shouted.

Please don't be dead. Please.

Silence greeted my arrival. I checked the sitting room, the library, and the dining room. Then, I hurried upstairs and checked the bedrooms.

In Jorge's room, I found a prone figure lying on the floor with a stake protruding from his chest. Horror numbed my body, freezing me in place as I crouched over Jorge's body.

"No," I breathed. Red-hot anger bled through my vision again, and my fingers clenched into fists. "*No!*" I roared. Red magic exploded from my hands and ricocheted off the walls. The sharp stench of dark magic crackled in the air.

Suddenly, Jorge sucked in a breath, his legs twitching.

My arms dropped, and the magic faded. My blood thrummed with shock. I glanced down, hovering over Jorge's chest, and found the stake was slightly to the right of his heart.

Whoever stabbed him had missed.

"Merciful Lilith," I breathed. With a swift movement, I yanked the stake out, and Jorge gasped loudly. The stake fell from my grip with a clatter, and I grasped Jorge's shoulders. "My friend. You're alive. You're all right."

Jorge grimaced and grunted as he tried to rise. "The wolves—"

I shushed him and nudged him back down to the floor. "Don't speak. You need to rest."

Jorge shook his head weakly. "He bested us, Leo. I . . . I don't know who's left."

"He took Brielle," I said in a hoarse voice. "He's in the Castillo de Coca."

Jorge went still, his dark eyes pinned on me. "You cannot go there alone, Leo."

"I have no choice."

Jorge's eyes narrowed as he scrutinized me, no doubt taking in my ragged appearance. He frowned as if he sensed something off about me. Something the red magic had done to me.

"He attacked you too," Jorge whispered.

I nodded.

"Why?"

"I found him with Brielle in an alley yesterday. I fought him. I think this is his retribution."

Jorge shook his head again. "No . . . this is bigger, Leo. He planned this."

I went very still, my eyes fixed on the wood panels of the floor. *He's right,* I realized. This hadn't been some impulsive act of revenge. This had been calculated. Planned. Estrella had been in on it—perhaps for some time.

"He planned this all along," I said in a hushed voice. "Ever since he arrived in the city. He always meant to attack us."

"As you suspected."

I slammed my fist on the floor. "I was a fool. I should've imprisoned him the moment he set foot in my city. He spoke of alliances and promised I had a fortnight to decide. Of course he would attack before then, catching the entire coven off guard."

Jorge grabbed my wrist. "Leo, promise me you won't go to the castle alone."

"Who else is left?" I asked. I didn't have time to search through every house in my coven. By the time I found all my people, Brielle could be dead.

"Brie?" bellowed a voice down below. "Are you here?"

I froze, my blood pumping furiously within me. Jorge's eyes met mine, his gaze darkening.

"Brie!" the voice shouted as it drew closer. A familiar scent filled my nose, and I shot to my feet.

Brielle's father, Oliver, appeared at the open door. His eyes were wild with fury, and his blond hair was ruffled. His gaze took in Jorge's limp figure and my defensive stance. "What happened?" he asked.

"Benito de Vargas," I said gravely. "He—he took Brielle."

"*What?*" Oliver roared, surging toward me with venom in his eyes.

Suddenly, Jorge jumped up, standing between me and Oliver. I blinked and clasped Jorge's shoulder when he teetered.

"Don't," Jorge said weakly. I couldn't tell if he spoke to me or Oliver.

"Your family?" I asked Oliver.

"They're fine. We split up to search for Brie."

"Have you seen any others?" I asked. "Anyone else from the coven?"

Oliver shook his head. "It's dead outside. Like a ghost town."

I frowned, confused by the phrase, though it seemed appropriate enough. It certainly did seem as if the inhabitants of my neighborhood had been killed.

"I'll bring her back," I said firmly. "I swear it."

"You're not going without me," Oliver growled, his jaw rigid.

I cocked my head at him, considering. He *was* a demon, after all. I could certainly use his abilities. "Your wife and daughter?"

"They'll remain here. Angel is no huntress, and Desi must protect her."

I blinked. "No," I said slowly. "Bring Angel here. Send for Riker Wilkinson."

"What?" Oliver's head reared back, his brow furrowing in confusion.

"He'll protect her, along with Jorge. We'll need Desi's help with this, Oliver."

Oliver's scowl remained, but, slowly, he nodded. "Very well."

I hadn't expected him to give in so easily. Perhaps he already knew how close Riker and Angel had grown.

I strode toward the desk in the corner and withdrew Jorge's knives. After handing one to Jorge, I slid another in the hilt of my belt. Then, I leveled a hard gaze at Oliver. "Let's go rescue Brielle."

16

BRIELLE

A SPLITTING PAIN IN MY HEAD WOKE ME—FOLLOWED by the all-consuming burn of fire within me. I jerked, my chest heaving as flames devoured my insides. A piercing shriek burst from my lips, echoing in the darkness.

Brielle, a voice whispered in my head.

I coughed. "N-Nix?" Though I barely breathed her name, my voice still blared against my eardrums. Wherever I was, it was somewhere big. A dark, musty scent assaulted my nose, bringing an onslaught of sickening and disturbing memories.

Knives cutting through me. Screams and moans surrounding me like ghosts. Fire, blood, and death.

I scrambled to my feet, blinking in the darkness. Metal bars surrounded me, and fear gripped my chest like a vise.

"No," I whispered.

I was back in the dungeons of the Castillo de Coca.

"Nix," I said quietly. "Are you hurt?"

I am well, Nix said. *But I feel Lilith everywhere, Brielle. I feel her more strongly than my connection to you.*

My blood chilled at her words. If Lilith was stronger than our bond, then what prevented her from taking over Nix completely?

"Can you still access my magic?" I whispered.

Nix was silent for a moment. *I feel it faintly. I'm not sure how much power I would be able to use. Brielle, I am not certain if I can help free you or not. I may not be strong enough.*

"That's okay," I said automatically, though her words knifed through me with the realization that I was on my own. "We'll figure something out."

The smell of dog wafted through my nostrils as soft footsteps approached. I squinted in the darkness, trying to make out the figure drawing near. Though I had a sneaking suspicion I knew who it was.

"I knew the moment I touched your body," hissed a familiar voice, "that there was a presence within you. It called to my wolf."

I gripped the metal bars so tightly my fists shook. Slowly, Benito emerged from the shadows, his yellow eyes gleaming like a light in the dungeon.

"You are no ordinary mortal," Benito purred. "The animal within you stirs the beast inside me. Do you not hear how they call for each other?"

He lies, Nix hissed, her voice an angry growl in my head. *I have felt his wolf, and there is no connection there. His wolf is a monster intent on destroying.*

"You bastard," I said through clenched teeth. "I'm not yours. And I don't give a damn about your wolf."

Benito laughed, revealing his long, pointed teeth. "Oh, Brielle. It doesn't matter what you think. All that matters is that I've found you."

An icy shiver rippled through me. My heart rate skittered, and I struggled to keep a fierce expression on my face. "What're you talking about?"

Benito slid two fingers through the bars of my cell to snatch a lock of my hair. I jerked away from his touch as nausea swelled within me. "Your disguise as a mortal was convincing," he said softly. "After all, I could smell no magic on you. But my wolf has a stronger sense of smell than I do. And you may not realize it, but your creature has a *very* distinct smell. It awoke the wolf within me. I had no choice but to succumb to it."

I spat in his face, and he stiffened. "Asshole," I snarled. "You had no choice but to assault me? Unlock this cell and I'll show you just how *uncontrollable* I can be."

Benito only grinned at me, his eyes glinting with desire. "Oh, I'm sure I would enjoy that immensely. But my lady has other plans for you."

Horror chilled me to the bone. "Lilith," I whispered, my

hands shaking against the prison bars. I shook my head slowly. "Benito—whatever she's promised you, it—"

"My bargain with the Dark Lady is no concern of yours," Benito said in a clipped tone. "But rest assured I am getting everything I hoped for in exchange for turning your beast over to her."

"Benito, you *can't*! She'll use the phoenix to destroy *everyone*!"

Benito chuckled and cocked his head at me like I was a petulant child. "Oh, Brielle. It warms my heart to hear you sound so concerned. But you seem to be confusing me with a kinder, gentler soul. You see, I don't *care* about anyone else. It just so happens that where I'm going, the Dark Lady's power cannot touch me."

Confusion swirled in my mind, and my brow furrowed. *Where is he going?* I wondered.

Nowhere on this Earth, Nix said in my head. *The Underworld perhaps?*

But why—

I sucked in a breath and leaned closer to the rusty metal bars. "You've lost someone."

Benito went very still, his yellow eyes sharpening.

"Who was it?" I went on. "A lover? A brother? A friend?"

In a flash, Benito's face was in front of me, his sharp teeth bared. Gray and white fur sprang along his jaw and arms, and a savage rage blazed in his eyes. "You know *nothing*," he spat. "Do not patronize me, girl."

"If Lilith promised to bring you to a lost loved one, it won't be the same," I said in a hasty voice. "They'll be different—altered. They won't know you, Benito." It was one of the many subjects I'd researched as a kid when I'd been trying to access my powers. Necromancy was the darkest of magical arts. It was very different from those who communed with the souls of the great beyond. The dark casters who practiced necromancy were essentially reani-mating corpses. Like zombies.

"It will be different in the Underworld," Benito said in a soft voice, his eyes distant. "If I bring her here, then yes, she will not know me. But if I go to her—"

I shook my head, feeling sick. "Benito—"

"*Stop!*" he roared, slamming his hand against the bars. I shrank away, flinching. "Do not address me as if you know me. As if we are friends. I do not care for you, and you do not care for me. Let us not pretend otherwise."

"Please—" I begged.

"I grow weary of your blathering." Benito waved a tired hand, but the fury and pain in his eyes told me I'd struck a nerve. "My lady wishes you to be weak. I will return when the hunger has set in." He flashed his teeth in a wicked smile before vanishing in the darkness.

"Benito!" I shrieked, banging my fists against the bars.

The metal sound echoed in the dungeon, but no one responded.

With a frustrated groan, I slid to the grimy floor and rubbed my forehead. "Nix, are you still there?" I whispered.

Yes.

"Have you been to the Underworld before? Is there anything I can tell Benito to convince him this is a terrible idea?"

Nix was silent for a moment. *I have not been there,* she said slowly. *But . . . occasionally a spirit will cross over to the Astral Realm where I sleep. I dream of them. Communicate with them. But it doesn't happen often.*

"What are they like? The spirits?"

They are in agony, Nix whispered. *Lilith is the Lady of the Underworld, and she tortures her souls.*

"But Benito said she doesn't have power down there."

She doesn't. But she is the only being who is free. The only one not imprisoned. In a sense, that is the greatest power of all.

"So, Benito will only travel to the Underworld to find his girlfriend is being tortured for an eternity," I breathed, my body chilling with horror.

Yes.

I ran my hands through my messy hair. "Okay," I said to myself, rising to my feet and wiggling my limbs to wake my magic. "I can do this. We can get out of here. I'm assuming you're in the Astral Realm now?"

Yes . . . but it is different. Colder.

"What do you mean?"

Ordinarily I rest here because it is warm, and my body prefers warmth. But lately it's become colder. Less comfortable.

A bolt of realization shot through me. "Nix, does Lilith have any power in the Astral Realm?"

Nix remained silent for so long I thought for sure I'd lost my connection to her. Then, she finally said in a frightened whisper, F*or most of my life, I have never felt her there. But recently, even when I rest, I cannot escape her. Since our battle against Lilith, I have felt her with me. Constantly.*

I quelled the rising panic in my chest and cleared my throat. "If I fall asleep, can you take over? Can you come here and rescue me?"

I don't know.

I took a deep, shaky breath and glanced up and down my cell, muttering to myself. "The bars are enchanted. Last time I was here, I couldn't use magic to escape. But last time, I didn't have *you*, Nix . . ." I rubbed my chin, racking my brain. My gaze drifted upward to the rocky ceiling above me. I gasped. "Nix, can you crash through the ceiling like you did the day of the battle? When you rescued me and Angel?"

Once again, Nix took a long moment before responding. *I don't know, Brielle.* Her voice was much fainter now. *I am weak. So much weaker than before. And when I rescued you and your sister from the caves, I perished afterward and was reborn in the ashes. I fear I don't have the strength to recover quickly enough. I fear that Lilith—*

"Is waiting for you to die," I whispered. "If you're reborn, you'll be powerless to stop her."

I already feel powerless, Brielle.

"But why?" I said angrily. "What did I do wrong? We bonded!"

Something unusual happened during our fight with Lilith, Nix said slowly. *I felt her dark magic penetrating through our bond. Perhaps . . . she marked me somehow.*

I froze, my blood running cold. Something in her words resonated with me, and a memory resurfaced. When my parents had first tried to cast spells with me and Angel as kids, Dad's magic hadn't worked as well with her. Mom had said it was because he was a demon. Dark magic couldn't bond with light magic.

"Nix," I said, struggling to keep my voice even. "Do you use dark magic? Are—are you a demon now?"

The silence in my head screamed at me like a warning bell that something was terribly wrong. I remembered Lilith's blood-red magic practically suffocating me as I used Nix's powers against her. The way it flooded my nose and mouth like I was drowning . . .

If my suspicions are correct, Nix said in a horrified murmur, *then, yes—I am a demon.*

17

LEO

CREEPING TOWARD THE CASTILLO DE COCA AS DUSK approached was reminiscent of my days during the time loop when I led my coven to attack the Count. But this time, my unlikely comrades were Brielle's parents. The smell of Desi's light magic was jarring against my nostrils, and the back of my neck prickled with the presence of casters I didn't trust. How I longed for Miguel, Jorge, and Guadalupe's aid, their comforting scents and the trust we shared.

But for all I knew, Miguel and Guadalupe were dead. The thought sent waves of agony pulsing through me, and red clouded my vision again.

Calm yourself, Leo, I thought. The red magic was growing stronger within me, and with each burst of power I became more frightened of it. Where had it come from? Why was it here?

And where was my own black magic? Even after being staked, my body should have recovered by now.

I couldn't shake the chilling voice in my dream after being staked: *I am yours now, Leo Serrano.*

I had a disturbing hunch I knew who had spoken to me. I wanted to be wrong, but I couldn't deny the way the clues slid together in my mind. The way Brielle reacted when we touched. The way her firebird feared me and claimed I was Lilith.

But no, I thought as I crept through the forest toward the castle. *I'm not a Nightcaster. And even if I were, Lilith only possesses witches. It isn't possible.*

But so many things seemed impossible before now. Such as time travel. And light witches living among a coven of vampires.

And a demon falling in love with a light witch.

"Are you sure about this?" Desi hissed, breaking through my thoughts. "The place looks abandoned."

I followed her gaze to the castle surrounded by shadows. The grounds were covered in darkness, and the absence of light did indeed suggest it was unoccupied.

Or occupied by those who preferred the dark.

Before I could respond, Oliver said, "They definitely came this way. I can smell the wolves." He looked at me. "What's the best way inside?"

"There's a secret entrance through the moat," I said. A

smirk spread across my lips, though it felt emptier than usual. "We may have to do some swimming."

Desi groaned and tied back her mane of curls while Oliver raised his eyebrows at her.

A few minutes later, we crept up the stairs to the court-yard—the same spot where Brielle had interrogated me a year ago. The memory sent a mixture of emotions through me: amusement, pride, and the smallest sliver of fear.

What if he's killed her? I wondered. *Or bitten her?*

But then I remembered how capable she'd been during that interrogation. She'd summoned me from a few drops of my blood and stood her ground when my demons surrounded her.

She could handle herself against Benito de Vargas.

Oliver, Desi, and I crept through the gardens, using the massive hedges to conceal us from view. After several tense minutes, we reached the moat, whose depths sparkled in the moonlight.

I waved a hand toward the water. "Shall we?"

Without preamble, Oliver jumped in. Desi gasped, her eyes wide, before she looked at me. I flashed her a grin before diving in after Oliver.

The water was cooler than I remembered, but the chill soothed my weary body. The aches and hunger that had been pulsing through me quieted for a moment, and all I felt was the swirling water around me. Nothing but peace.

A splash next to me indicated Desi had jumped in as well, and I snapped back to the mission. I waved my hand toward the concrete foundation of the castle just in front of us. Then, I propelled myself forward, sensing Oliver and Desi following. I swam lower and lower until I found the tunnel my men had gone through many times last year. My feet and arms moved faster and faster. Though I could last an eternity in the water, I knew Desi and Oliver would need to breathe soon.

At last, the tunnel opened up to a cavern underneath the castle. I broke through the surface and climbed onto the concrete landing. Oliver and Desi gasped when they emerged from the water, and I helped them up.

Desi looked up at the damp and musty cave and wrinkled her nose. "It looks like a sewer."

I frowned, and Oliver laughed. "Which way?" he asked.

"Before we proceed, can one of you cast a cloaking spell?" My voice was soft, but the sound of our whispers still echoed in the vast chamber.

Desi nodded and stepped forward, raising her hands. They glowed blue as she uttered the spell.

"Magic above and powers that be,

Conceal us from our enemies."

The sickly-sweet smell of light magic stung my nostrils as it swarmed around me. The red magic flickered to life within me, roaring in fury as Desi's spell embraced me. I shoved the foreign power away and clenched my fingers into fists.

Oliver's shrewd eyes shot to me, and his brow furrowed. "You all right?"

My nostrils flared, and I exhaled as the fury within me subsided. "I'm fine. Thank you, Desi."

Desi nodded, sharing an uncertain glance with her husband.

I led the way toward another tunnel, and we followed the narrow path until we reached the dead end.

"What—" Oliver said, but I raised a hand to stop him.

Stepping forward, I raised my hands and felt along the cracks in the wall until my fingers met a familiar crevice. I hoisted myself up, using the hidden footholds to climb.

Oliver's head reared back in surprise, but he and Desi quickly joined me in scaling the wall. The higher we climbed, the stronger the smell of wolf filled my nose. Fury pulsed through me, and red clouded my vision again.

Stay calm, Leo, I told myself. *Brielle can handle herself. She'll be fine.*

I focused on my breathing, but all I could think about was what Benito might be doing to her. All because I'd failed to protect her.

When we reached the top, a grate sealed the entrance. I pushed against it lightly, but it wouldn't budge.

"Damn," I muttered.

"What is it?" Oliver hissed from below me.

"Someone has sealed it since I was here last," I said.

"Move aside," Desi ordered.

Oliver and I leaned sideways as Desi lifted one hand, her limbs trembling from the effort of maintaining her balance. With a grunt, she thrust her arm forward. Blue magic crackled in the air, and the grate crashed open with a thunderous sound that echoed in the cavern.

When the dust settled, I said, "Move. *Now.*"

Oliver and Desi didn't hesitate. We all scrambled out of the cavern and found ourselves in a cellar filled with crates and dusty furniture. Loud footsteps echoed nearby, and we darted behind a grand piano. I held my breath easily, but Desi and Oliver panted as if they'd sprinted for hours. I shot them a warning look, and their mouths clamped shut.

The footsteps slowed and drew nearer. I flexed my fingers, sensing the pull of my magic. But as it flowed through me, I knew it wasn't my own, but the foreign red magic.

Lilith's magic.

Where did my magic go? It was as if when the stakes had been removed, they'd taken my magic with them. Now all that remained was Lilith's presence within me.

I can fight her off, I told myself. *Just as I fight off the beast within me every day.* After all, I hadn't fed in several days. The hunger hadn't even bothered me.

The footsteps stopped short, and then someone hissed under their breath. Frantic footsteps pounded up the stairs as the visitor dashed off, no doubt to inform Benito of the broken grate.

"She's most likely being held in the dungeon," I said hastily as we emerged from our hiding place. "I don't know where it is, though. I was never able to find it during my time here. I suggest we split up. I'll be faster if I shift."

Oliver and Desi nodded, and I closed my eyes, reaching inward for my shadows.

Nothing happened.

Panic raced through me, and I tried again. Still nothing.

"What's wrong?" Oliver asked.

I shook my head and gritted my teeth. "Something is wrong with my magic."

Desi and Oliver shared an alarmed look, and irritation prickled through me.

"I will be fine," I growled, drawing my dagger. "I can still fight. Come, I'll show you to the main hall."

They followed me up the stairs. When we reached the huge oak door, I pressed against it gingerly, peering through the crack toward the hallway. After one moment of tense silence, I pushed it open all the way, and a mighty groan echoed through the castle. Ushering Oliver and Desi out, I hurried behind them and pulled them into an alcove to hide. The shadows concealed us from view as more footsteps echoed throughout the castle.

My blood hummed through my body, and the powers within me swirled with anticipation. An array of wolfish smells wafted through my nose, and a disturbing hunger rose within me. Not the usual hunger for blood I normally fought, but a foreign hunger. A hunger for death and blood-shed. A hunger for destruction.

Unease rippled through me, but I couldn't focus on it now. Brielle needed us. She needed *me*.

I jerked my head toward the hallway once it was clear, and the three of us crept along, pausing with every echoing sound. The familiar smells of the castle and its previous occupants brought on a wave of memories and trauma. My siblings had died here. I'd fought battles here.

And now this wretched place had come back to haunt me once more.

I paused at the foot of the stairs leading to the guest quarters. My gaze shifted around the grand hallway. This was as far as I'd come during my last attack.

"Here," Desi whispered, pulling a corked vial from her tunic. She shook the concoction and muttered a spell under her breath.

"Magic above, gather near,
And find the soul we seek here.
Use this potion to lead the way,
So we can find her straight away."

Desi uncorked the vial, and a shimmer of blue light erupted from the glass. It spun in the air until a bright blue ember hovered in front of Desi.

A locator spell. Of course. My eyebrows lifted in surprise at how well-prepared Desi was.

The three of us followed the ember down the hall and

toward the magnificent entrance doors. Frowning, I opened my mouth to say we were going the wrong way, when the ember suddenly took a sharp right, floating downward toward what looked like another alcove. When we followed it, I sucked in a gasp.

Not an alcove. But another set of doors.

Using her Telekinetic powers, Desi broke open the door, and we hurried through.

The smell of black magic filled my nose as the dungeon's darkness swallowed us. Desi and Oliver hesitated, but my vampire vision allowed me to see clearly. Rusty cavern walls surrounded a narrow staircase, and far below us were the metal bars of prison cells.

I took the lead and guided Oliver and Desi down the steps. Before we made it to the bottom, a growl echoed in the dungeon. The stench of wet dog filled the air, and I knew several of the wolves had shifted to beast form.

"Get ready," I muttered to Oliver and Desi.

Claws clicked on the concrete steps. A wolf lunged for me, and I ducked and rammed my blade into its fur. It whimpered but snapped its jaws at Desi, who grunted and slammed the wolf backward with her magic. The wolf tumbled down the steps, and we hurried after it, eager to avoid a battle on the staircase.

"Brielle?" I shouted frantically, knowing it was no use keeping my voice down. We'd already been spotted.

Another wolf bounded toward us. Oliver summoned a

gust of wind that swept the creature back and slammed it into the metal bars with a loud clang.

"Find her!" Oliver yelled at me. "We'll fight them off!"

I nodded and hurried toward the row of cells, peering briefly in each one.

Empty. Empty. Empty. Then, I stopped, my heart lurching. A small figure was huddled in the corner of a cell, her grimy blond hair matted with blood and dirt.

I sucked in a breath. "Brielle?"

When she turned to face me, her eyes were all black, and her teeth were covered in blood. Her face, while so familiar to me, was lit with a foreign and sickening glee. "Sorry, dear," she whispered in an ethereal voice. "Brielle's no longer here."

18

LEO

My body felt numb as I stared, horrified, at the girl I'd come to rescue.

But it wasn't her at all. Lilith had taken over. I recognized her voice. I'd heard it in my head as well.

Which meant Lilith had control over more of us than we'd feared.

"Brielle," I whispered, pressing my face against the bars. "It's *me*. It's Leo. Your parents are here."

Brielle simply stared at me, her mouth stretched wide in a malicious grin. Her black eyes seemed to drink in everything all at once.

"Where—where is Nix?" I asked loudly. "Where is your firebird?"

Brielle threw back her head and laughed. "The firebird is *mine*. It cannot save her now. Nothing can."

The phoenix saved her once, I thought, my head spinning. *It can save her again. But how do I summon it?*

My body suddenly went still as I remembered what happened whenever we touched. The lustful moment we'd shared in my home earlier—when she'd completely burst into flames.

"Brielle," I tried again, trying to ignore the scuffling and shouts echoing behind me. "Come. Let me free you." I felt around for the door and found it bolted shut. Cursing, I lifted my hand, trying to summon my magic.

Brielle cackled. "You are mine too, dear. You can't free her without my magic."

My hands shook as I strained to bring my magic forward, but nothing happened. Then, in desperation, I thought of the red magic still festering within me, hoping I still had access to it. Something faint crackled beneath my palm, but still, nothing happened.

I slammed my hand against the bars and grunted in frustration. Brielle laughed again.

Think, Leo, I said to myself. *If she were your enemy, how would you bring her closer?*

I took a breath and cocked my head at her. "It's a bit pitiful, dear Lilith, for you to possess the body of a mere child. Isn't it?"

Brielle's smile faded, and her eyes narrowed. "You know best she isn't just a *child*, now, is she?" A slow smile spread across her face, and she raised her eyebrows.

She knows. She knows how I feel about her.

I swallowed and forced an easy smirk on my face. "Perhaps not. But Benito? Myself? The *silversmith*? It all seems a bit desperate." I leaned back and crossed my arms. "Surely you, the Dark Lady, Lucifer's Whore, can do better than that?"

Brielle's mouth twisted in fury, her bottom teeth showing as she snarled. Slowly, she crawled toward me.

Closer, I urged. *Closer.*

"You know nothing," she spat, her face so contorted with rage that I didn't recognize her anymore. "You foul, useless demon scum. You think you know power?" She laughed without humor. "I can show you *true* power. But I must access it first. And if you knew even a taste of the power in store for me, oh, you would sink to the lowest of depths to reach it, just like me."

I raised an eyebrow. "I don't believe you."

Brielle's nostrils flared.

I shrugged. "I think you have *no* power in the Underworld, *my lady*. In fact, I think you are so overcome with boredom that you find yourself desperate to possess the lowly mortals of this earth. Perhaps you found it amusing to inhabit the mind of a common silversmith. Was it fulfilling, to be covered in grime and sweat? To labor and waste away your days pandering to the needs of the locals?"

Brielle roared and lunged for me, but I was ready for her. I shoved my hand through the bars and grasped her wrist before she slammed into the cell wall. My fingernails dug into her skin as I clung to her, gritting my teeth as she thrashed.

"Let me *go*," she grunted, thrashing against my grip. My fingernails dug into her skin as I held fast.

"You know me, Brielle," I whispered. "You know my touch. My skin. The heat between us." With my other hand, I reached through the bars and brushed my thumb against her cheek.

Brielle suddenly went still, her wide, black eyes fixed on me.

"Wake up, Brielle," I said. "Bring the fire back. I need you."

Brielle's head twitched, and her whole body shuddered. A strangled moan ripped from her throat, and I resisted the urge to back away from her.

A howl pierced the air behind me, but I kept my gaze on Brielle. *Desi and Oliver can handle it.*

"Come back, Brielle!" I cried over the sound of her grunts and gasps. Her body twisted and writhed, and her skin burned against my fingers. A familiar heat scorched me, but still I held her wrist. The red magic within me exploded to life, and fire raged so violently my bones quivered. My vision blurred, and I staggered, barely managing to cling to Brielle's wrist. With a groan, my head slumped against the cell bars, and the coolness of the metal on my face jolted me from my haze.

Focus, Leo, I told myself. *Stay alert. Bring her back.*

I shook my head, but the redness still crept into the corners of my eyes. The magic within me churned and roared like a rapid river bursting free from a broken dam.

The fire against Brielle's skin grew hotter. Closing my eyes, I bellowed, "Nix, come out! I need you!" When nothing happened, I slammed my palm against the cell bars again. The sound rang in the cavern. "*Now!*" I roared.

Then, Brielle's entire body burst into flames. Something heavy crashed through the cavern ceiling above us, and I stumbled backward in shock. Boulders and large rocks rained down from above, and I darted out of the way before I was crushed.

"Brielle!" I shouted against the avalanche.

A burst of blinding light seared my eyes. I shielded my face from the burn of the phoenix's flames, trying to ignore the panic within me. Had Brielle been crushed? Had she burned up?

She's fine, I thought. *Nix will take care of her.*

Slowly, the dust settled. Brielle's cell was empty. A gaping hole in the ceiling revealed a glimpse into the hallway above.

Suddenly, a heavy force slammed into me, and I collapsed to the rocky ground. Dizzily, I climbed to my feet and found Benito standing before me with a smug smirk on his face.

I cocked my head at him. "Pleasure to see you again,

Benito. You've been conspicuously absent from the festivities down here."

Benito's mouth stretched wide in a feral grin. "You released the firebird."

I remained very still, keeping my face arranged into a carefully neutral expression. "Yes, I did." I didn't like the glee in his eyes. Like releasing Nix had been part of his plan all along.

Benito clapped his hands and roared with laughter. "Excellent. I couldn't have done it without you, Leo."

My blood ran cold, and I suddenly put the pieces together. Brielle had told me she'd felt disconnected from Nix. Then, I'd come down here and found her possessed by Lilith.

Releasing the phoenix had given Lilith exactly what she wanted: access to the firebird.

More grunts and shouts echoed behind me. A wolf growled and then whined, which I took to be a good sign. Hopefully Desi and Oliver were holding their own against Benito's wolves.

Beneath my cloak, I carefully fingered the pistol I still carried. *Keep him talking, Leo.* "And what interest would you have in a firebird?" I asked calmly. "You are no Nightcaster."

Benito chuckled, shaking his head. "That always your problem, Leo. You never saw beyond what was right in front of you. There's a bigger plan at work. Bigger than just you and me."

My skin prickled at his words, and alarm blared in my head.

He can't be working with Lilith. He can't be. What could he possibly gain?

I scrutinized him. Behind the eager glint in his eyes stirred something else. Something tortured as it ate away at him.

I recognized it all too well. Grief.

"Paloma," I whispered, suddenly remembering the lover he'd lost years ago during the battle with my coven.

Benito's smile faded. "You cannot stop this, Leo. It is beyond your control."

My fingers gripped the pistol and slowly drew it from my holster, keeping it hidden beneath my cloak. "Perhaps you're right," I said quietly.

Benito frowned, his brows furrowed. He looked me over as if sensing a trap.

"Benito," I said, stepping closer to him. He tensed at my movement. "Whatever you hope to accomplish, it won't bring Paloma back."

Darkness stirred in his eyes, and the grief in his face morphed into fury. His fingers clenched into a tight fist. "I won't bring her back. I plan to—"

I aimed the pistol and fired into his chest. His words

choked off with a sickening gasp. He staggered backward, his face draining of color. Blood pooled from his chest, and a white glow emanated from the wound. An effect of the silver bullet.

I strode toward him with the pistol still aimed at him. Then, I froze.

Benito stiffened, his body quivering. Fur sprang on his arms and face, and his teeth lengthened into sharp fangs. A roar burst from him. Red magic poured from his hands and swirled around his chest.

I stumbled back, gaping in horror. Lilith's magic consumed him like a fog, and a tiny clatter rang in the cavern. The bullet had fallen to the ground.

Oh, no, I thought, taking another step back. My eyes were wide as I watched the red cloud disperse. Within Lilith's magic was a large, white wolf. Benito's black eyes drilled into me, and a low growl raised the hair on the back of my neck.

"Oliver! Desi!" I shouted, turning on my heel and fleeing from the predator. His paws padded against the ground as he chased after me.

Come on, I urged myself. *Shift! Now!* I tried summoning my magic, but it wasn't there. Even the red magic was inaccessible.

As if Lilith wanted Benito to finish me off.

Several figures grappled in front of me. I surged toward them, drawing my dagger as I ran. Oliver and Desi saw me first and sprang apart. With a shout, I pummeled into their assailant—a man with matted blond hair that fell past his shoulders. His yellow-rimmed eyes fixed on me for a moment before I tackled him to the ground, letting Benito soar over my head. I plunged my dagger into the man's shoulder and rolled off him, looking for Desi and Oliver.

"Where's Brie?" Oliver demanded.

"The firebird took her," I panted. "Move. *Now!*"

Oliver shared a look with Desi and then rushed forward, following me toward the staircase. We took a step, and then a mass of white fur shot forward, slamming into Oliver and knocking him to the ground.

Desi screamed and flung her hands in the air, smashing the wolf into the wall with her magic. While she held the wolf, Oliver jumped to his feet and fired a ball of fire into Benito. The wolf howled in pain, and the smell of singed fur stung my nose.

"Go!" Oliver shouted, still shooting fire at Benito.

Desi and I turned just as Benito's comrade staggered to his feet, his side bleeding freely from my blade. Desi shoved him back down with her magic and scrambled up the stairs with me close behind. A quick glance over my shoulder indicated Oliver still held Benito at bay.

"Oliver!" Desi cried.

"Oliver, move!" I shouted, aiming my gun again. "I have him."

Oliver dropped his hands and jogged wearily toward the stairs. I fired, and the sound rang in the cavern. Benito slumped sideways, half his fur a mangled mass of blood and ashes. But I knew it wasn't over. Oliver climbed up the stairs and joined us, and we kept running, though I had my pistol ready.

A burst of red magic surged in the air. The wolf groaned and climbed to his feet.

I fired again, and he fell over once more.

I didn't wait for him to recover. Oliver, Desi, and I flew up the stairs as fast as we could. When we reached the hallway, we barreled through three of Benito's men with a flash of fire, blood, and Desi's blue magic. We threw open the great entrance doors and sprinted toward freedom.

19
BRIELLE

Fire consumed my dreams. Faintly, I heard Leo's voice shouting my name. I tried to speak, but my mouth was glued shut. I couldn't move. Couldn't breathe.

My eyes flew open. A deep rumbling shook the ground. *An earthquake?* Frowning, I sat up and found myself on a wide, rocky cliff. Peering over the edge, I saw boiling lava hundreds of feet below me.

I yelped and scrambled to my feet, my pulse thundering in my ears. The air was filled with smoke and ash. The volcano below me churned and boiled, and a breeze whipped my hair in front of my face.

"Hello?" I shouted. My voice echoed, surrounding me with my own terrified plea.

"Brielle," a voice whispered.

I whirled around as a figure approached. Through the smoke, I made out the shape of a large bird—bigger than any I'd ever seen before. Then, a burst of fire momentarily blinded me. I shielded my eyes as the creature came into view.

She was breathtaking. The most beautiful thing I'd ever seen. She resembled a falcon with orange and yellow feathers that glowed with her flames. Her deep brown eyes seemed to pierce right through me. Her wings were folded behind her, but she still stood almost as tall as me.

"Nix," I whispered, my eyes wide. "How—"

"We are no longer connected, Brielle," the voice murmured. The creature's beak wasn't moving, but it was different from when she spoke in my head. Now it sounded like a soothing voice echoing next to my ear. My mind felt strangely blank without her inside me.

"What do you mean?" I asked, trying to quell the panic rising inside me.

"Saving you broke our connection," Nix said. "I tried keeping my distance so our magical bond wouldn't snap. But when Leo touched you . . ."

I gasped, suddenly remembering the events as if they'd been a bad dream. A darkness smothering my mind, taking over completely. *Lilith.* And Leo had been trying to reach me. But I hadn't been there. I hadn't been present at all.

"How—how did Lilith take control of me?" I whispered in horror, trying to shake the disgusting feeling of her being inside my head.

"She's been summoned," Nix said. "She has more power

here in the mortal realm than in the Underworld. She did not realize how disconnected we were until Benito imprisoned you. When she found out, she took control."

I swallowed as bile climbed up my throat. "Is she—will I —" I couldn't finish. I didn't even know how to word my question.

"She will not possess you as a cursed witch," Nix said. "She can only do that from the Underworld. No, her ability to possess is quite limited, from what I observed from Benito. She can only possess the bodies of others for a short amount of time."

I stared at Nix, who watched me with eyes that seemed to see everything—past, present and future. Those eyes looked a thousand years old. "You got me out," I said in a broken voice. "You—you shouldn't have done that."

"Lilith would've killed you. Or Leo. I couldn't let either of those things happen."

"She wouldn't kill Leo. Not if—" I stopped, realizing Nix had been right. If Lilith could possess anyone, even Benito, then she'd taken hold of Leo too.

"She *can* if he proves to be an obstacle in her plan," Nix said grimly. "I imagine she will try to find a way to use him, but if he proves to be difficult . . ."

Leo? Being difficult? Imagine that. "He'll fight her," I said. "And she'll kill him."

Nix didn't say anything. Her silence confirmed my fears.

Another earthquake shook the ground, and my hands

flew out as I teetered. "Where—where are we?" I glanced warily over the edge of the cliff again.

"The Astral Realm."

I stiffened and gaped at her. "What? I thought I couldn't come here."

"When we were bonded, that was true. I didn't know mortals could come here either. I believed it could only be inhabited by ancient magical creatures."

"I'm not a mortal."

Nix shook her big, beautiful head slowly. "It is the best way to describe you compared to a creature like myself."

"Is this—is this place real?"

"Yes and no. The location of the Astral Realm changes based on its occupants. I prefer warmth, so I often come here to this volcano. But sometimes it is a large cave. Or a desert. The Astral Realm adapts and alters itself through time and space."

My brows furrowed. "So we could be in a different *time* right now?"

"Yes, but you must think of this as another dimension. If we were to encounter other mortals or creatures here, they would not see us. Because our presence here is temporary. It is only a holding place while we are between layers of consciousness."

My head spinning, I nodded, though I still didn't quite understand. "What will happen to you, Nix? What can I do? Can we bond again?"

Nix hesitated. "I do not know. This has never happened before. All Nightcasters before us have either bonded with their phoenix or become possessed by Lilith. Never in our history has a witch bonded with her phoenix and then broken that connection."

A lump formed in my throat, and guilt flooded my mind. *My fault, my fault, my fault.* "Is this because you're infected with dark magic? I shouldn't have fought her so hard, Nix. I'm sorry."

"She would have killed you and possessed me," Nix said. "I would rather perish than be controlled by her. But our broken connection has brought me clarity. I *am* a demon, Brielle. And a demon cannot be bonded to one who possesses light magic."

I opened my mouth to respond when another rumble shook the ground so violently I fell backward on my rear with an "oof." Cracks formed in the cliff, and chunks of rock floated down toward the lava.

"Um, Nix?" I said uncertainly.

"Our time is almost up," Nix said quietly. "I hope to see you again, Brielle. Good luck."

The earth quaked again, and rocks cracked and crumbled. I gasped, trying to scramble away from the cliff's edge. But as I moved, my mind swirled, blurring my vision. Dizziness overcame me, and I fell backward. I crammed my eyes shut, expecting a heavy impact against my head. But a weightless sensation overcame me like there was no gravity, and something soft met my head.

My eyes flew open and saw a vast, decorative ceiling. Startled, I sat up quickly. Too quickly. My head spun, and I raised a hand to my forehead. "Ow," I groaned.

"Brie!" a voice yelped by my ear.

I winced and hissed as another slice of pain shot through my head. Blinking, I looked around and found myself in the guest room at Leo's house. Angel sat next to my bed, her eyes bloodshot and rimmed with dark circles.

"What happened?" I croaked, trying to rise.

Angel shoved me down. "You've been out for two days, Brie. Take it easy."

My eyes widened. "*Two days*? But Benito . . . Lilith . . ." I broke off, sputtering. Then, my blood ran cold. "Leo! What happened to him? Is he—did I—" The last thing I remembered was bursting into flames with him still grasping my wrist. Had I hurt him?

"Leo's fine," Angel said, and the tightness in my chest loosened slightly. "He's currently scouring the city for the remaining members of his coven."

I stared at her as a lump formed in my throat. "Remaining members?"

Angel's lips pressed together, her eyes grim. "Benito's wolves attacked the coven. At least half the vampires and Donors are dead."

Bile rose in my throat, and I suddenly felt lightheaded.

Sitting back against the headboard, I covered my mouth and shook my head. "This—this is all my fault."

"Your fault?" Angel's brows pinched, and she cocked her head. "It isn't your fault that someone else attacked the coven, Brie."

"But it is." I looked at her sharply. "Benito wanted access to Nix. He's working with Lilith."

The blood drained from Angel's face as I filled her in on what Benito and Nix had told me.

"So—so your phoenix is just *gone*?" she whispered. "Where did she go? Does Lilith have her?"

"I don't know," I croaked. "But Angel, she said she can't be bonded to me while she possesses dark magic. I think—I think I need to—"

A knock at the door interrupted me. Angel raised a finger to stop me and jumped to her feet to answer the door. I frowned, squinting as I tried to make out the figure on the other side of the door. Whoever it was had a deep voice, but Angel blocked him from view. Then, she cast a nervous look at me over her shoulder, and I caught a glimpse of bright red hair.

I stiffened. "Riker, what the hell are you doing here?"

Angel jumped and grimaced in my direction. With a sigh, she pulled open the door to allow Riker inside. I self-consciously drew the blanket further up to cover myself.

Riker offered a nervous grin and set a tray of fruits, cheese, and bread on the table next to me. "I heard you talking. Thought you could use some food." He stood back and clasped his hands in front of him, his face red. He shared an anxious glance with Angel.

"You never answered my question," I said.

"I was here with Angel while your parents were rescuing you," Riker said.

My eyes widened, and my nostrils flared. "You were here . . . what, to *protect* her?" I scoffed. "Well, that's rich. Especially since my parents were rescuing me from the very same place *you* abandoned me."

Regret swarmed in Riker's face. "Brielle—"

"You need to leave," I snapped. "I don't want you here."

"Well, I *do* want him here," Angel said, lifting her chin.

My gaze slid to her, and I frowned. "Angel—"

"No, Brie, I've had enough of this. Riker made a mistake, and it's been a *year.* Since then, he's done nothing but help our family. Are you saying you've never made a mistake? That if you'd been in his shoes, you wouldn't have done the same thing to protect the people you cared about?"

I fell silent, stunned by the harshness of her words.

"Do you still have feelings for him?" Angel asked abruptly.

My face burned, and I dropped my gaze. "Angel—"

"Come on, Brie, everyone in this room knows what went on between you two." Angel waved a hand. "Tell me, do you still have feelings for him?"

"No," I sputtered. "But—"

"Then, what's the problem? You guys don't have to be best friends or anything. And for Lilith's sake, you forgave *Leo* for attacking you, so why—"

"Because he's with *you*, Angel!" I shouted, gesturing at them with my hand.

Silence filled the air. Angel gaped at me, and Riker, his face beet-red, looked like he wanted to bolt from the room.

"You're my sister," I said, my face still on fire. "I've always felt overprotective of you, especially here in the eighteenth century among a coven of demons. I would die before I saw you tortured in the same way I was, Angel. And if you had been here, if you had *seen* what the Count did to me, I don't think you would've been so quick to forgive him, either." My voice broke at the last word, and I couldn't stop my lower lip from trembling. *Dammit, Brie, pull yourself together.* I bit my lip and dropped my gaze.

The three of us remained silent for several, long moments. My hands itched to move or reorganize something, and my stomach growled loudly. I stared hungrily at the food next to me, and suddenly Riker snorted.

My gaze snapped to him, and he quickly covered his mouth. "Sorry. Sorry, it's just—you two just had this awkward shouting match, and meanwhile there's a beast in Brielle's stomach just roaring with hunger, and then I see you eyeing that food like a predator watching her prey, and . . ."

Angel's shoulders shook with silent laughter, and her

lips twitched as she tried to remain composed. My own face split into a grin, and we all started laughing. Though our faces were red, and Riker and Angel still stood there stiffly like they were waiting for me to explode, for a while we just shared the humor of the moment. With everything going on, we certainly needed the laughter. My stomach felt weightless with my chuckles, and I hadn't realized the knots and unease that had gripped my body until they released.

When our laughter faded, Riker smiled warmly at me and gestured to the open door behind him. "I'll just, uh, go tell your family you're awake." He turned to leave.

"Riker," I said, and he stopped. My throat felt tight, and my words came out in a rush. "I'm sorry for being such a bitch to you. Angel's right. You don't deserve it."

The corners of Riker's mouth spread as if he wanted to laugh again, but he bowed his head toward me. "I don't blame you in the slightest, Brielle. But I appreciate your apology."

I offered a tight-lipped smile as he left and closed the door behind us. Slowly, Angel approached the bed and sat on the edge. It wasn't until she grabbed my hand that I finally met her gaze.

"I get it now," she said quietly. "You weren't mad at him —you were mad at *me*."

My eyebrows rose. "What? Angel, no—"

"It's okay, Brie. You've always been so protective of me

that you wanted me to be the same with you. You wanted *me* to hate him for what happened to you."

My mouth clamped shut as truth rang from her words. Suddenly, I could see my anger as clearly as if I were holding a magnifying glass. Riker and I hadn't seen much of each other since the battle with the Count, but the few times we had, my anger had only unleashed when he'd been with Angel. When I'd seen them being so friendly with one another.

I always thought it was just my urge to shield her from him, to protect her from what he might do. But what hurt me the most was the warmth between them—as if he *hadn't* doomed me to die in that castle. Or as if Angel didn't care what he'd done to me.

Heat burned in my throat, and I swallowed. "I didn't"—I cleared my throat—"Angel, I'm so sorry. I didn't realize . . . Lilith, I'm so stupid."

"Brie, it's *fine*," Angel said in a soft voice, leaning closer to me. "The air is clear. Riker has no hard feelings toward you. If anything, he wants you to punch him in the face because he thinks it'll help the situation."

I laughed and sniffed, my eyes feeling hot.

"Besides, didn't I break the first rule of girlfriends?" Angel asked, raising an eyebrow at me. "He's your ex. I shouldn't have even gone there."

I grimaced in distaste at the word "ex." "Ew, don't call him that. We kissed once and didn't even date. He was just . . . a crush. That's all. If you really like him, you have my blessing to ride off into the sunset and make lots of beautiful redheaded babies."

Angel slapped my arm, her face reddening. "Brie!"

We both laughed, and I felt more at ease than I had in months. Slowly, Angel's face sobered, and she stared at the brown blanket under her hand. "Brie, there's something else."

My smile faded as I watched her warily. "What?"

"Riker is here for another reason. We've been collaborating with our visions to see if there are any similarities. He's taken extensive notes about the visions he remembers, and I've added to them." Angel paused and took a breath. "Leo recently went to see Riker to look at his notes, and that was when Riker realized they're all connected." Her eyes met mine. "Brie, the visions are about *you*. You and Lilith."

20

LEO

"If you stay here much longer, I should have your things sent for," Jorge said from the doorway of his study.

I looked up from my notes, eyebrows raised. "Oh, Jorge, I'm flattered, but what will the neighbors think?"

Jorge chuckled without humor and hobbled into the room before easing into the seat opposite me. I shifted uncomfortably as guilt coursed through me. Jorge was barely strong enough to walk after being staked. I had been staked *twice* and felt perfectly fine.

A small part of me knew why: because Lilith's power was still flowing through me.

"You're avoiding her," Jorge said, fixing a sharp gaze on me.

"I'm avoiding *everyone*," I muttered darkly, sifting

through papers again. One phrase kept popping up in Riker's notes: *The wolf triumphs when the silver demon falls.*

It wasn't terribly difficult to discern what that meant. My silver-rimmed eyes meant *silver demon* could refer to me. And the wolf, obviously, was Benito. But when would it happen? When would Benito kill me?

"It wasn't your fault, Leo," Jorge said quietly.

"Oh?" I looked up at him. "Is someone *else* in charge of protecting my people? Someone I've overlooked?"

Jorge fixed a flat look at me. "We only lost seven. It could have been much worse."

Seven. I knew them all by name. Francisco, Tulio, Pilar, Raul, Santiago, Cesar, and Eduardo. Eduardo, my soft-spoken soldier, had been Second Tier like me. Like Jorge. And yet he'd been killed.

"Doesn't that strike you as odd?" I murmured.

Jorge frowned. "What?"

"All of us were staked. But only seven were killed. It was more than just luck, Jorge. Those wolves *know* how to stake a vampire properly."

Jorge's brows knitted together. "Yes, I thought that was odd too. But why would they want our coven to survive? How does that benefit them?"

I thought of Lilith's voice in my head and suppressed a shudder. "I don't know." I set the papers down on the desk with a bit too much force and rose to my feet. "I must return home. But I'll be back shortly."

Jorge shakily stood as well. "Will you finally speak with her then?"

I forced a smile. "If you insist, *Father*." I patted him lightly on the shoulder while he rolled his eyes. Then, I grabbed my cloak and left the house.

My true intent was to find Riker. I knew he spent most of his time with the Gerricks, especially since the attack. Perhaps he and Angel had some theories about the phrase I'd been rereading. Maybe one of them had had another vision that might provide clarity.

I slipped into the servants' quarters. My maids were so accustomed to this that they didn't even glance up from stitching my clothes. I tried not to stare at the shirt—it was the one I'd worn when I'd been staked.

And when Lilith had sent her powers into me. I had no doubt I'd be dead if she hadn't saved me. But *why*? Did she want to use me somehow? With Brielle now disconnected from her phoenix, as Oliver had told me, she was no longer at risk. I couldn't deny the relief I felt knowing she was free from Lilith's influence.

But I wasn't. So I had to keep my distance. Brielle had already been a target of Lilith's before. I didn't want to give Lilith another reason to pursue Brielle.

I kept my hood down as I crept down the hallway and toward the study where Riker and Angel worked. Low murmurs and an array of familiar scents surrounded me. I almost reached the study when I stopped short. A familiar ocean scent filled my nose, swelling within me and sending my mind spiraling. Then, I heard her voice.

". . . doesn't make any sense. I'm not a Nightcaster anymore."

I lingered by the door, listening hard.

"But Nix is still out there." I recognized Angel's subdued voice. "She must think she can take the phoenix somehow."

Leave. Now. The urgency racing through me drew me backward a few steps. Out of habit, I tried summoning my shadows to shift to bat form, but as usual, nothing happened. Instead, blood-red magic pulsed within me like a festering wound. Waiting.

My cloak swished as I turned from the study, intent on barricading myself in my room if I had to. At some point, Brielle would have to eat or sleep. Maybe I could catch Riker on his way out.

You're a fool, Leo Serrano, a voice chided in my head.

I knew that. But I was also a fool who was a danger to everyone. The only reason I hadn't fled yet was because my coven needed me. Leaving them without a leader would be a death sentence, especially after such a devastating attack.

As soon as I ended Benito, I would leave forever until Lilith's influence ran its course.

I crept toward the staircase, feeling ridiculous and weak without my shapeshifting abilities. Suddenly, the doors to the study were thrown open, and Brielle's scent wafted down the hall.

Damn. I froze and sighed, drawing back my hood.

"You're back," Brielle said coldly when she found me poised at the bottom of the stairs like a thief.

"I am." I straightened and tried to appear less guilty. The fire in her eyes told me I was failing. "Are you . . . well?"

Brielle snorted and crossed her arms. She wore a tight tunic belted at the waist and trousers that made me want to draw her close and run my hand along her thigh. "I don't see why you'd care. Especially since you haven't bothered to check on me *once* since I was kidnapped."

I resisted the urge to flinch at her words. *Kidnapped, tortured, imprisoned.* All because of me. It was painful for her now, but it would be even more so if I was around her for too long. If Lilith didn't take her, someone else would. Benito or any number of my enemies would use her to get to me. I should've been mindful of that long ago. When my coven started to notice how I felt about Brielle, that should've warned me not to get close to her.

I rubbed the back of my neck. "Your father has kept me informed."

"Good for him." Brielle's tone was icy enough to freeze the room.

I swallowed and forced myself to meet her hard gaze. The longer I stared into the depths of her caramel-colored eyes, the more I saw. Anger was at the forefront, but behind it was pain and confusion.

I dropped my gaze before her emotions suffocated me.

Forcing an easy smile, I jerked my head toward the staircase. "Forgive me, but I have coven business to attend to."

I climbed up the stairs and sensed Brielle following me. *Damn her.* I strode into my room as if I hadn't noticed and went to the desk, shifting papers around as if I'd intended to come here.

The back of my neck prickled when Brielle entered the room and slammed the door shut with such force the frame rattled. "What the *hell* is your problem?" she demanded.

I straightened and turned to face her, realizing what a frustrating predicament this was. I had to keep my distance from Brielle because of Lilith's influence. But Brielle was never one to let something go if it was bothering her.

I crossed my arms and raised my eyebrows. "I'm not sure what you mean."

"Don't patronize me, Leo." Brielle took a step toward me, her jaw rigid. "You came to rescue me, you *saved* me from Lilith, and now you can't even look me in the eye! Why? Did I do something to piss you off? Did I—" She stopped, her mouth clamping shut as hurt flashed in her eyes. "Was it because Lilith possessed me? Did that frighten you?"

My eyes widened. "What? Of course not!" With a laugh, I added, "I've seen truly disturbing things in my lifetime, Brielle. I was *more* concerned she wouldn't relinquish her hold on you."

"Then, what is it? With Estrella gone, I know you need a

Donor. Is that it? Are you trying to avoid drinking from me? Or is it because your last Donor betrayed you?" Understanding filled her eyes, and she staggered back a step. "That's it, isn't it? You're worried I'll betray you like she did."

"Brielle—"

"I *knew* it," she cried, her face reddening. "You've never trusted me, have you? I mean, I know I can't blame you, but how long will it take for you to—"

"Brielle!" I shouted, drawing closer and grasping her shoulders. I ducked my head to look her in the eye. "I trust you with my life."

Her eyes narrowed, and the regret on her face was enough to crush my soul entirely. "Then, what's wrong? You can tell me, Leo. I've seen my fair share of horrible things too. I'm not afraid."

I laughed, but the sound was hollow. "You are the most fearless person I know, Brielle. You don't have to convince me."

Brielle swallowed, and I felt her blood pulsing within her. The anxiety in her eyes and pain in her expression made me realize there was more at stake here than I'd thought.

I'd hurt her by keeping my distance. She thought I didn't care for her.

With a groan, I ran a hand through my hair. The truth,

then. Brielle deserved nothing less. "It's Lilith," I said quietly. "Your firebird was right. I feel her inside me."

Brielle's face drained of color. "What? How do you know?"

"My magic is red now. I can't access my usual shapeshifting abilities, and sometimes I . . . *hear* her. In my head."

Fear flickered in Brielle's eyes, followed by something else. Something like *relief.* But it was gone before I could get a closer look. "So you've been avoiding me because—"

"Because I don't want her to take you again," I whispered.

Brielle's gaze locked onto mine, and I stepped closer to her, drawn by the pull of her eyes. Heat churned between us, but in a flash, anger filled her face again. "You thought I couldn't handle it?"

I blinked. "What?"

"You don't have to *hide* from me, Leo. I don't need your protection."

Irritation flickered within me. "Your time in the dungeon suggests otherwise."

Shock and rage blazed in her eyes. "You bastard. I've proven myself *more* than capable over the past year. And I've shared *everything* with you. We worked together to fight Lilith before! Why is this any different?"

"Because she's *winning*, Brielle! She's taking over my coven! Half my men are dead, and my enemy has struck a bargain with her. Now she has a hold on me too! It's only a matter of time before *everyone* I care about is slaughtered because of her!"

"Then, you'll need all the help you can get!" Brielle shouted. "Let me *in*, Leo! Let me help!"

"I can't!"

"Why not? Because you don't trust me?"

I scoffed, my blood boiling from her accusation. "I trust you with my life, Brielle."

Her eyes narrowed. "But not with this?"

"I didn't say that," I said through clenched teeth.

"Then, why? Why are you pushing me away?"

"Because Lilith knows how I feel about you!" I roared. My cheeks were flushed, and my blood pulsed with energy and need. I longed to hold Brielle and bring her body against mine, but I shoved the desire away and locked it up.

Brielle's face slackened, and her jaw dropped. The color drained from her face, and she stared at me with wide-eyed horror.

Horror. She was horrified to hear I had feelings for her.

Smack. My head swiveled to the side, and for one disorienting moment, I had no idea what happened. Then, I realized Brielle had *slapped* me. Slowly, I turned to face her. Her eyes were blazing, and her face was pink.

"Don't you dare," she growled.

My eyebrows shot up. "Dare what? To care for you? To love you?"

Brielle gasped as if I'd uttered a filthy word. She raised her hand to slap me again, but I caught her wrist before she could. "Stop it," she hissed. I couldn't tell if she meant to stop grabbing her or to stop professing my love. She thrashed and writhed in my grip, but I held her steady. I took a step closer to her, and she inhaled sharply. Fear shone in her eyes, but it mingled with something hot and palpable—something I could feel down to my bones.

"Brielle," I murmured, drawing even closer to her. "I love you."

She licked her lips and shook her head. "No. No, you *don't*. That's not love."

I laughed. "And how do you know?"

"It's just our blood connection. It's my *blood* you want, Leo. Not me."

I raised an eyebrow. "Though I can't deny that your blood *is* alluring, Little Nightmare, I know for certain I would love you even if no blood flowed through your veins. Even if you were nothing more than a spirit haunting me with your stubbornness and anger, I would still love you."

Desire stirred in her eyes, but she shook her head again. "You can't do this to me," she said in a broken voice. "You *can't*—" She placed a hand on my chest as if to push me away, but her fingers lingered against the fabric of my shirt. Her hand traced up to my collarbone, and her eyes darted to mine. "You make me weak," she whispered. "I don't like being weak."

I leaned close to her, close enough to smell the saltwater scent emanating from her pale skin. Her brown eyes were speckled with flecks of green. A dusting of freckles coated her nose and cheeks.

"Tell me to stop," I said in a throaty voice, "and I will."

Brielle's breath hitched, and her gaze flicked down to my mouth. She caught her lower lip between her teeth, and a low groan climbed up my throat.

She made no objection, so I drew closer until my chest was touching hers. Redness bloomed across her cheeks, and her body tensed as if poising for a fight. But she didn't pull away from me.

My eyes bored into hers, and she looked up at me with fear and longing. *I should stop,* a voice within me warned. *I should back away from her and keep my distance. Even if it hurts her.*

But being close enough to taste her warmth and her breath, I couldn't move away unless she wanted me to.

"Tell me to stop, Brielle," I said again.

Her eyes held mine. I sensed her blood racing, and my own blood pulsed desperately in response. *Want, want, want,* my blood seemed to say.

Then, ever so slightly, Brielle shook her head. "Don't," she breathed. "Don't stop."

21

LEO

WHEN BRIELLE UTTERED THE WORDS, MY BLOOD raged in triumph and drew me forward. With my finger, I traced a line from her ear down her jaw before cupping her chin in my hand. Her lips parted, and her eyes closed. She wanted this.

Just like I did.

I waited for the fire to consume her as it had before. But though her skin was warm to the touch, there were no flames. It was only her heat and mine.

I leaned in and brought her mouth to mine. A small, shaky sound escaped her lips when we kissed, and I almost drew away. Then, her fingers clutched at the fabric of my cloak, pulling me closer. Her lips moved urgently over mine, and the soft, velvety touch of her mouth suddenly turned hot and desperate. My body tensed as I anticipated the fire to stop us as it always had.

But it didn't.

Her body arched into mine, and her hands traveled up my shoulders until her arms were around my neck. Her fingers tangled in my hair.

My blood pounded loudly until it was all I could hear. *Want, want, want.* The beast within me roared to life, sensing Brielle's proximity and lusting for her blood.

I broke the kiss, ducking my head and pressing my lips together. A dull throbbing split through my head as I kept my hunger at bay. Brielle's panting only aroused me further, and I closed my eyes, trying to block everything out.

"I'm sorry," Brielle gasped.

I opened my eyes to frown at her. "Whatever for?"

Her mouth opened and closed, and her cheeks flushed. "I—I don't know. I just assumed I wasn't very good at this." Her mouth clamped shut, and her face reddened even more. As if she hadn't meant to admit that.

My eyebrows lifted. Her face seemed so small. So innocent in that moment. Like she was laid bare before me in all her weaknesses.

I ran the pad of my thumb along her lower lip, and her breath caught. "You are perfect, Brielle," I murmured. "But I don't trust myself."

Confusion swirled in her eyes, and then she blinked, suddenly understanding. "My blood."

Slowly, I nodded.

Brielle exhaled and dropped her gaze. When she looked

at me again, her eyes were hardened with determination. "You can drink from me, Leo."

I stared at her. Surely, she couldn't mean that. She'd fought me so hard when I'd exchanged blood with her. She'd made it quite clear how repulsive the idea of being my Donor was.

"I'm serious." Brielle gathered her hair until it swept over one shoulder, leaving the side of her neck exposed. The hunger within me lurched in response, and my body seemed to boil with need at the sight of so much of her skin.

I couldn't tell if I yearned for her blood or her body more.

"Go ahead," Brielle urged. "You can bite me."

My fangs emerged of their own accord. I almost closed my mouth to shield them, but something in Brielle's eyes ignited at the sight. As if the prospect of sharing blood aroused her as much as it did me.

I drew closer to her, waiting for her to stop me. Her breathing turned ragged, but she leaned into me, inviting me closer. Slowly, I sank my teeth into the exposed part of her throat. She gasped, and then her sweet blood filled my mouth. I moaned and grabbed her waist, pulling her closer. She threw her head backward to give me better access as I gulped down more of her blood.

Take care, Leo, I reminded myself. The thought sent a bolt of clarity through me, staving off my bloodlust. I slowed down and pulled back before I sucked her dry. Her hands clung to my cloak, trying to pull me closer.

"Your turn," I rasped. Raising my hand, I pressed my fangs into my wrist until I drew blood. Then, I brought my wrist to her mouth.

Brielle's eyes were still closed in rapture, and a trickle of blood dripped from her neck. When I pressed my arm to her lips, she drank freely as if it was routine. As if she knew exactly what to do. A brief flare of exhaustion pulled at my body as she drank, but when she moaned, I drew closer, desperate for her to have more. Her chest pushed against mine, and my free arm curled around her back to bring us closer.

When white spots danced in my vision, I gently pulled my arm away. Her lips were stained with my blood, and when her eyes opened, a white gleam shone in them. She blinked up at me, disoriented. I grinned.

"Did you enjoy it, Little Nightmare?" I asked, brushing her hair behind her ear.

"I want more," she croaked.

My stomach lurched at the desire in her voice, but I shook my head. "We can't. Not yet. Give our bodies time to adjust."

"No," she said breathlessly. "More of *you*."

She snatched my belt until her hips were against mine, and then she kissed me again. A startled noise rose up my throat, but then desire took over. I tasted my blood on her lips and teeth. Our mouths moved more urgently this time, consumed by heat and desperation. She caught my lip between her teeth and pulled gently. I growled, pinning her to the wall until my body was pressed up against her. She grunted from the impact of her body hitting the wall, and I felt her heart skittering from underneath my chest.

"Leo—" she gasped, and my name was like a plea on her lips.

I silenced her with another kiss, my lips moving down her chin and jaw until I reached her neck. I licked up her blood lingering from my feeding, and the taste of the sweet, tangy substance against her hot and delicious skin was almost more than I could bear. My hands moved from her waist to her thighs, and I hitched up her legs until she straddled me.

"Oh," she whispered, her eyes flying open in surprise. She drew away, her face becoming even redder, if possible. "Leo, I—I can't—" She swallowed, gasping for breath.

My body ached for her, but I slowly lowered her legs and nodded. "Right. Of course. Forgive me, I—"

"It's not that I don't want to," she said in a rush, her eyes wild as she looked at me. "It's just that I've never—never done it before." Chagrin filled her eyes, and she dropped her gaze.

Warmth spread through my chest, and I tilted her chin up so she met my gaze. "Brielle, it's nothing to be ashamed of." I paused and pressed my lips together. "I wouldn't dare presume—if you don't want me to be your first—"

Brielle pressed a kiss to my mouth. "I do," she murmured against my lips. "I want you." She pushed against me until we both staggered backward toward the bed. My chest felt weightless as I fell over with her on top of me. The bed creaked under our weight, and my hands found her hips again as she drowned me in her sweet kisses.

"Are you sure?" I broke apart for a moment, but she silenced me with another kiss. More insistently, I touched her face to draw her away from me. "Brielle. Are you sure?"

She sat up, her legs wrapped around me, and slowly loosened the belt at her waist. Then, she dropped it to the ground so her tunic fell loosely around her shoulders. Loose enough to spill onto the floor if I shifted it the right way.

My throat felt hot, and I swallowed. "Brielle—"

"I'm sure if you're sure," she whispered, her eyes alight with energy.

Merciful Lilith, I've never wanted anyone more in my life. I took a breath and traced a finger along the length of her jaw. She leaned over me, giving me full view of the beautiful, bare skin underneath her tunic. I kissed her neck, moving down to her shoulders and collarbone. I gently ran my teeth along the skin of her shoulder, and she gasped, her hands tightening on my chest. She unfastened my cloak with shaking fingers and then worked on the buttons of my shirt.

Sensing her anxiety, I grabbed her legs and flipped her over. She yelped in surprise, and then I was hovering over her. Her face was red as she laughed. With quick movements, I unbuttoned my shirt and tossed it onto the floor.

Brielle's breath hitched as she looked me over, her eyes lingering on the scars that crisscrossed my chest.

"Most are from battles," I said softly. I pointed to the long, jagged scar over my heart. "This was from my mortal death."

Brielle's eyes widened as she looked at me.

I grinned. "I wasn't born a vampire."

She swatted my shoulder. "I know that. I just—I knew you were born into a coven of vampires, so . . ." She broke off with a shrug.

I offered a half smile and pressed gentle kisses along her collarbone. Her legs tensed, and she arched her head back. "Each of us prepares to Turn once we die," I murmured against her soft skin. "It happens differently for everyone." With my tongue, I traced light circles on the skin of her throat.

Brielle released a low moan. "You'll—you'll have to tell me that—that story sometime," she said in a strained voice. Her hips thrust forward against mine.

I laughed. "Is now not a good time?"

She laughed too, but it sounded hollow and raspy. I

raised my hand to her shoulder and slowly slid her tunic down. Brielle held her breath, her eyes widening. Fear and uncertainty filled her face, and I froze.

"Should I stop?" I whispered.

Our gazes held, and I raised my eyebrows. I kept my expression soft, hoping to convey to her it wouldn't upset me if we stopped. I would still love her even if she wanted to wait a hundred years.

Brielle swallowed and licked her lips. "No. Don't stop." She sat up so we faced each other on the bed. Then, with trembling hands, she pulled the tunic up and over her head, letting it fall to the floor. For a long moment, I drank her in just as she'd done me. Hunger and heat swirled in my head until I almost couldn't see straight.

Brielle's arms shifted as if she wanted to cover herself, but she fidgeted and kept them by her sides.

I reached forward and traced the length of her jaw, her shoulder, and then down to her stomach, my movements soft and feather light. Her eyes closed, her body leaning into me.

"You're beautiful," I breathed.

Her eyes opened to find mine. Flames flickered within the depths of her caramel-colored eyes, igniting the desire within me. Gently, I eased her backward so she lay on my bed like a porcelain goddess. With nimble movements, I slid off her trousers before removing mine as well.

I scooted forward and lay next to her. For a moment, we

simply gazed at each other. Our eyes traveled up and down our bodies, absorbing every imperfection and blemish, every private and secret part we kept tucked away from the world. Here we were, exposed for each other, laid bare with all our weaknesses. I'd never felt this deep a connection with any woman I'd bedded. Not even Estrella.

I hadn't loved her. I hadn't loved anyone until Brielle.

"You have scars too," I murmured. My fingers traced a white, jagged scar on left shoulder. Another smaller one on her stomach. A fresher pink scar rested just below her thigh, and when I brushed my fingers against it, Brielle stiffened and then giggled.

"Sorry," she muttered. "That tickles."

I grinned and leaned in to kiss her. Slowly, I positioned myself on top of her. Her fingernails dug into the skin of my shoulder, and I growled in response.

"Brielle—" A groan cut me off as her tongue flicked against mine. Heat burned between my legs, and I longed to finish, to dive into the pure ecstasy my body ached for.

But with Brielle, I wanted to take my time. This was her first. I wanted her to savor it.

Fire swelled in my body as I felt her chest rise and fall against mine. Her heavy breathing nearly drove me mad. Slowly, I eased my leg between hers and rubbed against her. She let out a strangled moan, and more flames burned within me until all I felt was heat. Redness crept in the corners of my eyes.

Brielle, Brielle, Brielle.

She was everything. My thoughts were consumed by her. Her breaths. Her moans. The way my name tore from her lips like a plea.

More redness clouded my vision until I could no longer see. Too late, I realized what was happening. Brielle's hands still reached for me as I drew back, stumbling off the bed.

"Leo—" she said uncertainly.

"Brielle, I don't—I can't—" I broke off as the heat within me raged like a monster. In my mind, I heard Lilith's laugh.

And then darkness took over.

22

BRIELLE

To be touched by Leo, to lie there naked with him, was like diving into ice cold water while completely on fire. It was like a presence within me stirring to life, awakened when his skin met mine. And the way his eyes burned with need and raw emotion made me want to hide and embrace him at the same time.

He loved me. I felt it in his gaze, in the careful movements of his hands along my body, in the desperate way his lips and tongue caressed my skin. But did I love him?

I knew he hadn't missed that I hadn't said it back. But he didn't seem to mind.

I didn't even know what love was. My only romance had been with Riker, and look at how that turned out. My body certainly felt like it loved Leo. And when he spread my legs and rubbed against me, I wanted to scream, *love, love, love.*

Just when the fire in my belly churned so intensely I

wanted to cry out, Leo pulled away. My body felt the absence of his heat like a chill, and I suddenly wanted to cover up.

Blinking and incoherent, I slowly sat up. My hair was a ruffled mess on top of my head, and my body ached to go back to what we were doing.

"Leo—" I stopped short, and my blood ran cold. All the arousal from earlier fled from me when Leo turned to face me. His eyes were all black, and a foreign and malicious grin spread across his face.

Lilith had possessed him.

I was suddenly painfully aware of how naked I was. And judging by the way Lilith's smile widened, I knew she was too.

"I do hate to interrupt this passionate moment," Leo said in a voice layered with whispers and hisses that raised goosebumps on my skin. "But I have need of your shapeshifting bloodsucker."

I bent over and dug through the mess of clothes until I found an athame still strapped to my belt. I wielded it toward Leo, who laughed at me.

"Stab me, Brielle?" he crowed. "If you attack me, you attack *him*."

"He can heal from this," I said through clenched teeth. "But it's an athame infused with light magic. It'll be painful for him—and you too. You're the goddess of all demons, after all." I cocked my head and narrowed my eyes, trying to avoid the way my stomach churned seeing such evil in Leo's eyes.

It's not him, I reminded myself over and over. *Be brave.*

"I bet there's a very small bond tethering you to his consciousness," I said. I sauntered closer to Leo, pretending like I wasn't mortified by my nudity or the fact that Lilith had probably watched the entire thing like some leaked sex tape. "Leo is the strongest demon I know. But if I stab you with this"—I wiggled the athame, and Leo stepped away from me—"I imagine it'll hurt so much that Leo will regain control and kick you out." I raised my eyebrows at her. "Care to test that theory?"

Leo's nostrils flared. "Don't challenge me, girl. You know *nothing* of my abilities. I can summon an undead army in an instant. I can penetrate through even the strongest of curses. And I can certainly defeat a pitiful thing like you."

"You failed before," I said.

Leo sneered at me. "Only because of your firebird. And . . . where is the precious creature?" He looked around in mock surprise. "Don't you ordinarily burst into flames in moments like this?" He gestured to my body, and I crossed my arms, feeling nausea swirling in my stomach.

The way Leo's black eyes glinted told me Lilith already knew this. She'd been testing me. Watching. Waiting.

And now she knew Nix was gone.

Rage pulsed through me, and I gritted my teeth. In a

quick movement, I hurled the athame at Leo. It sank into his chest. He fell to his knees with a groan, hunching over on all fours. Regret pulsed through me, but I couldn't dwell on it. I lunged and pinned him to the floor as blood welled from the wound. Pressing my arm into his throat, I shouted, "Leo! Leo, come back!"

Leo's eyes closed, and his head turned left and right. A strangled yell tore from his throat, and I pressed harder against him.

"Leo, it's me!" I cried. My eyes burned, and I blinked rapidly. *Don't cry now, you idiot.* "It's Brielle. Come back to me!"

His back arched, and he released a chilling roar of agony that seemed to rattle my bones. I resisted the urge to shrink away from him. The walls and floor quaked from his cry, and I glanced around nervously, waiting for the roof to collapse.

Then, everything went still. Leo's head still twisted back and forth as if he were asleep and trying to wake up. He murmured incoherently, his eyelids fluttering. His face drained of color, and his body suddenly went limp.

"Help!" I screamed, not caring who saw me naked. Leo could be dying. Lilith could've called my bluff and taken him from me. I had no idea what she was capable of, but I had no doubt she could kill whoever she possessed. "Someone *help!*"

The doors burst open, and Jorge hobbled forward, his

face strained from the movement. His eyes found me, and a blush exploded across his face. He quickly looked away from me and hissed, "For Lilith's sake, Brielle, clothe yourself."

"Lilith possessed him!" I shouted angrily. "I didn't have *time*. He might be dying, Jorge. I need your help."

Cursing under his breath, Jorge grabbed a robe draped on the armchair and tossed it at me. I quickly slipped it on and backed away from Leo.

Jorge inhaled sharply and looked at me with fire in his eyes. "You *stabbed* him?"

"He can heal!" I sputtered, knowing my excuses were feeble. "Lilith said she needed him. I knew he would rather die than be her puppet."

Jorge stared at me, his gaze hard. Then, something stirred in his eyes and he offered a jerky nod. "You're right," he said stiffly.

Am I hearing things? I thought. *Did Jorge just* agree *with me?*

"Athames can't kill vampires," I said, crossing my arms. "Right?"

"No, they can't. But the presence of a summoned demon can."

My blood chilled, and a lump formed in my throat. *Did I just kill Leo?*

Jorge knelt by Leo's side and waved a hand over his body. Black smoke inked out from Jorge's fingertips and surrounded Leo's chest. Jorge closed his eyes, his brows furrowing in concentration. My heart raced, and my hands itched to move or help somehow, but I forced myself to remain still.

At long last, Jorge dropped his hand, his face paling.

"What is it?" I demanded. Fear rippled through me, making me feel nauseous.

"There's darkness in him," Jorge said in a grim voice. "His body doesn't recognize my magic. That's never happened before."

I swallowed, staring at Leo's ashen face. He looked so weak. Weaker than I'd ever seen him before.

"Do you know anyone who can perform an exorcism?" I asked.

Jorge's gaze snapped to mine. "A *what*?"

I rolled my eyes. "You guys don't know that word? You know, when a demon possesses—"

"I know the word," Jorge snapped. "I—Leo, he—" He broke off and exhaled through his lips. "We don't associate with necromancers."

Necromancers. Of course only necromancers could do it. In my time, anyone could pursue the art of exorcising demons—healers, light witches, even aurologists like Mom.

I suddenly froze and shot to my feet. "Wait here," I muttered before bolting from the room. I hurried down the stairs, glancing around for any sign of my family. But of course, they were nowhere to be found. If they'd been close, they would've heard me screaming.

I tore down the hallway, checking the study and the sitting room before I stopped short. Muffled voices drifted from the servants' quarters. Without preamble, I shoved open the doors with a loud bang.

Angel yelped and jumped to her feet. With wide eyes, I surveyed the room. Angel, Riker, and my mom surrounded the small table. In a corner, a maid stitched one of Leo's shirts.

"Brie—" Angel's brow furrowed. Her eyes moved up and down my body, no doubt taking in Leo's too-big robe that fell loosely over me.

Riker's face reddened, and his gaze darted away from me. I ignored him and strode toward Mom.

"I need your help," I said.

Alarm and unease crossed Mom's face. Then, she looked over my robe and grimaced. "Oh, honey . . . I—you really should've figured this out before you and Leo—"

"Holy mother of Lilith, *stop!*" I said, my face burning as I realized what she thought. "Not with that. Leo's hurt. Can you perform an exorcism?"

Mom's head reared back, her face paling. "*What?* Brie, what happened?"

"Lilith happened," I said darkly. "There's no time to explain. Can you do it? Jorge says in this time period, only necromancers can do it, and I don't think we have time to track one down."

"I"—Mom bit her lip and glanced at Riker and Angel— "I've never done one before, Brie."

"But you've seen Elias do them before, right?" I remembered Mom telling us about her boss doing exorcisms.

Mom blinked rapidly, her face growing even paler. "Well, *yes*, but—"

"Then, come on." I tugged on her hand. "We need you upstairs."

Mom yanked her hand from my grasp. "Brie! I—I don't have any tools or equipment. I could *kill* him."

"I may have already done that," I said, my voice breaking. "Please, Mom. You're our only hope. At least . . . examine him while Jorge sends someone to find a necromancer."

Mom's mouth opened and closed as she sputtered incoherently. She looked at Riker and Angel again, who looked equally horrified. Then, Mom exhaled and nodded.

Relief washed over me, and I led her out of the room, down the hallway, and up the stairs.

Mercifully, Jorge had draped a blanket over Leo's naked body, but Mom still blushed when she walked in. Her eyes traveled to the pile of clothes by the bed and the rumpled sheets. She raised an eyebrow at me.

My face grew hot, and I waved a hand. "Later." I pointed to Leo, whose chest was still covered in blood.

Mom crouched down next to Jorge, who shot a curious glance at me but made no objection. Mom's eyes closed, and she pressed a hand against Leo's chest. Her brow furrowed, and her face scrunched up in concentration.

"Wow," she murmured. "I don't even need my aura detector to sense another presence in there. It's practically screaming at me."

"Does that mean you can remove it?"

Mom winced. "The stronger the presence, the tighter the grip they have on their host. It'll be like removing a giant leech from a beating heart."

A lump formed in my throat, and I couldn't speak. I couldn't even move.

"What do you need?" Jorge asked.

Mom rattled off a list of potion ingredients as well as some tools that made me think she would cut Leo open like for an autopsy. I was only half listening. Numbly, I staggered to the pile of clothes by the bed and slowly dressed myself. When I pulled on my tunic, I remembered how Leo had deftly slid it off my shoulders, his eyes hungry with need.

His words rang in my head. *I would love you even if no blood flowed through your veins. Even if you were nothing more than a spirit haunting me with your stubbornness and anger, I would still love you.*

I ran my fingers over the tangled sheets on Leo's bed,

thinking of what would've happened—what we would've done—if Lilith hadn't interrupted us.

I expected to feel sick at the thought. It wasn't that long ago that Leo repulsed me.

Instead, I found myself filled with . . . *regret.*

I'd wanted to share this with him. Never in my life had I met a man I thought was worth losing my virginity to.

Until now.

Warmth tickled my throat, and I blinked rapidly as my vision clouded with tears. What if I never got to tell him how I felt?

Stop it, Brie. He'll be fine.

Suddenly, a bolt of magic shot through me as severely as an electric shock. I doubled over, clutching my stomach. Pain and anger coursed through me. My vision blurred, and then I saw Leo's face crumpled in agony. My blood boiled as he called to me. To my blood.

In an instant, the feeling vanished, leaving me cold and empty. My heart racing, I glanced over my shoulder. Leo still lay there, completely motionless. But I'd felt him. I was sure of it.

I'm his Donor, I realized. *We share a bond.* Leo had said something about how vampires and Donors had a connection that warned them when they were in danger.

I couldn't deny what I'd seen—what I'd *felt.* He was in trouble. He was in pain. And I had to do something about it.

I straightened and turned from the bed. Jorge was gone,

no doubt off to get Mom's ingredients. Mom murmured a spell, her hands glowing blue as she moved them up and down Leo's body like a scanner.

I strode toward the door. Mom didn't glance up as I passed, but she asked, "Could you send your father if you see him? I'll need his help."

I muttered a response before bolting from the room. My body pulsed with energy, my blood churning as determination fueled me.

There was another way to push Lilith out.

By giving her what she wanted.

23
LEO

Faint screams filled my mind. I vaguely registered Brielle's voice calling to me, but it was gone before I could respond. Darkness and red clouds flooded my vision. Thunder rumbled around me.

Then, suddenly, everything went still. I was surrounded by darkness. I tried shifting, but my body was frozen. A roar of fury built up in my throat, unable to release.

What the hell have you done to me, you viper? I wanted to shout at Lilith. I thought of Brielle, naked and waiting for me on the bed. What had Lilith done to her?

I will end you, I vowed. *Even if it takes my life, I swear I will end you.*

I wriggled and shifted, trying to break free of the vise that gripped me, but it was no use. It was as if my mind was floating in a vast and empty void—with no ties to my body at all.

Like my body wasn't mine anymore.
It was Lilith's.

24

BRIELLE

Before I could sneak out of Leo's house, Angel caught me. Of course. She stood in front of the door, her arms crossed and her eyes narrowed.

"Where are you going?" she demanded.

There was no point trying to fool her—I was already dressed in my cloak and fully armed.

"Don't get in my way," I growled. "You can't stop me, Angel."

"Brie, what're you going to do?" Angel asked, her face softening. "You have that look on your face."

"What look?"

"The 'I'm going to do something reckless and stupid' look."

I scowled at her. "Go ahead. Try and stop me. I'll fight you off if I have to, Angel."

"Brie—"

"Leo is *dying*," I said, my voice breaking. "And I have a way to save him. But you *have* to let me go. Please, Angel."

Angel stared at me for a long moment, her dark eyes full of sympathy and concern. "Let me come with you."

"No, Mom needs Dad's help. I need you to go find him while I take care of this."

"If you're going where I think you are, we can find him on the way. He's with Benito's pack."

I stiffened, my blood running cold. "Why?"

"Trying to mediate. Obviously, things have gotten out of hand. He thinks as a peaceful third party he can help smooth things over."

I swore and rubbed my forehead. When I looked at Angel, she was smirking. "What?" I snapped.

She shrugged, feigning innocence. "I just feel like I've seen that kind of behavior before. You know, running off on his own to solve everyone's problems and risking his life in the process." She raised her eyebrows.

I shoved past her toward the door. "I don't have time for your sarcasm, Angel." With a huff, I threw open the door and hurried down the steps of the porch. Then, I glanced over my shoulder. "Are you coming, or what?"

Angel closed the door, and we strode quickly down the road. The streets were eerily quiet. Ordinarily we'd find merchants and villagers bustling about, but it was like a ghost town. My skin prickled with suspicion, and I exchanged a worried glance with Angel.

"Stay close," I muttered.

She nodded, her eyes wide as we skirted down a dark alley, winding between buildings to avoid drawing attention. With the streets so empty, anyone keeping watch would notice us right away.

"Do you know how Lilith possessed him?" Angel asked in a whisper.

I shook my head stiffly. "He has Timecaster blood, though." My gaze slid toward Angel, and her face paled. I knew we were thinking the same thing.

"Lots of us here are Timecasters," Angel breathed.

"I know." I looked at her again. "Have you felt anything? Anything funny?"

She raised an eyebrow. "You mean like I'm being possessed? No, I haven't." Suddenly, her mouth twisted like she might be sick, and she flung out a hand to stop me. "Brie."

I shot her an irritated look and exhaled. "What? We can't stop."

"I'm not a Timecaster."

I blinked. Then, I remembered what Mom had said last year when I'd first found out: *You and I are Timecasters, but your dad and Angel aren't.* I hadn't thought much of it at the time. "Okay, so the gene doesn't always pass down or something? I don't know, it doesn't matter right now, Angel."

Angel's mouth opened and closed. She clenched her

teeth and dropped her gaze, then nodded. "Right. Of course. It doesn't matter right now." Her gaze grew distant.

In any other situation, I would've pressed her to know what she was thinking. But time was of the essence. We had to move.

I took her hand and led her down the narrow road, pausing occasionally to smell the air. A lingering stench of wet dog stung my nose, but it mingled with other disturbing scents—blood, ash, and black magic.

Something dark was happening to the city. A chill of foreboding swept through me.

Bring back Leo, then focus on the city. I repeated the words again and again to quell the mounting panic within me. My fingers itched to organize something, to busy myself with a mindless task. In the castle, I used to sneak into the library and arrange books by color. I couldn't say I missed those days, but I certainly missed that coping mechanism.

The wolves' smell took us toward the castle, and I groaned inwardly. Of course Benito would still be holed up inside. The last thing I wanted to do was go back to the place I'd been imprisoned and tortured. But if it was the only way to save Leo, then I had to do it.

We approached the courtyard in front of the castle. A pair of werewolf sentries stood by the front doors. I strode confidently toward them, and Angel's hand shook in my grasp.

"Are you sure about this?" she muttered.

I nodded, though uncertainty swirled in my stomach, making me feel sick.

Be strong, Brie.

The guards stiffened when they saw us approach, their yellow eyes gleaming with malice. Though they were only in human form, I felt a prickle of unease shoot through me. It didn't take much for these wolves to shift. When Benito had cornered me in the alley, half his body had morphed before I'd even registered it.

"You ladies must be lost," one of the men sneered, sharing an amused expression with his comrade.

I lifted my chin. "We're here to see Benito. I have something he wants."

"I'm sure you do." The second man's eyes roved over my body with disturbing slowness.

Rage flowed through me. I aimed a high kick in his chest and sent him sprawling. The first man roared in fury, but I drew my athame and held it to his throat.

"Let us enter," I growled. "Please." Beside me, I sensed Angel draw a dagger as well, though I hadn't even noticed she was armed.

"Unless this blade is made of silver," the first man hissed, "I'll just heal from this."

"True," I said. "But I'm sure it'll hurt like hell." I pressed the blade into his skin until a drop of blood oozed down his neck. "Care to test it?"

The man's body shook, and he clenched his teeth. "No." He looked to his comrade. "Let them through."

The second man's eyes widened as he glanced from his friend to me and Angel. "*What*? You—"

"It's *her*, Andre," the first man snapped. "You know what Benito said about her."

Suspicion quivered through my body, but I kept myself composed, my gaze flicking from Andre to the other guard. My grip on the blade never faltered.

Andre sighed. In a flash, he shifted to wolf form—a tall scrawny black wolf. He stood on all fours, back arched, and then raised his head with a fierce howl. The sound rattled my bones and chilled my blood. My eardrums burned from the shrillness of the howl. A lump formed in my throat as I exchanged an alarmed glance with Angel.

No turning back now.

The huge entrance doors opened, and I realized the wolf howl had been a signal to let us in. I dropped my arm, and the first man staggered away from me, his eyes burning with rage.

"You'll pay for that, bitch," he muttered, quiet enough for only me hear.

I glared at him and sheathed my blade. "It's been a real pleasure."

Andre led us through the entrance doors where another pair of wolves stood on guard. They nodded to Andre and watched me and Angel with unabashed curiosity.

We entered the massive foyer and strode toward the hallway. The statues and paintings shone as magnificently as if the servants had just cleaned them. For a moment, I was transported to a year ago when I lived here. I could almost hear voices floating from the dining hall and Riker's laughter from the alcove where we'd almost kissed.

My face burned, and I shoved the thoughts away. We passed the shadowy alcove that I knew led to the dungeons. A sick feeling swirled in my stomach. With a deep breath, I averted my gaze, determined to stay focused.

Find Benito. Find Dad.

When Andre continued walking with us, I realized we needed to alter our plan. We couldn't find my dad *and* Benito if we were guarded the entire time.

"Where is my father?" I demanded, stopping in the hallway.

Andre stopped and raised an eyebrow. "Your father?"

"Yes. He came here to negotiate with Benito, and no one has seen him since."

Andre smirked, his eyes gleaming. "He was a fool to come alone, girl. Benito treats prisoners as he sees fit."

Andre turned to continue down the hallway, but I stayed put. I grabbed Angel's wrist to keep her next to me.

Andre sighed and turned to face us again. "You aren't in any position to make demands, little girl."

My nostrils flared. "I have what Benito wants. I'm not giving it up until I know my family's safe."

Andre's jaw went rigid, and he stepped toward me. I resisted the urge to back away from him and instead looked up at him through narrowed eyes.

"You can make your demands to Benito," Andre hissed. His foul breath stung my nose, and the stench of wet dog surrounded me. "Now, follow me before he imprisons you again."

My fingers clenched into a tight fist, and Angel grabbed my arm. "Brie," she whispered warningly.

Gradually, my hand relaxed, and I lifted my chin, my eyes never leaving Andre. "Fine," I said through clenched teeth.

Triumph sparked in Andre's eyes, and he offered a smug smile that made me want to punch him in the face. "This way," he said, turning back to lead us down the hallway.

Bastard. I stared hard at the back of his head, hoping to slice it open with my eyes. I felt Angel's arm brush against mine, and I slowly tilted my head toward her. Barely moving my lips, I whispered, "When I distract him, you escape and find Dad."

Her arm stiffened in my grip. "Brie—"

"I'm the only one who can negotiate with Benito. Dad's probably in the dungeon." I jerked my head backward. "It's in that shadowy alcove there. Find him, get him out, and get home."

"I'm *not* leaving you."

"I have what Benito wants." I widened my eyes at her. "And I'm giving it to him. I'm not expecting to leave here."

Angel stopped short, her mouth falling open. "*Brie—*"

"What's the problem?" Andre snapped, glancing back at us.

Angel's mouth clamped shut, her eyes shifting to Andre. I nodded at her, hoping to reassure her, but her brows bunched together in concern. I knew she wouldn't drop this.

But I needed her to. She *had* to get Dad out. I wouldn't be able to live with myself if he was hurt or killed all because Lilith wanted my phoenix.

"Everything's fine," I said, striding forward confidently. Andre raised a suspicious eyebrow at me as I continued down the hallway with him.

Nearby, I noticed a familiar alcove with a shelf full of elaborate ceramic vases. Perfect.

Over my shoulder, I met Angel's gaze and nodded slightly. Then, I stumbled forward into the vases. They shattered with an earsplitting sound that echoed in the vast hallway.

Andre whirled on me, his eyes blazing. I lay in a crumpled heap on the floor, moaning pitifully. He jerked me up by my elbow.

"Watch your step, you clumsy whore," he spat, yanking me up forcefully. When he turned back around, Angel was gone.

I bit back a smile. *Way to go, sis.*

Andre swore and darted up and down the hallway. Black fur sprang on his arms, and panic welled inside me.

"Stop!" I shouted, waving my hands. His transformation halted, but he was still covered in fur. His hungry yellow eyes drilled into mine. "Take me to see Benito. *Now.*"

Andre bared his fangs at me and stepped toward me. A low growl built in his throat. "You planned this."

I jabbed a finger into his chest. "So what if I did? I have what Benito wants—the reason he struck a bargain with Lilith in the first place. I'm offering my *phoenix* to him. And if you take off trying to hunt down my sister, I'll withdraw that offer. I don't think your boss will be too happy if you mess this up. Especially after all the careful plans he's made."

Andre stiffened. Rage emanated from him so thickly I felt like I was suffocating. But I held my ground. As I stared into his eyes, I saw a flicker of fear piercing through his anger before it vanished.

Andre leaned close enough for his breath to sting my nose. "I'll deliver you to Benito. And then I'll hunt down your sister and make sure she pays for your trickery."

Worry and fear swirled in my chest, but I clenched my fingers into fists, trying to quell my emotions.

Our staring contest only lasted a moment longer before Andre turned on his heel and continued down the hallway. I followed him in silence until he led me to the large throne room. I'd only been in this room a handful of times while exploring the castle. It was flanked by two grand thrones and a wide space for courtiers to congregate, no doubt. Benito, in all his glory, sat on the king's throne leafing through papers. He was lounging backward as casually as if he were chilling on a couch at home.

"What a douchebag," I muttered.

Andre shot me a filthy look over his shoulder.

Benito glanced up from his papers, his expression almost bored. "Are you here for another prison cell, little witch? Was the first one not to your liking?"

Don't take the bait, Brie, I told myself. Shouting at him wouldn't solve anything. My voice was stiff as I said, "I've come to make a deal with you."

Benito scoffed and handed Andre his stack of papers before rising to his feet. Though he towered over me, I stared at him, never breaking eye contact.

"Is that so," he murmured. It wasn't a question.

My nostrils flared, but I kept my expression composed. "Yes. I've come to offer you my phoenix."

Benito went very still, though something unreadable flickered in his eyes. His gaze slid to Andre as they communicated wordlessly. Then, Benito looked at me, his eyes wary. "Really." His voice was dripping with sarcasm.

"Yes. In exchange for Lilith's safe return of Leo Serrano."

Benito threw his head back and laughed, his voice

bouncing off the magnificent walls. I crossed my arms and chewed on my lower lip, impatiently waiting for him to stop. When he finished milking it by wiping an imaginary tear from his eye, he looked at me with a satisfied smirk. "You must think me a fool, Brielle."

"Among other things."

Andre shifted behind me, muttering foul curses under his breath. Benito raised a hand, and Andre went still.

"I know what you mean to Leo Serrano," Benito said, moving closer to me. My skin crawled from his nearness, but I held my ground, trying to shove away the growing nausea inside me. "But I also know he serves a greater purpose for the Dark Lady. Forgive me if I don't believe you, Brielle. Besides, Her Ladyship has indicated to me that you no longer have control over your firebird." He spread his arms as if he'd caught me in his trap. "You have nothing to offer me."

"I no longer have control over the phoenix because she has been infused with dark magic," I said in an even voice. "Lilith's magic. Since I am a light witch, we are no longer connected." I paused, knowing that once I said it, I couldn't turn back from this plan. I took a breath and said, "But if I become a demon, then the phoenix and I will be bonded once more. She will be mine to command."

Silence rang in the room from my words, and I heard Benito's sharp intake of breath. His eyes widened a fraction before he composed himself. "You're bluffing. You would never turn yourself over to dark magic—and you would never turn over your firebird, either."

I took a deep breath. "I would . . . for Leo."

Benito's eyes narrowed, and he laughed again. "As heartwarming as your charade is, little witch, I'm afraid I don't believe you." He nodded at Andre, who drew forward and grabbed my arm.

I shook him off with a grunt and stepped toward Benito. "I *am* telling the truth. And if you don't accept my deal, then I'll become a demon on my own and bond with my phoenix. Then, I'll use her to destroy you and free Leo myself. I'm sure Lilith will be thrilled when I come to her directly and tell her you refused my offer of what she wants most."

Benito paled slightly, his eyes flashing. "Don't threaten me, girl."

"I think we're long past that," I growled, my blood boiling as I remembered the way he grabbed me in the alley.

Benito stared at me, his jaw ticking back and forth as he contemplated this. Then, he pointed at me as if just realizing something. "You said *become a demon on your own*? If I agree to your terms, what exactly are you asking of me?"

No turning back, I reminded myself. My heart raced, but I kept my body composed. Lifting my chin, I said, "I want you to bite me."

25
LEO

Face me, I roared in my head. *Face me, you coward!*

But as always, Lilith remained silent, and my mind was nothing more than a vacant void. Weak. Powerless.

Think, Leo, I urged myself. I felt restless, which was bizarre because I couldn't feel my body at all. I saw nothing but darkness. Terrifying emptiness.

I needed to offer something that Lilith would want. But she wanted Brielle's firebird. What could I possibly offer her?

Horror and realization clawed at my mind as an idea formed. The emotions swirled within me, warring with each other, until my panic and desperation won over.

I'll do it. For Brielle. I had no other choice.

Lilith! I roared in my head again. *I have something you want. Come and face me so we can discuss a trade.*

I expected her to ignore me as usual. Just as I resigned myself to think of something else, a flash of red magic burst against my vision. I wanted to flinch or shy away from the brightness of the light, but I still had no access to my body.

Then, I saw her. Lilith stood before me with wild curly dark hair and eyes completely consumed with black. She flashed her sharp, jagged teeth at me in an eerie smile.

"Hello, darling bloodsucker," she crooned, cocking her head at me. "What is this trade you speak of?"

I blinked, my jaw dropping—and then realized I had my body back. I glanced at my legs and hands. I wore nothing but a loose, satin robe, and my chest was covered in blood, though I felt no pain. Squinting, I looked around. We were in my room—the bed was still unmade from my heated moment with Brielle.

"Jorge!" I shouted, rushing toward the door. "Brielle! Where are you?"

A red forcefield slammed into me, and I staggered backward, my head spinning. Rubbing my forehead, I whirled to face Lilith. "What have you done to them?"

"I haven't done anything," Lilith said, her eyebrows lifting in an almost innocent expression. She spread her hands wide. "We are in the Astral Realm. No one is here but us."

My eyes narrowed. "You're lying."

"This is where the little witch and I fought long ago."

Lilith smirked. "When she vanished for months, she was here with me."

I went very still. I remembered those months of torture when I feared Brielle wouldn't wake. And when she did, it seemed no time had passed for her at all.

The same thing had happened to my sister, Lucia.

Does this mean I won't wake up for weeks—even months? My blood chilled at the thought. Judging by the blood on my chest, everyone would think I was dead.

I can't be killed by a blade, I thought frantically. *Only a stake.*

"Yes, but they know I possessed you," Lilith said, her eyes flashing with malice. "They will have assumed I took your soul." She cocked her head and smiled again. "And I plan to take it, unless you have a better offer for me."

I swallowed and drew myself up, fighting off the fear and anger burning within me. "I offer myself to you—willingly. As your slave."

Lilith stared at me, her black eyes piercing through me. Then, her lips stretched wide to reveal dark, stained teeth as she laughed. "You are such a fool, Leonardo Serrano. This is no offer. It is a pitiful attempt to distract me. How can you offer yourself when you are already mine?"

I clenched my teeth. "Yes, I am already yours. But you have taken my body by force. You should know better than anyone that a fighter like me can resist demonic possession. In fact"—I gestured around us and smirked at her—"I'd wager *that's* why we're here. Because I fought you off. You said you had plans for me?" I crossed my arms and raised my eyebrows. "Well, by all means. Execute those plans. Use me for your purposes, Lilith. What are you waiting for?"

We stood there staring at each other for a long moment. Then, Lilith's eyebrows lowered as she glared at me. "How dare you—"

"No, how dare *you*?" I growled, stepping toward her. "You dare to presume I am yours when you are just as trapped as I am?" I took a breath and said in a calm voice, "But if you accept my trade, I will give myself up willingly. You can take me for your own and use me however you like."

Lilith pressed her lips together, considering. "And in exchange?"

"In exchange, you spare my coven. Remove your servant Benito so my people will not perish."

Lilith's mouth stretched in another cruel smile. "Sadly, I cannot influence Benito or his pack anymore. My work with them is complete. Their bodies are their own now."

I shook my head. "You're lying."

"I am being earnest," she said. "I influenced them to do my bidding, and the work is done. They have made their choices, and I cannot change their will without killing them. I must save my strength for my other plans." Her smile widened.

Other plans. Rage and panic burned inside me until I

was filled with the urge to wrap my hands around her throat.

Keep calm, Leo. You have her here. Find a way out. "Then —then spare Brielle. Spare my coven from your influence."

"I have already made my mark on your coven as well," Lilith said softly.

A chill rippled up my spine. *Who? Who has she influenced?*

"But," Lilith went on, clasping her hands in front of her, "I can retreat from your people and spare them from any *further* influence of mine. I do not need them anymore. My work with them is complete, after all. I was *hoping* to amuse myself by causing turmoil among your people, but with you here offering yourself so willingly . . ." She grinned again. "Well, how could I resist?"

I swallowed. "Then, let me return to help my people face the threat. Let me fight alongside them. And then I am yours."

Lilith chuckled, shaking her head. "I am no fool, Leonardo. If I free you, you will not return to me willingly."

"I will. I swear it. I will make a blood bargain to prove it."

Lilith froze, watching me. Scrutinizing me. I held her gaze, resisting the urge to fidget and shift my weight. Her dark eyes bore into mine like she was sifting through my words, reading my very soul.

Then, she cracked another smile. "I see your intent is pure, Leonardo. I agree to your terms."

"You will remove yourself from my people?" I verified. *Get her to say the words.*

Lilith inclined her head. "Yes. And I will restore your body after you perform a blood bargain with me. You have until the end of the battle with your coven before I summon you to the Underworld."

The Underworld. A dark sense of foreboding fell over me like a shadow, warning me this was wrong.

I will never return. If she takes me to the Underworld, I will have no way to return.

But for my people—for Brielle—it was worth it. I couldn't let Benito's pack destroy them. And I had the sneaking suspicion that Lilith had more horrors planned for my people. I had to protect them. I had to fight for them.

I nodded. "Very well." I stretched my hand toward her, and Lilith raked one of her long, claw-like fingernails down my palm. Pain flared against my skin, and blood oozed from the wound. Then, she dragged her nail against her own skin, drawing blood. We clasped hands. My blood burned against hers, and red magic swirled around our hands.

"I, Lilith of the Underworld, the Dark Lady and Mistress of Darkness, vow to you, Leonardo Serrano, shapeshifter and vampire coven leader of Segovia, Spain, to remove my influence from your coven and return you to your proper form until the battle has finished."

White hot pain erupted in my palm, and I gritted my teeth, struggling to hold on, though her magic scorched me. My voice never wavered as I spoke. "I, Leonardo Serrano, shapeshifter and vampire coven leader of Segovia, Spain, vow to you, Lilith of the Underworld, the Dark Lady and Mistress of Darkness, to willingly turn myself over to you as your slave to perform your bidding as soon as the battle is finished."

The heat between us intensified. I bit down hard on my lip, tasting blood. My hand shook in Lilith's grasp, and her eyes gleamed as if she knew the pain I was in.

At long last, the agony subsided, but still I held on. My eyes were level with hers. *I am strong,* I reminded myself. *I am fierce. I will not be weakened by her.*

Lilith chuckled, and I knew she read my mind. She dropped my hand and sighed. "Oh, Leonardo. I will do so much more than weaken you."

Before I could respond, she waved her hand. Her red magic swirled around me, suffocating me and obscuring her from view. I coughed, closing my eyes against the sting of her foul dark magic. Nausea stirred in my stomach, and I clenched my fingers into tight fists.

A gasp tore from my throat, and my eyes flew open. My gaze settled on the ornate dome ceiling of my bedroom. Blue magic flashed before me, and a low voice murmured a spell.

Pain stabbed through my chest, and I cried out. Someone yelped next to me, and the blue magic vanished.

"Leo!"

Disoriented, I blinked, trying to see clearly. "I—Brielle?" I tried sitting up and groaned as dizziness clouded my vision.

"Shh," the woman said, pushing me back against the bed. "Rest. You're still healing."

My vision cleared, and I saw Desi standing above me. Her hair was wilder than normal, and dark circles rimmed her eyes. In her hand was a long, jagged knife dripping with blood.

My blood.

I jerked forward, tumbling out of the bed and collapsing in a heap on the floor.

"Leo—"

I scrambled to my feet, raising my hands to ward her off. *She has Timecaster blood. Lilith could have influenced her.* "Stay back," I warned.

Desi's eyes widened, and then her gaze shifted to the knife. She gasped and set it down on the ground. "I—I was performing an exorcism. I had to extract your blood from the wound. And"—she broke off with a nervous chuckle—"it appears to have worked."

I opened my mouth to correct her but then stopped. *It's better if she believes this. It's better if no one knows of my bargain with Lilith.* My mouth clamped shut and I nodded. "Thank you. I, uh—where is Brielle?"

Desi's face paled, and she dropped her gaze.

I stepped toward her, fear chilling my bones. "Desi. Where is she?"

She finally met my gaze, and her terror matched my own. "She went to see Benito. To barter for your life."

26

LEO

IN A FLASH, I DRESSED IN MY ARMOR AND HOLSTERED my pistol. Then, I gathered my shadows around me to shift. To my surprise, my familiar black magic poured from my fingertips and surrounded my body, engulfing me in an inky cloud. The smell of my own magic filled me with warmth and comfort like a lost friend found.

The relief was short lived, though, as I realized Lilith would only have withdrawn her red magic from me if she was certain she would have me later. The absence of her power haunted me like a dark cloud hanging over me. A grim reminder of my fate.

Not now, Leo, I told myself. I couldn't dwell on it now.

Once I was out the servants' door in the back, I shifted to a hawk and took off toward the Castillo de Coca. The wind whipped against my wings and feathers, but I kept my eyes fixed on the castle ahead.

If he kills Brielle, this has all been for nothing. I have *to save her. She must be safe.*

Though my great wings flapped, pushing miles behind me, it felt excruciatingly slow. While I flew, I imagined horrific things happening to Brielle. More torture. Physical assault. Brielle's screams ringing in the dungeon.

Fear and panic swirled within me. *Why the hell would she go to him? How could she be so foolish?*

As I landed in front of the castle courtyard, I was reminded of when my brother, Ronaldo, had recklessly stolen into the castle against my wishes.

The Count had killed him.

But I'd be damned if I lost Brielle the same way.

I shifted back to my vampire form and charged toward the sentries posted outside the doors. Before either of them could speak, I lunged and tore open their throats with my teeth, leaving them bleeding out on the concrete. I knew they would heal and wake later. But I didn't care. My pistol would be too loud and draw too much attention.

I pulled at the doors, but they were locked. I rammed my fist repeatedly against the wood, not expecting a response.

For Lilith's sake, don't make me swim through the moat again.

Fire burned in my chest, and I sucked in a breath before shifting again, this time to a beetle. I shook off the disorientation of squeezing myself into a creature so small and wriggled through the cracks of the giant entrance doors. When I was free, I shifted again, teetering slightly from the dizziness of so much shifting.

An array of voices surrounded me, but my head wasn't clear yet. Hands grabbed my collar and threw me against the wall. Stars danced in my eyes.

Dammit, Leo, focus!

My vision cleared, honing in on the snarling faces of the guards assaulting me. I smashed my head against the werewolf closest to me, and he stumbled backward with a groan. Then, afraid another shift would render me useless, I drew my sword and drove it into the stomach of the second guard. When he crumpled, I bolted down the hallway, faltering for a moment as I considered where Brielle would be.

Benito would've imprisoned her on the spot, I thought. *Or . . . taken her straight to his bedchamber.* I suppressed a chill at the thought, trying to shove down the white-hot rage that filled my mind.

Dungeon first. I had to assume Brielle had fought him off and Benito had imprisoned her in self-preservation.

I wouldn't let myself consider the alternative: that Benito had assaulted Brielle and killed her when she didn't comply.

Remembering stealing into the castle with Brielle's parents, I stopped at a shadowy alcove that led to the dungeon staircase. I pulled open the doors and crept soundlessly down the stairs, trying to ignore the stifling smell of demon blood that surrounded me.

Familiar scents tickled my nose. My brows furrowed as I tried to place them. Some were old, but some were fresh and pungent.

Oliver. Was he here now, or was I smelling him from when we were here previously? I smelled faint traces of Brielle, as well as a fresher whiff of her sister, Angel.

My blood chilled. *No.* Brielle must've brought her sister. How could she be so foolish? Why hadn't she taken Jorge or Miguel?

I gritted my teeth, reminding myself that my anger wouldn't solve anything. Especially if Brielle was already—

Don't think it, Leo.

I followed Angel's scent, sensing her nearby. Something rattled against the metal bars, and then all was silent.

They know someone's down here.

I stopped, remaining absolutely still. A hushed whisper echoed, followed by more metallic rattling. Frowning, I inched closer. If they were Benito's men, why were they whispering?

I stiffened as two figures came into view. One was inside the prison cell while the other was outside it, fiddling with the lock.

"Angel?" I hissed.

Angel dropped the lock against the cell with a loud clang, looking up at me with wide eyes. She pressed a hand to her chest. "Mother of Lilith, Leo, you scared me half to death." She looked me over, her face filled with concern. "You're all right!"

"Thanks to your mother." I glanced at the prison cell and made out Oliver's features through the bars. His face was beaten and bloody, but his eyes blazed with the familiar fire I often saw. "What happened here?"

"Dad came to negotiate an armistice with Benito," Angel said grimly. "They imprisoned him."

Panic coursed through me. "And . . . where is Brielle?" I squinted, glancing through the nearby cells as if I could make out her hunched figure like when I'd rescued her before.

Angel swallowed, her gaze darting to Oliver for a moment. "She's . . . with Benito."

"*What?*"

"She had a plan!" Angel said quickly, raising her hands as if that would calm me. "She was going to offer up her phoenix in exchange for you."

"She doesn't *have* her phoenix anymore," I growled, my chest twisting with rage. "Are you saying she marched in here to offer Benito something she *doesn't have*? She's bluffing? Against an entire pack of wolves?"

Angel's face paled, and Oliver slammed his fist on the bars. "Stop arguing and get me the hell out of here!" he hissed. Though anger laced his tone, I could read the panic in his eyes.

He feared for his daughter, just as I did.

I snatched the pins in Angel's hands and picked the lock, my fingers shaking with fear and rage. It took me multiple attempts before it finally sprang open. The cell creaked as Oliver pushed it open, and then the three of us flew up the stairs.

The hallway was eerily quiet. Where the hell was everyone? Aside from the guards I'd attacked, I hadn't encountered anyone.

I sniffed deeply, sensing Brielle's presence in the air. Then, I surged forward, following her scent. We hurried down the hall toward the throne room. When I threw open the doors, a crowd of werewolves turned to face me.

The wolves were gathered in a circle in their human form, though some sprouted fur and claws as if they couldn't help it. Candles were lit around the circle of wolves, and within the circle was an inert figure I recognized.

"Brielle!" I cried, hurrying to her.

Benito stepped in my path. White fur lined his jaw and arms, and the yellow of his eyes gleamed even more prominently. He bared his fangs at me. "Stay back, Serrano. You're interrupting a sacred ritual."

My blood chilled as I glanced from Benito to Brielle. Then, anger darkened my vision, and I shoved Benito backward before landing a blow on his jaw. He staggered, and several of his men rushed me.

My fangs emerged, and I used them as knives, tearing through the flesh of my assailants. I tasted skin and bone, but I kept fighting them off. A few of them shifted to wolf form and leapt for me.

"Get Brielle!" I roared, but Oliver was already fighting off wolves to get to her. A blast of fire exploded in the air as Oliver used his powers to ward off the pack.

Pain tore through my shoulder as a wolf raked his claws through me. I shifted to bat form and flew high above them, circling the ceiling until I floated to the ground to where Brielle was. When I shifted, my vision darkened, and I collapsed on the floor next to Brielle.

"My love," I murmured, dazed, trying to reach for her.

The stench of wet dog filled my nose as a wolf grabbed me. I felt his furry hands on my throat, but my blurry vision prevented me from responding.

"You *did* warn me that terrible things happen when a vampire is infected by a wolf," a harsh, familiar voice said in my ear. "Let's test it, shall we?"

Benito leaned in. I felt his teeth scrape against my throat when he was suddenly blasted backward by a burst of red magic. In an instant, my vision cleared, and I was on my feet, facing an array of shocked and angry wolves.

Lilith's magic. Of course she would protect me.

Because she still needed me.

"Leo," gasped a voice.

I dropped my gaze and found Brielle sitting up, watching me with wide, horrified eyes.

She'd seen the red magic. She must have.

"Later," I muttered before scooping her up in my arms.

Oliver shot more fire from his hands, and several wolves dived out of the way to avoid getting scorched, creating an opening in the crowd. I sprinted through the wolves and toward the door. Oliver's face was bleeding and Angel clutched a wound on her arm, but they were well enough to run with me. Benito's roar of fury echoed in the throne room as we tore down the hallway and away from our enemies.

27

BRIELLE

WHATEVER DRUG BENITO HAD GIVEN ME LEFT ME feeling groggy and confused like when I'd gotten my wisdom teeth taken out two years ago. I tried to shake off the numbness, but it lingered, clouding my vision.

Had I seen Leo use *red magic*?

But . . . he was *here*. Which meant Mom's exorcism had worked, right?

Leo's spicy scent filled my nose, making me feel even dizzier. My skin felt hot in all the places he touched me, and I couldn't help but remember the unfinished business we had in his bedroom.

Then, my disoriented mind fogged again, and my head slumped backward. I jostled in Leo's arms, the rocky motion making me feel nauseous as we ran down the hall and past the unconscious guards at the door. Dad heaved open the door, and the brightness of the sun burst against my eyes.

Leo's arms tensed as the sun beat down on him, but still he carried me.

"I . . . can walk," I rasped. "Put me down."

"No," Leo growled.

I gazed up at him, blinking against the sunlight, and found his jaw rigid and his eyes blazing. He wouldn't look at me.

Is he angry with me?

Well, I couldn't blame him. Benito and his wolves had been about to bite me so I would Turn.

"Leo, the sun—" I said.

"I'm fine," Leo snapped.

"I'll take her." Dad stepped forward and took me from Leo's arms. His arms were softer and more familiar, and the heat swarming in my head subsided slightly.

Yes, it was better that Dad carried me. Being in Leo's arms was too distracting.

Angel's raspberry scent wafted through my nose. *Thank Lilith she's safe.* She muttered close to my ear, "Brie, what did they do to you?"

I shook my head dizzily. "Turning . . . ritual."

Dad stiffened, his body jolting from my words. "They were going to *Turn* you?" he roared.

"Dad," I hissed, blinking against the lights flickering in my vision. When would my vision clear? How long would the effects of the drug last?

"But it's not a full moon," said Angel quietly. "It's not even nighttime."

"There are other ways to Turn someone," Leo said darkly. "You need a full pack and a blood ritual to do it."

"Brie, are you *insane*?" Dad said through clenched teeth. "Why would you agree to that?"

"Nix," I mumbled. "She's a demon. I had to bond with her."

Silence followed my words. I pressed my face against Dad's chest, ready to fall asleep, when suddenly, he spoke again.

"Brie, *I'm* a demon," Dad said. "If you wanted to practice dark magic, why didn't you come to me?"

"No time," I said. "Leo was in trouble."

I heard a sharp intake of breath and knew it was Leo. But at that moment, the sluggishness of my brain took over, and I slumped against my dad, falling blissfully into unconsciousness.

When I awoke, I was in the guest room at Leo's. I groaned and sat up, wondering bitterly how many times I'd wake up from being trapped in that damn castle.

I was an idiot. An ignorant, stubborn, idiot.

Thankfully, the fog in my head had subsided, though a splitting headache took its place. I sat up, looking around for a pitcher of water, when I noticed movement against the wall. I stiffened, feeling around for a weapon, but I was dressed only in my shift.

When the shadows peeled off the wall, I realized it was Leo. My body relaxed, but only slightly. Just the sight of him —*in my bedroom*—made my pulse race.

"You're here," I said stupidly as he stepped toward me. Then, I noticed the hardness in his gaze and the tightness in his eyes.

He was angry.

I swallowed, drawing the blanket around me to cover myself. *Though it's not anything he hasn't seen before,* I thought, and a confusing array of heat, shame, and longing swept over me.

His silver eyes flashed in the afternoon light filtering in through the window. He crossed his arms, his nostrils flaring. "Care to explain yourself?" His voice was dangerously quiet, and for some ridiculous reason, I would've preferred him to yell at me.

I shifted slightly on the bed. "You were dying. Lilith had you, I"—I choked on the words and cleared my throat—"I had to do *something*, Leo, I—"

"And going to Benito, asking him to Turn you was the answer?" he snapped, the volume of his voice rising.

My mouth clamped shut as anger whirled in my chest. "What would you have done, Leo? If it were me?"

He went very still, and his eyes suddenly grew guarded. Something unreadable crossed his face, but it vanished quickly. "There are other, *safer* ways for you to become a demon, Brielle, if that's what you wish."

I nodded. "I know. But I didn't have time to perform blood rituals."

Leo spread his arms wide, smiling without humor. "You *live* among a coven of vampires, Brielle."

"I *know*," I said again sharply. "But I also didn't have time to let the vampire venom infect me. Plus, I'd have to be killed, but I needed to ensure I had enough venom inside me first." I shook my head. "Besides, I didn't want—" My mouth snapped shut again. *Dammit, Brie.*

Leo's eyes narrowed, and he drew closer to me. "You didn't want what? To become a monster like me?"

"No," I said quickly. "*No,* I didn't mean that. You're not a monster, Leo."

Leo chuckled wryly. "I most certainly am. But I don't blame you, Brielle. The hunger, the maddening thirst for blood—I wouldn't wish that on anyone." He paused, his eyes darkening. "But you would have the same problem as a werewolf."

"I know."

"Do you?" Leo snapped. "You keep saying that, but I don't think you *do* know. If you had submitted to that Turning ritual, Benito would've claimed you as part of his coven. He would've been your Alpha—your *leader.* And you would've been bound to serve him."

"I couldn't just let you die!" I shouted, fury rising within me. How could he not understand the position I'd been in?

"Then, why didn't you speak to your father? To *anyone*

315

in my coven for help? Why did you seek out Benito on your own, *knowing* what he wanted to do to you?"

"I knew anyone in your coven would try to stop me," I said quietly. "Because they would suffer your wrath if anything happened to me."

Leo's eyebrows lifted, and he frowned slightly. "Well, that *is* true."

"And Leo, I—" I broke off, closing my eyes for a moment. *Just say it, Brie.* I remembered how ashen his face had looked when he was unconscious. He looked like a corpse. *Don't let another moment pass without you telling him.* I opened my mouth, and the words came out in a rush. "I didn't want to become a vampire without you."

Leo blinked, his brows furrowing. "What?"

I dropped my gaze. I couldn't look at him when I said this. "You and I have shared blood. And it was the most . . . exhilarating thing I've ever done." *Well, besides almost having sex with you.* "I—I didn't want to share that with anyone else. I knew that in order to become a vampire, I would have to exchange blood several times with another vampire." I took a breath. "If I were to do this, I would want that vampire . . . to be you." Slowly, hesitantly, I raised my gaze to meet his.

Conflict warred in his eyes. The anger still stirred, but it mingled with regret and desire. Then, his expression softened, and he approached the bed. My body tensed, and my heart skittered at his nearness. But instead of caressing me or laying me back or pinning me down like I thought—and secretly hoped for—he knelt on the floor. He placed his hands on my knees, and heat swirled in my stomach.

"Brielle," he said in a low, soft voice that made my toes curl. "You are the only person I want to share blood with too."

I gaped at him. "But Estrella—"

"She betrayed me," Leo said in a harsh voice. "Her loyalties lie with Benito now. And . . . I don't want another Donor. I want only you. If you'll have me."

My pulse roared in my ears so loudly I couldn't hear anything else. I swallowed, my mouth suddenly feeling dry. Then, I leaned close to him and ran my fingers through his dark curls. "If it weren't for Lilith, I would've had you already," I murmured.

Heat stirred in his eyes, and half his mouth curved upward in a devilish smile. He leaned in, but before our lips met, I breathed, "I love you."

Leo froze, his lips inches from mine. Startled, he drew away from me, his eyes wide. "What?"

I couldn't let him kiss me—I couldn't let him do *anything else*—before I told him. "I—I love you, Leo."

Our eyes locked for a moment as Leo stared at me, his face blank with shock. Then, a wide grin lit up his face, making him look for a moment as young as me. He always seemed so much older and wiser and seasoned for his age, but in this moment, he could've been one of the goofy jocks at my high school. His eyes crinkled, and joy emanated from his face so thickly I could almost feel it burning against my skin. I couldn't help but smile back, my heart lifting at the light in his face.

"Brielle," he whispered. He laughed in disbelief, tucking loose hair behind my ears. "I—I don't know what to say."

I leaned closer to him. "Then don't speak."

A deep sound rumbled from his throat, igniting the fire within me. His hand curved around my cheek, his fingers trailing down my jaw, my neck, and then my shoulder. His thumb traced circles along the bare skin of my shoulder as he brushed aside the sleeve of my shift.

My breath hitched, and he caught my lips with his. His mouth traced over mine hungrily, and I felt sucked in by the fierce passion of his movements. His hand tangled in my hair, pulling me almost violently toward him. His lips and tongue caressed mine with desperation, and I responded with the same enthusiasm. A moan pulled from his lips, and I drew it from him with each kiss, with each gasp of breath. His hands moved to my knees and climbed higher and higher, slowly pushing up my shift until my insides spiraled and I was shaking with need.

Suddenly, something powerful circled between us like a foreign presence, and I went still. My blood chilled, and I pulled away from him. When he looked at me, his eyes were wild, but they were still his own.

I swallowed and shook my head. *She's gone, Brie. She's not here.*

"Are you all right?" Leo said breathlessly, running a thumb along my lower lip.

I nodded. "I just keep feeling like she's going to take you again."

"She won't."

I frowned. "How do you know?"

Leo hesitated before responding. "Your mother succeeded in removing Lilith from my body. I'm free now."

Suspicion prickled along my spine. "Leo, I saw you," I said slowly. "I saw you use red magic earlier. *Her* magic."

Leo said nothing, but he held my gaze. His face was a blank mask.

I jerked my head back, stung. He was hiding something. He wore the same apathetic expression he used when facing his enemies—when facing people he didn't want seeing his true face.

Why is he using that face with me?

"You don't have to hide from me, Leo," I whispered, touching his cheek. "You can tell me."

A forlorn look crossed his eyes, making him look so lost and innocent that I leaned closer, placing both my palms to his cheeks. "Leo, please," I whispered, brushing kisses along his forehead. "Let me in."

His hands found my waist, and he placed his head against my chest. "Brielle, I—"

A frantic pounding on the door silenced him, and we both jerked upright in alarm. My heart skittering, I snapped, "Go away!"

"Brielle, it's me," said a frantic voice I recognized immediately.

"Izzy?" I stood, snatching a robe off the armchair and wrapping it around myself before I opened the door.

Izzy's eyes were wild and crazed, and her white hair was a tangled mess. A long bloody cut ran from her eyebrow to her jaw.

My jaw dropped. "Izzy, what happened to you?" I stood back to let her in, and her eyes moved to Leo.

"Oh, good, you're here too." Izzy raised a shaking hand to her forehead. "It—it's Harrison." Her frightened gaze moved from me to Leo. "I think he's possessed."

28
LEO

A STUNNED SILENCE FOLLOWED IZZY'S WORDS. MY initial reaction was doubt. *Lilith promised. She made a blood bargain with me.*

But then I remembered her words: she would remove her influence. But she couldn't change the choices her victims would make.

What if Harrison had already made a choice that was irreversible? How could we stop him if Lilith wasn't possessing him anymore—if it was only a shadow of her influence making the decisions for him?

"Where is he now?" Brielle asked, moving to the wardrobe to find a fresh outfit.

"I left him back—back at the house." Izzy rubbed her face, her hands still shaking.

I gently touched her shoulder and gestured to the armchair. "Come and sit."

Izzy tried to wave me away, but I tugged on her arm, and she relented. I sat on the edge of the bed and faced her, trying to ignore the sounds of Brielle dressing herself behind me.

"What happened?" I asked Izzy.

"I—I don't know, we were performing a spell together to try to calm down our flames, and he went crook on me!"

I frowned and cocked my head.

"She means he got angry," Brielle said from behind me.

"Yeah, but not just angry," Izzy went on. "Like, he wasn't himself. His eyes turned all black. And he attacked me." She gestured to the bloody cut on her face. "I managed to knock him out with a vase, and then I came straight here."

I sensed Brielle approaching and assumed it was safe to face her. She was dressed in a blue tunic cinched at the waist and riding trousers. I raised my eyebrow at her, and she nodded grimly, crossing her arms. "Lilith," she muttered.

Izzy's face turned ashen. "Crikey, I was afraid of that. How do we free him? How can we fix this?"

"My mom performed an exorcism on Leo," Brielle said. "I can ask her to do the same for Harrison."

I went very still. Dread coiled within me, and I sighed. "It won't work."

Izzy and Brielle looked at me. I felt the intensity of Brielle's gaze on me, but I refused to meet it.

"Why not?" Brielle demanded, her voice filled with suspicion.

"Because the exorcism didn't bring me back." I composed my face into a carefully neutral expression and looked at her. "I struck a bargain with Lilith."

Brielle's face paled, and she staggered back a step. "You *what*?"

"It had to be done," I said firmly. "And if I hadn't, you'd be a werewolf under Benito's control right now."

Izzy blanched. "Wait, what?"

Brielle shook her head. "No, you can't pin this on me. What did you offer her, Leo?"

I stood. "It doesn't matter now. What matters is what I learned from her. We struck a blood bargain, and she swore to remove her influence from my coven."

Izzy's mouth twisted as if she were ill. "But Harrison isn't a part of your coven."

Brielle and I slowly looked at her.

"We were trying to form a light coven together, remember?" Izzy whispered.

Brielle suddenly straightened, her eyes widening. "Juan, Abe, and the others . . ." She trailed off and covered her mouth in horror.

Izzy nodded.

"Where are they?" I demanded, trying to remember how many others had lived in the castle with Izzy and Brielle. No more than a dozen, I thought. But even so, every single one of them had fallen through a time portal, which meant they were Timecasters. Lilith had access to them.

"Abe and Juan moved to Madrid," Izzy said, ticking off the names on her fingers. "Alexei and Jacques sailed for France. Riker's here. Chris, Samson, Wes, and Elias died in the battle last year."

Brielle suddenly grabbed my arm, her fingernails digging into me. "Is Riker a part of your coven, Leo?"

My mouth opened and closed. "I . . . presumed so." The response sounded feeble in my ears. "But knowing Lilith, she would use his light magic as a loophole, claiming he wasn't a true member of a vampire coven."

"Light magic," Brielle whispered faintly. "No—*no!*"

Without another word, she fled from the room, her frantic footsteps thudding down the stairs. After exchanging a bewildered glance, Izzy and I tore after her.

Brielle's voice echoed in the foyer. "Where are Mom and Angel?" she demanded. "And Riker—I need to find them *now.*"

"Angel and Riker were in the study last time I checked," came Oliver's low rumble. "I don't know where your mother is. The maid said she went out to gather spell ingredients, but that was a while ago."

I reached the bottom of the stairs and hurried to Brielle's side. Oliver's jaw was rigid, his eyes filled with fear and determination.

"What's going on?" he asked, his gaze shifting to me.

"Mom might be in trouble," Brielle said, her voice trembling slightly. "I need you to find her. I'll take care of Riker and Angel." She turned to Izzy, who was looking paler by the minute. "You go next door and find Jorge. He can send some men to go with you to take care of Harrison." Brielle's eyes moved to me. "Come with me."

My head reared back in surprise, and I wasn't the only one. Oliver's jaw dropped, and Izzy's eyebrows lifted.

"What?" Brielle snapped, waving her arms impatiently. "Go! Now!"

Oliver blinked and grabbed his cloak before bolting out the door, followed by Izzy. Brielle took me by the arm and led me toward the study, her steps slow and careful.

"I need you in case they're both possessed," she whispered as we approached the closed door of the study.

I smirked. "You don't need to explain yourself, Brielle. I still believe you're a fierce warrior, even if you do occasionally need help from a dashing vampire."

Brielle snorted and shot me a flat look. She moved closer to the door and pressed her ear against it. I closed my eyes, focusing on my enhanced hearing. A few mutters, an occasional step or two . . . Nothing out of the ordinary.

Brielle looked at me and nodded once before opening the door.

Angel and Riker were standing above the desk, their heads bent together as they perused a book. Angel frowned when she saw Brielle, who no doubt looked ready to lead an army. Angel straightened and approached her sister. "What is it?" Her gaze flicked to me.

"Lilith is possessing Timecasters," Brielle said, glancing briefly at Riker. I watched him too. His blue eyes were wide and concerned, and he seemed fairly normal.

But I knew too well Lilith could take over at any minute.

"Brie, I told you, I'm not—" Angel hissed.

"A Timecaster, I know. But it's in your blood, Angel. We can't be too careful."

Angel shook her head. "Brie—"

Riker suddenly bent over, groaning. His arms circled around his stomach as he collapsed to the ground.

"Riker!" Angel hurried to him and touched his face, which had turned pale and clammy.

"Get away from him!" Brielle tugged on Angel's arm, but Angel shook her off.

"It's a vision, Brie!" Angel shouted, flinging her arm out to keep Brielle away. "Give him some space."

Riker started trembling violently, his whole body thrashing. His eyes rolled back until they were all white. My mouth fell open as horror cut through me. It was so similar to when Lilith was in possession . . . but also so different.

Riker inhaled with a rattling gasp and then spoke in a deep, throaty voice that sounded like it was layered by a dozen other voices. "The wolf will triumph when the silver demon falls. And the demon will respond when the Dark Lady calls. The city will burn. The witch will Turn. And infected mortals will walk through walls."

Riker's chest shuddered, his back arching as a howl of agony burst from his lips. The walls seemed to quake from his cry, and my skin prickled with the presence of magic.

Then, Riker exhaled slowly, his body becoming limp against the floor. Angel lovingly swept a lock of red hair from Riker's sweaty forehead and then looked up at me and Brielle.

"He'll be all right. But he's passed out."

Brielle looked at me. Darkness and suspicion filled her eyes, but the pallor in her face told me she was still afraid. *"The demon will respond when the Dark Lady calls,"* she recited. Anger mingled with fear in her expression. "You surrendered to her . . . didn't you?"

I held her gaze, but I couldn't speak. Betrayal and pain emanated from her eyes so intensely that it burned into me, searing right through my skin.

You lied to me, her eyes seemed to say. *You betrayed me.*

"Brielle—" I said in a broken voice, stepping toward her.

She drew back, flinching away from me. Her eyes swelled with hurt, agony, and regret. The emotions lanced through me as severely as if I could see into her soul. I knew the bond between our blood made me feel her reaction more acutely, but even without the bond, I read the grief plainly on her stricken face.

It ripped through me, carving a hole in me that throbbed and festered with all the devastation and torment I felt when I'd lost Lucia and Ronaldo.

Because in that gaze, I saw what Brielle wasn't telling me.

I opened up to you.

I offered my body to you.

I became weak. For you.

And you gave yourself up to her.

I wanted to shout that it wasn't like that at all. That I'd done it to *save* her.

But I knew Brielle as well as I knew myself. She'd exposed herself, leaving her naked and vulnerable before me just as when I'd almost bedded her. She'd given herself to me completely. Body and soul.

And I was leaving. Worse than that, I'd freely offered myself to the monster who had been torturing Brielle for most of her life.

In the split second when our gazes met, she realized I was no longer hers.

I was Lilith's.

"Brielle," I said again, but with resignation. Because I knew no excuse was enough.

"I would've found a way," she whispered, her eyes brimming with tears. "I would've brought you back."

A knot formed in my throat, choking me. I couldn't

breathe or speak. I could only gape at her. My eyes stung with tears that would never come.

I closed my mouth and swallowed. Breathing deeply through my nose, I nodded. "I know. But I couldn't let you do that."

Anger flared in her eyes. "Let me?"

"Guys," Angel said sharply.

I blinked, suddenly remembering there were others in the room with us. I turned to find Angel peeling back the curtain to gaze out the window.

"What is it?" Brielle blinked rapidly and wiped her nose before facing her sister.

"Look." Angel's voice shook as she pointed out the window.

Brielle and I drew closer, and my blood ran cold.

Dozens of people were in the streets fighting. And not just mortals—casters. *My* people. Guadalupe and Miguel were dueling with their black magic. There was Harrison Porter, exploding in a burst of flame as he rushed a were-wolf I recognized from Benito's coven.

"Who are they?" Brielle asked, pointing to several figures at the end of the road clad in blue and white striped uniforms.

"Damn it all," I growled, running a hand through my hair. "It's the coven from Madrid."

"What coven?" Angel asked. "The Council?"

I shook my head, remembering what Brielle had told me

of the magical body of government in her time. "The dark coven that governs the country. From what I understand, they eventually join the Council in Barcelona, but since the Count's death, I'm unsure how that has changed things."

"Why are they here?" Brielle demanded.

"Lilith has been summoned. People are being possessed —even mortals." I sighed and turned from the window before shuffling through my desk drawer in search of weapons. I handed daggers to Brielle and Angel and then holstered my pistol in my belt. "I feared this might happen if the situation worsened. I'd hoped we could resolve it before they intervened."

"I don't understand," Brielle said, her tone sharp. "What does this mean? What will they do?"

"They're here to quiet the civil unrest in the city. And I'm sure if Benito or his pack are questioned, they will assert that they were not the cause—that rogue demons were wreaking havoc in the city before they even arrived."

Brielle raised an eyebrow. "Well, technically that's true."

My nostrils flared. "If the Madrid coven takes control, my own coven will be disbanded. My people will be imprisoned or executed."

Brielle fixed a cold gaze on me. "But you've already given up on us, haven't you, Leo? You won't be here for much longer anyway."

My mouth fell open, and my insides turned to ice at her words. Before I could speak, she brushed past me and left the study. I felt Angel look questioningly at me, but I didn't glance her way. My body felt numb.

Get ahold of yourself, Leo, I ordered myself. *She will get past this in time. One day she will. She's angry now, but at least she is alive. At least she will be safe.* My gaze shifted to the fray outside the window, and doubt crept into my mind.

But will she be safe? Will anyone be safe?

29
LEO

I DONNED MY ARMOR AND STRAPPED MY SWORDS TO my back. I couldn't afford to be staked again—not if my people depended on me.

And we are already so few in number.

I racked my brain, trying to deduce some sort of clue that anyone else in my coven might have Timecaster blood in them. Guadalupe was a given since she was a blood relative of mine. But the others? How would I know?

After ensuring my pistol was loaded with silver bullets, I hurried outside. Shouts and screams pierced the air. Gunshots exploded, and the street reeked of blood and dark magic.

I smelled Lilith. *Everywhere.* Something powerful rose up inside me in response to her presence, but I shoved it down. *Not yet*, I told myself angrily. *She can't summon me yet.*

Brielle's words rang in my head. *You've already given up on us.*

I shook my head, trying to rid myself of the thoughts that sent icy tendrils of dread coiling through me. Instead, I focused on the battle before me. Black and blue magic crackled in the air, stinging my nose. My gaze shifted over each individual, searching for any mortals. I frowned.

There *were* no mortals. Everyone on the street possessed magic. To my left, Andre the werewolf battled Jorge. Harrison Porter attacked Izzy. Guadalupe was still engaged with Miguel, her black eyes glittering with malice. A few Madrid casters sparred with a pair of vampires in my coven, but all of them had clear eyes—no sign of Lilith.

I hurried toward Guadalupe. She was a vampire and a member of my coven. If Lilith had honored her bargain, then her influence could easily be removed.

I hoped.

I slid between Guadalupe and Miguel just before Guadalupe sank her fangs into his throat. I rammed my elbow into her face, and she stumbled backward.

"I've got her," I said to Miguel. "You rally anyone else from the coven who isn't possessed and take cover."

Miguel nodded, his face bloody and bruised, and then darted away.

Guadalupe lunged for me, her long fingernails raking down my forearm. Thank Lilith I'd worn armor, otherwise she would've sliced through my entire arm. My fingers itched to draw my swords, but I didn't want to harm her.

If it isn't a stake, she'll heal, I reminded myself. In a swift movement, both my swords were drawn, and I faced her. Her teeth were bared, and darkness clouded her face. She looked unrecognizable.

"You *know* me, Guadalupe," I said loudly. "It's me, Leo. I'm your family."

Guadalupe went still, but the darkness in her face remained.

I edged closer to her. "Your favorite scent is snow in the forest. When we were children, we used to sneak into our parents' quarters when they were feeding to see what it would be like. Before you Turned, you fancied Jorge."

Guadalupe blinked, and a violent shudder shook her frame.

Yes, I urged, stepping closer.

"My mother died because she didn't have enough vampire venom to bring her back," I went on. "You were there for me when I grieved." I was now close enough to touch her. I stretched out my hand and pressed my palm against her cheek. Her skin was hot to the touch. So unlike the cool emptiness of a vampire's body.

"Wake up," I said quietly. "I need your help, cousin."

Guadalupe cocked her head at me, her black eyes mildly curious. For a moment, we held each other's gazes. Then, her eyebrows lowered, and she roared before lunging for me again.

I swiped my sword just in time, nicking her shoulder. She pivoted away from me before I could bring my other sword down. Her foot slammed into my face, and blood poured from my nose as I stumbled back a step. I swung my sword again, but she kicked me in the chest. I collapsed on the ground with a loud grunt. Pain exploded from the back of my head, and lights danced in front of my eyes.

Guadalupe pounced on top of me, her sharp fangs bared. She looked positively feral with a wildness in her eyes that couldn't be tamed. I struggled against her grip, but something within me thrummed at her nearness. At first, I thought it was Lilith, but then I went still as a familiarity rang within my blood.

My blood. Of course. It runs in her veins too.

As she leaned in to drink from me, I let her. I didn't resist. Her teeth pierced the flesh of my throat, and I stiffened. Agony and discomfort swirled sickeningly within my body until I thought I'd retch. Vampires feeding on each other was nothing like the relationship between a vampire and a donor. Guadalupe's vampire venom flowed through me, tainting my bloodstream and warring with my own venom. I shuddered, my body rejecting her poison, but still I let her drink from me.

With a gasp, Guadalupe broke away, staggering backward on all fours. Her head shook violently, and she blinked and moaned in agony.

My body thrashed against the venom in my body as it tried to clear it out. Dazed, I glanced up and down the street, trying to find some savior, some way to heal from this. Time could heal any wound, but I was short on time at the moment.

I needed a Donor. *My* Donor.

As if hearing my blood's cry, I felt a pair of caramel eyes land on me. I turned my head to meet her gaze. She was halfway down the street and sparring with a werewolf. She kicked him in the face before surging toward me with fire in her eyes. Her long blond hair swung behind her in a braid, and dirt and blood were smeared on her face. She held a dagger in each hand and also wore armor, though I hadn't seen her grab any. As she strode toward me, dodging blow after blow and occasionally stabbing an assailant who got in her way, I marveled at her beauty. She was a warrior. A vision.

And Lilith help me, I loved her.

A figure approached from my left, and I tensed, trying to rise. My arms shook as I sat up to face my attacker, but then I went still.

It was Guadalupe, and her eyes were back to their normal warm brown. Her face was paler than normal, and she looked as if she might faint.

"Leo." She raised a hand to her head and groaned. "What happened?"

"It's a long story," I groaned, swallowing down bile. "If a possessed caster attacks you, let them drink from you." I gulped down a breath of air, my body shuddering again. "It helps them remember."

Guadalupe balked. "You let me *drink* from you? Leo—"

"I know, but I had no choice! Be wary of the light casters. There might not be a way to bring them back. But try not to kill if you can help it."

Guadalupe touched my shoulder. "What can I do for you, Leo? You can't stay like this."

A werewolf roared and dived for Guadalupe, but she ducked and tore through the creature's fur with her fangs. The wolf whined and went limp.

Guadalupe spat hair from her mouth and gagged. "Foul things." Running a hand over her mouth, she looked at me in concern again.

"I'll be fine." I looked at Brielle as I said it. She was closer now. Only a pair of Madrid warlocks stood in her way. Relief swelled within me. Regardless of how angry she was, she was still coming for me. I read it plainly in the determination of her gaze.

Guadalupe followed my gaze and nodded slowly before jumping to her feet.

I grabbed her wrist before she darted into the fray. "Try to rid us of the Madrid coven if you can."

Guadalupe's eyes widened, and she looked around until she found the men dressed in blue and white. She swore and gazed skyward for a moment as if praying for strength. "Take care, cousin." She snatched a dagger from the ground and lunged for a nearby werewolf.

I slowly straightened and grabbed my swords. A Madrid warlock approached me, his bearded face covered in sweat and blood. His eyes roved over me, and recognition flickered in his eyes. "You are Leonardo Serrano."

"The same," I said slowly, cocking my head at him. He didn't appear possessed. Perhaps if I kept him talking, he wouldn't engage. I certainly needed the break. I still felt Guadalupe's venom coursing through me. My stomach churned, and I felt certain I would vomit.

The man stepped closer, his dark eyes narrowing. "You are under arrest for exposing our kind to civilians and inflicting unnecessary harm on the mortals."

My eyes widened. "What?"

Quieting magical unrest was one thing. But I knew for sure my coven had followed the proper protocols around the mortals.

This had to be Benito's doing.

"My coven has done nothing of the sort," I said in a rush. "The werewolf pack from *your* city has brought devastation—"

"We have witnesses!" the man roared. "Your people have spouted the same lies and excuses. It's over, Serrano.

You have been stripped of your title and your coven is henceforth disbanded." He brandished his knife and stepped closer to me. "Come quietly, or we will be forced to execute you on the spot."

Like hell. Darkness swelled within me, and fear briefly glimmered in the man's eyes as he read the power and strength in my gaze. Lilith's magic crackled to life inside me just as the man attacked. Drawing on Lilith's strength, I ducked to avoid his blow and sliced my sword through his thigh. The man roared and spun to avoid another cut from my sword. He kicked me in the leg, and I slammed my head against his with a loud crack. His fist collided with my stomach, and he jerked his knee upward. I groaned, hunching over as he slammed the hilt of his dagger against my head. Stars danced in my eyes, and Lilith's power receded. Nausea and agony filled my body until I started trembling again.

"I am truly sorry for this," the man said quietly, and the regret in his eyes was undeniable. He drew a stake from his belt. In the moment that he raised his weapon, I knew he was a man of honor and duty, bound to follow orders. And I held no ire for him.

I smelled her before I saw her. The warm saltwater scent filled my nose just as Brielle stabbed the man in the back. Blood bubbled from his lips as he slumped over motionless.

Brielle extended a hand and helped me to my feet with surprising strength.

"Thank you," I rasped.

Brielle watched me, her eyes unreadable. I sensed concern there, but also something guarded—something she didn't want me to see.

Perhaps it was the pain that still lingered from what I'd done.

"Are you all right?" She looked me over and frowned. "You look terrible."

I laughed hoarsely. "I let Guadalupe drink from me. It cured her of Lilith's possession, but . . ." I groaned and shuddered again as nausea roiled through me again. "Her venom—my body is rejecting it."

Brielle's face paled, and she glanced up and down the street. Several bodies littered the ground, though there were dozens of casters still fighting. "We should feed," she said in an undertone.

I looked at her. "Are you certain?"

"Yes. We could both use the strength."

I held her gaze for a long moment. Emotion stirred in her eyes, hot and desperate. A reflection of the longing I felt for her as well.

"As you wish," I said quietly.

After a quick glance at the fray, I took her arm and guided her to the porch of the house closest to us. We climbed the steps, and I backed her up against the door.

Her eyes widened, and a blush crept into her face. "Here?"

"We don't have time to find a more romantic or intimate spot, I'm afraid," I said with a weak chuckle. "I'll have to make this quick." The sounds of swords clanging and gunshots bursting behind me made my neck prickle. Shouts and screams blared against my ears, reminding me that my people were fighting and dying.

Yet here I was, about to indulge with Brielle. I felt like a selfish ass.

Brielle touched my cheek, her eyes full of sympathy. I had no doubt she read the self-loathing in my face. "You can't protect them if you're weak."

I nodded. I knew this. Jorge often said it to me as well when I pushed myself too hard.

Brielle gathered the loose strands of hair from her braid and pushed them off to the side, exposing her throat to me. "Ready when you are."

I swallowed, my mouth suddenly dry. Licking my lips, I leaned in and plunged my fangs into her neck. Her sharp gasp and the sudden stiffness of her body only ignited the monster within me. Then, the numbness of my venom took over, and she slackened and leaned into me. Her long, slow exhale made my head spin with yearning. Her arm circled around me, and her hand raked down my neck. Heat burned within me, begging, *More, more, more.*

But I summoned my strength and drew away, savoring the last few drops of her blood as I swallowed. Strength returned to my limbs, but I still sensed the poison of

Guadalupe's venom within me. I wiped away a trickle of blood on Brielle's neck and brushed her lips with my knuckle.

"Your turn," I murmured.

She blinked at me, dazed. Her eyes were filled with a hazy longing, and half her mouth quirked upward in an alluring smile. Her hand traveled down my chest and waist, lower and lower until I stiffened and cursed, jerking away.

"*Brielle,*" I hissed, my stomach clenching with need. I snatched her wrist, and she laughed.

I've taken too much of her blood, I realized as her head lolled slightly. I quickly raised my wrist to my teeth and bit down before bringing my blood to her mouth.

"Drink," I urged.

Brielle resisted at first until she tasted the drops of my blood trickling down my wrist. Then, she grabbed my arm, pressing it closer to her mouth. I tried to ignore the heat of her mouth on my skin or the way she gulped my blood down hungrily with a moan that made my body ache for her.

I gave her an extra moment to drink before I carefully pulled away from her. I caught a drop of blood dribbling from her lips and wiped it away.

Brielle's eyes opened slowly, and they shone with energy and power. Something crackled in the air between us, solidifying our bond as vampire and Donor. I felt her blood thrumming and could read the emotions in it. Excitement. Need. Hunger.

Brielle's brows pinched as she looked me over. "What *is* that?"

I swallowed, trying to push the crowded emotions from my thoughts, but still they circled within me. Passion. Confusion. Panic. Alarm.

"Our bond," I said. "The connection between our blood is sealed as vampire and Donor."

Brielle's eyes widened. "I thought it already had."

"Every Donor is different. Some only need a few feedings, and others take several before the bond sets in. But we will be connected from now on, even when we're apart." I dropped my gaze as uncertainty filled my chest. "I am sorry if this isn't what you wanted."

Brielle stared at me silently for so long that I looked at her. Her eyes were unreadable, but I sensed no anger there. She pressed her lips together, her gaze contemplative. "You didn't have a choice, Leo." Amusement sparked in her eyes. "I don't mind being bonded to you."

A grin tugged at my lips. "Does this mean you're no longer angry with me?"

Her face sobered, and she swallowed. "I don't know." She paused and took a deep breath. "I understand why you bargained with her, but . . ." She trailed off and shook her head. "It feels like you chose her over me. It's ridiculous, I know, but you gave yourself up to her when you had just pledged your love for me, and I felt like you . . . you *chose* to leave me." Tears sparkled in her eyes, and she blinked rapidly.

Regret and anguish washed over me, dragging my heart down to my knees. I cupped her face in my hands and brought her mouth to mine. Her lips trembled as she responded with the faintest of kisses before pulling away.

"I will choose you every time, Brielle Gerrick," I whispered, pressing my forehead against hers. "I am yours. For all eternity."

She looked up at me, her eyes shining. My body felt drawn to hers, pulled by some invisible force. I knew if I didn't leave now, I would never be able to part from her.

Before she could respond, before I did something reckless like run away with her, I turned and strode down the porch steps. I felt her agony pulse through my blood as I dived back into battle.

30

BRIELLE

I couldn't stop the tears from streaming down my face as I watched Leo cross swords with a dark warlock. He thrust and kicked at the man, easily overcoming him before moving on to the next assailant. The way his arms moved lithely—the way he slashed with ease as two other attackers jumped for him—took my breath away.

But I felt the tortured emotions along our bond ringing through me like an echoing chime that never ended. The rush of battle overpowered him, but layered underneath was the deepest sorrow he'd ever known. It tugged at me, drawing me toward him, and I knew it was his blood crying out to me in pain. Donors were often alerted when their vampires were in danger.

This was Leo alerting me. His movements were smooth and effortless, but inside, another war waged with his emotions. A battle between the bargain he'd made and the deepest desires of his heart.

Why Leo? I wanted to scream. *Why did you have to do it?*

Even if we won this battle, even if we saved the city, he would still go to her like a faithful puppy. He was hers and he could never be mine.

I angrily wiped the tears from my face, cursing myself for being such a baby. My eyes roved over the battle, noting the figures that had fallen to the ground. There were only a handful of casters with black eyes, which meant we were winning. But the warlocks from Madrid outnumbered us, and they would surely arrest the coven.

I didn't see Angel or my parents in the street. I had to find them.

I drew my daggers and hurried down the steps, stabbing a werewolf and slicing at a possessed warlock along the way. Blood sprayed on my arm, but a foreign energy fueled me as I spun to avoid the bite of another werewolf. Magic crackled just past my ear, and I ducked and rolled as a warlock cast a spell toward me. My body felt twice as fast as it had been before my bond with Leo had solidified. Exhilaration pulsed through me, and I felt the insane urge to grin with excitement.

Get a grip, Brie, I told myself before rushing toward my parents' house. I banged open the door, and an eerie silence settled over me. Suspicion prickled along my skin, and I went perfectly still.

Then, a loud crash made me jump, and something shattered on the floor. A weak, low groan echoed in the sitting room.

I ran forward, bursting into the room. What I saw froze me in my tracks. My blood chilled as I looked from the unconscious man on the floor to the black-eyed woman standing over him.

Mom was possessed. And she'd just knocked out Dad. A trickle of blood oozed from a head wound as he lay motionless on the floor. Slowly, Mom turned to face me, her feral eyes narrowing. Her lips spread in a wild, savage grin.

My heart stopped for a full beat. *I can't attack her. I can't hurt her.*

Then, she lunged.

I had my instincts to thank as I ducked to avoid her blow. My mind felt numb, but years of hunting demons was ingrained into my blood. My body took over as Mom flung her arms toward me, trying to Push me. I leapt out of the way and aimed a high kick in her chest. With an "oof," she staggered backward but straightened with another twisted smile.

How do I free her? I thought in a panic. *I can't kill her! Leo said he let Guadalupe drink from him, but Mom isn't a vampire! What do I do?*

Dodge, parry, block. I clutched at my daggers but didn't dare stab her. What if I killed her? Using my forearms to block, I defended myself against each of her blows until she caught me off guard with a blast of her magic. I soared backward and collided with the wall. Pain sliced through my head, and darkness clouded my vision. I collapsed in a heap on the floor, struggling to right myself before she finished me off.

"Mom, don't," I moaned weakly, trying to crawl away from her.

Mom stepped on my hand, and I screamed as agony shot up my arm. The dagger fell from my crushed fingers, and she swiped it with a triumphant gleam in her eyes. Crouching down to my level, she cocked her head at me as if toying with her prey.

"I'll see you in Hell, dear one," she hissed in a voice that wasn't her own. She raised the dagger.

Slice. Using my other hand, I cut her shin, and she cried out, her voice tinged with rage.

Go, go, go, I urged myself. I rolled over again and again until I staggered to my feet, my head still throbbing. Then, I brandished my dagger as Mom approached me, trying to ignore the blood dripping from my weapon.

"Would you really kill your own mother, girl?" Mom growled.

I suppressed a shudder seeing Lilith using my mother's body as a puppet. The woman who raised me. Who only ever looked at me with affection in her eyes.

And now she was approaching me, ready to send me to my death.

"Don't make me do this," I sobbed.

Something within me splintered and shattered like a dam had burst. Saying goodbye to Leo had taken all my strength, and I couldn't face this. I couldn't battle my mother, not if it meant one of us had to die.

She was here in Spain—in the eighteenth century— because of *me*. And now Lilith had possessed her.

I couldn't send her to her grave. I couldn't *kill my own mother*—not when she had come all this way just to protect me.

I can't. I can't do it.

The dagger fell from my grip, and I spread my arms wide. "You win," I whispered.

Mom faltered, her mouth falling open.

"Kill me," I pleaded. "I won't hurt you."

Mom blinked at me, and for a moment, I saw a glimpse of the woman I knew peeking through those dark eyes. But it disappeared, and she attacked.

My eyes closed as I waited for death.

Suddenly, a loud crash echoed in the room, followed by a heavy thump.

I flinched and opened my eyes. Mom had fallen over, surrounded by shards of glass as Angel stood over her with the broken remains of a vase. Angel panted, her eyes shining with tears, before she dropped the hunk of vase.

"Are—are you all right?" she said in a broken voice.

Mom moaned and shifted on the ground.

"I'm fine," I said quickly, grabbing Angel's hand. "Come on, let's go."

"Wait," she hissed, pointing to Dad's motionless figure. "We have to hide him. What if she kills him?"

Dread pooled in my stomach as I thought of Mom waking up from Lilith's possession and realizing she'd killed her own husband. I nodded.

Angel and I hefted Dad up by the arms and dragged him down the hallway toward the servants' quarters. It was empty, and I hoped the servants had gotten out safely.

"Does it concern you that the mortals have all disappeared?" Angel grunted as we dragged Dad over to one of the servants' beds. Gasping for breath, we both hurried over to the door and locked it. It wouldn't keep Mom out forever, but it would buy us some time.

"Yes," I muttered, wiping sweat from my brow. "But we have other things to worry about." I eyed her, suddenly suspicious. "You haven't been possessed?"

Angel groaned, rubbing her forehead. "*No,* Brie. I already told you, there's no Timecaster blood in me."

I blinked. "What? There *has* to be—"

"Brie." Angel faced me and took both my shoulders in her hands. "Mom and Dad adopted me."

I shook my head, uncomprehending. "Angel, what the *hell* are you—"

Angel gripped my shoulder firmly, her jaw rigid. "When I was ten, Mom and Dad told me where I really came from. That they adopted me. My parents died just after Mom and Dad got married, and they took me in as their own child."

I kept shaking my head, my brain too stunned to work properly. Adopted? *How*?

"I know I should've told you before," Angel went on, her voice tainted with grief. "But . . . I didn't want anything to change with us! We were already separated by our problems —my illness and your difficulties with your magic. I didn't want anything else to come between us. I didn't want you to feel like we weren't sisters because we *are*! That's all I've ever felt. My whole life, you've been my sister, Brie. I've never felt otherwise, so I didn't feel like I needed to tell you the truth. Not when it meant nothing."

As her words settled within me, something hollow took over, caving inward as my chest seemed to crumble in on itself.

More lies. More secrets.

How many times would other people make decisions for me? For what *they* believed was best for me?

How long would I have to stand by and let other people make the hard choices while I stayed in my naïve and ignorant little bubble?

Mom and Dad kept the secret of their time travel from me my whole life. Then, they came here and decided it would be best if we all moved to Cuba. Leo took it upon himself to shelter me from the possessed demons he found, plus he made a damn bargain with Lilith, offering his soul in order to protect me.

I was sick of it.

"That wasn't your decision to make," I said in a hard voice, my gaze distant as I stared at the door. "You can't just *decide* that it means nothing to *me*, Angel." The more I spoke, the louder my voice got. "You don't get to choose how I feel, how I react, how I *live*! You don't get to say, 'It's better for Brie if she doesn't know this,' because you know who gets to decide that? *I* do! For the love of Lilith, I wish people would *stop* hiding things to protect me! Stop making choices for me! Stop taking over my *life*!"

It wasn't until I stopped talking that I realized I was shouting. The echo of my words rang against the walls, and Angel's face drained of color.

"Brie—" she whispered, her eyes filling with tears. Her lower lip trembled, and she shook her head. Her lips pressed together, and a fat tear rolled down her face.

It wasn't her fault. I knew that. Angel had been open with me about everything—except this.

Perhaps that was why it hurt so much.

But this was the last straw. I couldn't take it anymore. I felt useless. Powerless.

Weak.

I ran a shaky hand over my face. I needed space—time to process this. But I couldn't leave her, not when Lilith was possessing everyone like some zombie apocalypse.

A loud pounding on the locked door made us both jump. A heavy weight pushed against the door, trying to break through.

Time was up.

I grabbed Angel's wrist, my grip a little too forceful. "Come on, we need to get out of here."

"What about Dad?"

I hesitated for a moment before throwing a blanket over him. "Leave the back door wide open. She'll be looking for us, not him."

We hurried out the exit, leaving the door open to lure Mom out, and circled around toward the alley that led to the street. Shouts and gunfire still rang in the air from the battle, but it was less chaotic than before.

As we crept further down the alley, Angel grabbed my arm and hissed, "Brie, *look*!"

I froze and followed her gaze. She was peering into our neighbor's window. Squinting, I stared through the grimy window until I found what she was looking at. A figure lay on a bed, twitching and thrashing violently. His arms jerked, and his head turned back and forth. A low moan poured from his mouth.

"Possessed?" I whispered.

"I don't think so," Angel said slowly. "But we haven't really seen what possession looks like in mortals."

Except for the silversmith, and he had died.

Suddenly, I remembered the passage I'd found in the book from the castle about opening the gate to the Underworld.

What if the gate had never shut? That was why Lilith could possess everyone.

And the mortals—who possessed no magic—were powerless against the spirits drifting in and out of the portal.

"We have to close the gate," I said in a hushed voice.

Angel turned to look at me with wide eyes. "What gate?"

In a hurried whisper, I filled her in on what the book had told me about sacrificing a mortal to open the gate.

"And you think to close it, it requires another sacrifice?" Angel hissed. "Brie, you can't just *kill* someone innocent!"

"The gate *has* to close!" I argued. "If it stays open, *every* mortal will die or be tortured by ghosts. What's one life compared to millions?"

"And who are you to decide who it should be?" Angel said, her eyes flashing. "Who died and made you executioner?"

My head reared back, and my mouth fell open. "Angel—"

"No, Brie. We find another way. Let's go in there and see if we can help him. If we can, maybe this city stands a chance *without* losing any more lives."

Before I could argue, Angel took off down the alley and climbed onto the neighbors' porch. After muttering a foul curse, I followed her.

31

LEO

Hours passed, and blood coated every inch of me like a second skin. My arms weighed down with fatigue, even with Brielle's blood coursing through me. Dozens of men lay dead on the ground, but Guadalupe and I had managed to wake up all of our vampires.

But Harrison Porter was still possessed.

And now, so was Izzy. And Riker. They advanced toward us like an undead army, their eyes blacker than ink. Behind them were the warlocks from Madrid. Among the dead, I recognized a few men clad in blue and white, but not many. Which meant the coven was still intent on arresting and possibly executing me and my coven.

My eyes found Jorge, who was hunched over, gasping for breath. His skin looked clammier than usual. He was still recovering from being staked.

"You need to go feed," I told him.

He shook his head. "The mortals are gone."

My blood ran cold. "What do you mean *gone*?"

"I mean no one can find them. And we haven't exactly had time to search the city for them."

I looked around as if to find a mortal strolling down the street like normal. But Jorge was right—everyone was gone. I'd noticed it when Andre had staked me.

I remembered what Alejandro had said—that the gate to the Underworld had been opened, and the spirits were restless.

How long had it been since we'd seen Ignacio possessed by Lilith? Several days at least.

It was far too long for the gate to be open. How would all of those spirits in the air affect the mortals? Would the civilians be possessed? Killed? Carted off to the Underworld?

Chaos surrounded me as the Madrid warlocks fought my coven—and the possessed casters fought *everyone*. A Madrid warlock kicked Harrison Porter to the ground and raised his sword. In a flash, I dived between them and raised my own blood-coated sword to block the warlock's.

"How else can we stop them?" the warlock growled between our clashed weapons.

"He's under my protection," I growled. "And he's possessed."

Harrison lunged, but I kicked him down. He crumpled just as Izzy roared and shot toward me. She barreled into me, tackling me to the ground. Her teeth were bared, and she shrieked in shrill fury. Her fingers clawed at my face until I managed to throw her off me. Slowly, she crept toward Harrison's prone figure as if trying to rouse him.

I suddenly went still, cocking my head at her.

Some part of her still cared for Harrison. Despite Lilith taking over.

I inched toward Izzy and Harrison, but Izzy turned to face me, hissing like some feral creature. I sheathed my swords and raised my hands in surrender.

"I won't hurt him," I said quietly.

Izzy froze, her mouth slowly closing. Her dark eyes stared at me blankly.

"You know him, don't you?" I asked, still creeping toward her. I sensed the Madrid warlock shifting behind me, but I glanced over my shoulder at him and shook my head slightly. My eyes widened at him before I faced Izzy again, hoping the warlock would heed my warning. "You care for him," I went on. "He calls to you. I know the feeling, Izzy."

Izzy blinked at me, her brows furrowing. Recognition stirred in her expression.

I crouched down beside her, and she shrank away from me, but her eyes tightened in fear, not anger. I cautiously touched her wrist and clasped her hand in mine.

"I need you to wake up," I murmured, glancing at Harrison, who still lay unconscious. "For his sake, Izzy.

Wake up and rouse him. I fear you're the only one who can."

Izzy looked at me, her face still conflicted. She shook her head with a light moan, then covered her face with both hands.

"We made a bargain," I hissed, changing tactics. "You swore to leave my people alone. Now *let her go.*"

A violent shudder rippled through Izzy, and she hunched over. She exhaled long and slow, then straightened to face me with her black eyes glinting.

"Oh, Leonardo, you know it isn't that simple," she crowed in an ethereal voice.

I suppressed a shiver. *Lilith.*

"She is under *my* protection," I said in a hard voice.

"But she's a light witch," Izzy said, cocking her head. "How can she belong to your coven?"

I gritted my teeth and leaned close enough to see the dark magic emanating from Izzy's skin like a faint fog. "If you want to find loopholes in our bargain, then I will too. You think I didn't plan for this? Why do you think I swore to surrender to you *after* the battle finished?" My arm flew forward and snatched the collar of the Madrid warlock, who'd been trying to sneak up on Izzy. He grunted as I hauled him forward, dragging his body on the ground until he was lying next to us.

"All I need to do is pick a fight with someone," I said, my gaze still fixed on Izzy. "I can keep this battle going for days.

Weeks even. And in that time, I will find a way to be free of you. I will close the gate to the Underworld, Lilith. All I need to do is sacrifice a mortal. Then, your reign will end."

Fury clouded Izzy's expression, and she lunged for me. With my free hand, I smacked her face until her head swiveled. Blood dripped from her lip, but she grinned widely at me.

"You play a dangerous game, Leo," she growled. "I can end this pitiful witch's life in an instant."

"Do that, and I swear I will carry on this battle until someone stakes me. And then you won't have anyone to perform your bidding as your slave." My mouth quirked up in my usual smirk, though my insides roiled with unease. *She's right,* a part of me shouted in a panic. *She can kill everyone I love right now without blinking.*

But I held her gaze, keeping my face stoic and my expression blank.

At long last, Izzy hunched over again, her body trembling from head to toe. Dark magic oozed from her like a vapor, and it swirled in the air, stinging my nose with the scent of blood and death. Then, with a rattling gasp, Izzy straightened, her eyes clearing to their usual brown. She blinked, dazed, before her eyes found Harrison lying next to her.

"Harrison!" she cried, lurching forward to clutch his face in her hands. "Wake up, my darling. Wake up!"

Harrison groaned, his head turning. Relief spread

through me, and I released the Madrid warlock, who rose on all fours to stare at me. His chest heaved with sharp breaths, and his expression slackened in horror.

"What devil bargain have you made?" he rasped. "Have you set a demon lord loose on this city?"

I leveled a gaze at him. "I struck a bargain to *save* this city. If I wanted this to continue, why did Lilith retreat? Why did I negotiate with her to remove her presence from my people?"

The warlock went still, watching me with guarded eyes. He was still suspicious, I could tell. But he couldn't deny that I'd just released Lilith from Izzy's body instead of killing her.

With a grunt, I shifted and rose to my feet, then offered my hand to the warlock. He scowled at me for a moment, looking like a child intent on sitting on his rear on the ground rather than admit he was wrong. Then, he sighed and accepted my hand as I hoisted him up. Several other Madrid warlocks looked over at us warily, and a few even stepped closer as if I were about to attack without warning. But the street was quiet. Bodies lay on the ground, most of which were dead. A few wolves moaned and shifted, and I knew they would rise soon.

Suddenly, a low growl echoed on the street, and I stiffened. The hair on the back of my neck prickled as I turned to face the new threat.

A huge, white wolf loomed toward me, his teeth bared

and stained with blood. I recognized the creature. It was Benito.

Rage pulsed through me as Benito stepped over the fallen soldiers as if they were nothing but dust under his paws. I stretched my arms wide and yelled, "Why?" My voice echoed down the street, and the few casters standing suddenly went still. "Why destroy my people?" I roared. "My *city*? All to get Paloma back? Do you think she will be satisfied when she sees what you've done?"

The wolf stopped and raised his haunches, his fur standing on end and his eyes wild with fury. In an instant, he shifted to his human form, though the white fur still coated his arms and neck as if the beast could call him back at any moment.

Stepping closer, he jabbed a finger toward me. "You didn't care for *my* people when she died!" Spit flew from his mouth as he drew even nearer.

I straightened, raising my chin to see over his head. I was taller, but not by much. His arms were much meatier than mine, so I knew he made up in strength what he lacked in height.

"You came to my coven," I said in a soft voice. "*You* started a riot when you tried to usurp my brother. The deaths of your people are on *your* hands, Benito. Just as they are tonight too."

A low, feral growl rumbled from his throat. "Your people were unhappy, Leo. They were suffering. Under my protection, they could've been something more. Something powerful!"

"That power was for *you*!" I shouted, waving a hand toward him. "Not for my people! We do not enforce blood bargains here. Anyone who desired more was free to leave; they knew that. If they were unhappy with Ronaldo's leadership, they could have left!"

Benito chuckled without humor, shaking his head at me like I was a petulant child. "You are so naïve, Leo. So foolish to believe everyone thinks as you do. It makes it all the more satisfying to see your little coven crumble. What a terrible misfortune to befall the city." He rubbed his chin, frowning with mock sorrow. "Innocent civilians slaughtered. Casters turning on each other. The mortals vanishing completely!" He spread his arms, gesturing to the quiet houses around us. A wicked smile lit up his face. "Such a shame the city fell into the hands of an incompetent demon leader."

My body quivered with anger that roiled through me like a thunderstorm. The gleam in Benito's yellow eyes told me all I needed to know: *he* had summoned the Madrid coven. He'd pinned all these misfortunes on me and my coven. And I had no proof that he was the one responsible.

With a roar of fury, I swung my sword at him. Just before my blade landed, he shifted back to his wolf form and pounced on me. His claws tore through my flesh, and I cried out. But the adrenaline and rage pulsing through me numbed my senses, and I felt nothing as blood poured down my body. I kicked at the wolf, knocking him sideways before I sliced my sword against his back. Blood spurted, and the wolf howled in agony. With my free hand, I drew my pistol and pulled back the hammer before aiming at him.

Benito lunged, pinning me to the ground. His hot, foul breath blew in my face, his sharp teeth just inches from my eyes. I thrashed, but his heavy paws kept me pinned.

My shadows gathered around me and I shifted just before he bit me. In bat form, I flitted high above him before shifting again, landing right on top of him. He whimpered against my weight and swiped a paw at me. His claws raked down my throat, and I grunted, gritting my teeth as white-hot knives cut into my skin.

I pressed the barrel of my pistol deep into his fur. He struggled, but I held him firmly, ignoring the throbbing pain in my cheek and neck. "Join your lover, Benito," I hissed before pulling the trigger.

The gunshot exploded in the air, and Benito's eyes widened. His body went rigid, and a low, weak moan escaped his mouth. I rolled off him as he started convulsing, his giant body twitching and thrashing. A blinding glow spread from his bullet wound, igniting the street as brightly as midday. I shut my eyes against the sting of the light, rolling away from him so it didn't burn my face.

I tensed, waiting for Lilith's magic to save him as it had

before. But either she was honoring her bargain with me or she didn't need Benito anymore. No red magic came to his aid.

Then, in an explosion of ash, Benito vanished. His remains drifted away with the wind, leaving nothing behind but a lingering smell of canine and blood.

32

BRIELLE

Angel and I slowly crept into our neighbors' house. The floorboards creaked with each step, and the silence within the house screamed at us that something was wrong. Outside, the noises of battle stopped, and I tried to let that comfort me.

But I knew Leo would go to Lilith soon. If he hadn't already.

I'd know, I told myself, searching inward for our connection. My blood pulsed, and, distantly, I felt his own blood thrumming with energy. With life.

He was still here. For now.

The wolf will triumph when the silver demon falls. I remembered Riker's vision. I'd assumed *silver demon falls* referred to Lilith's death. But what if it referred to Leo falling into Lilith's clutches? Or falling to the Underworld . . . forever?

A soft thumping echoed in the house, jolting me from my thoughts. Angel pointed toward the bedroom we'd peered into earlier, and I nodded. Carefully, we inched forward until we were close enough to peek into the room.

The man still thrashed on the bed, moaning and grunting. His eyes rolled back until they were all white, and his face was covered in sweat.

Angel grabbed my arm, her fingernails digging into my skin. "It's Diego."

I frowned and stared at the man. He had a thick mustache and dark hair speckled with gray. The more I watched him, the more familiar he seemed. Then, I remembered: he was a merchant I'd seen often in the marketplace. He sold cloth and fabric with his wife. I looked around as if I might find her somewhere nearby.

"What's wrong with him?" Angel whispered, crouching next to the bed and reaching for Diego.

"Don't touch him." I surged forward and snatched her wrist. As I drew closer, I felt darkness emanating from him like a low vibration that tickled my skin and rattled my bones.

Lilith. It has to be her.

"Is he possessed?" Angel asked in a hushed voice.

I shook my head. "His eyes are white. He's resisting it perhaps?"

We both fell silent, staring helplessly at the man. How could we help him if we didn't know what was wrong?

A flicker of flame surged to life in my chest, and I gasped.

Angel looked at me in alarm. "Brie?"

The faintest of voices tickled my ear like someone was shouting at me from a mile away. I closed my eyes, my brows furrowing as I strained to hear the voice. Magic thrummed through my body as the voice continued, beckoning me.

"Brie," Angel said again, her voice more urgent.

I froze, and my eyes flew open. I found myself leaning over Diego with my hands hovering over him. My instincts told me to move away, but something pulsed within me, reaching for the man. A voice within me sang for him. Wept for him.

My magic was calling to him. My hands itched to reach forward, to touch and heal.

Which was ridiculous. I was no healer.

And yet . . .

I took a breath and pressed my hands against Diego's chest. Angel gasped next to me. The man suddenly went still, his back arching and his chest rising as if to meet my palms. I gently pushed him back so he relaxed against the bed. He exhaled long and slow, his body going limp. His head lolled sideways.

My magic rose to the surface of my body, pouring from my hands like liquid. A blinding blue light engulfed the room, and I squinted against the luminosity. My hands thrummed from the power emanating from me. The flame I'd felt earlier roared to life within me, and I suddenly felt another presence alongside me.

Nix.

I closed my eyes, picturing my firebird. Her magnificent wings. Her dark sentient eyes. Her powerful fire.

Nix, I thought. *Can you hear me?*

She didn't respond.

Perhaps we were still disconnected by her dark magic. But I felt her power pulsing through me as plainly as I felt the floor under my knees.

Beneath my hands, I felt the man's heartbeat waver. His pulse slowed as the life left his body.

No, I thought. *Come back. Bring him back.*

I pressed my hands more firmly against him. Fire raged through me, summoned by the call of my magic. Ash and smoke permeated the air, and I felt as if the fire stung my face and cheeks. Like the whole room was on fire.

Slowly, the light of my magic faded, as did the smells. When my power diminished, my forehead was covered in sweat and I was panting like I'd run a marathon.

As soon as I removed my hands, ash sprinkled to the ground. Frowning, I gazed down at my hands and found them covered in soot.

Suddenly, Diego inhaled a rattling breath that sounded like his first breath in days. He choked and wheezed as he struggled to breathe.

Tears pricked my eyes, and I wiped my brow, unable to stop the relieved smile from spreading across my face.

Diego coughed and slowly rolled to face us. His weak eyes narrowed as he stared at us. "Miss—Miss Gerrick?" He frowned, looking around. "Where is Silvia?"

I swallowed and exchanged a glance with Angel, who stared at me with wide stricken eyes. Her face was clammy and ashen, and she looked at me as if she'd never seen me before.

"What do you remember?" I asked in a hoarse voice.

Diego blinked, shaking his head. "A—a dream. It must've been."

"Tell me about it," I urged. "What did you see in the dream?"

"A . . . mountain of some sort? No, a volcano. And a small dragon. Fire everywhere." He shuddered. "The darkness called to me, Miss Gerrick. I tried to resist, but Silvia was there. I couldn't leave her."

My blood chilled, and goosebumps erupted over my skin. I knew exactly where he'd been.

The Astral Realm. With Nix.

But *why*? And how? Even casters couldn't get to the Astral Realm, so how did this mortal end up there? Was that where all the other mortals had vanished to?

"Was anyone else there?" I whispered.

Diego frowned. "I—I'm not sure. I heard voices. Echoes. Whispers I tried to ignore." He swallowed, suddenly looking ill. "I—" He stopped, breathing heavily. "I must find my wife." He tried to rise, but his face turned a sickly green, and I pushed him back down.

"You're still recovering," I said. "You need to rest. My sister and I will find your wife."

I felt Angel's gaze on me, but I couldn't look at her. My heart was racing, my mind spinning as I tried to sort through what had just happened.

Had I healed Diego? Or just summoned him from the Astral Realm?

But the ash—it was almost as if he'd been reborn just like Nix.

As if he'd *died* . . . and my magic had brought him back.

An idea formed in my mind, and I straightened. "Is there something of your wife's I could use? Like a hairbrush?"

Diego looked at me in bewilderment, but he seemed too weak to argue. He weakly jerked his head to my left. "On the vanity."

I nodded and strode to where he'd indicated, finding a brush resting on the small wooden vanity. A few dark hairs coiled on the bristles, and I plucked one free.

Angel drew close to me and hissed, "What're you doing?"

"Summoning his wife back."

Angel snatched my arm, her grip firm and unyielding.

In a hushed voice, she said, "Brie, you'd better tell me what the hell is going on. What did you do to that man?"

I froze, staring at the hair in my hand. "I can't explain it. I felt Nix's power. She brought him back." My gaze met hers. "I can bring his wife back too. I'm sure of it."

"Brie, this doesn't feel right. What if it's Lilith?"

"It's not," I said sharply. I stared at her, pleading with my eyes. "Angel, I can *feel* it. I know what Lilith's magic feels like, and this isn't it. I—I need you to trust me. Okay?"

Angel stared at me for a long moment, her lips pressed together. For the first time, she looked like my older sister. The one making wise decisions, the one with the level head. And I felt like the puny little sister asking for permission.

I wasn't sure when our roles had reversed. But I suddenly felt like I *needed* her on my side. Like I needed her approval and support. It felt odd to be so exposed and vulnerable, to ask her for help when ordinarily it was the other way around.

Perhaps because I now knew we weren't truly sisters after all.

But it made the relief so much sweeter when she nodded, her eyes shining with affection and trust.

"Okay," she said.

I nodded too and pressed my palms together, covering the hair of Diego's wife. Then, I closed my eyes.

Nix, I thought. *I don't know if you can hear me, but I*

know you're there. Show me what to do. Show me how to bring her back.

I waited, the air silent except for our breaths. I felt Diego and Angel watching me, and I tried not to fidget under their scrutiny.

Suddenly, the tiniest flicker of a flame ignited in my chest. I clung to it like the dying embers of a fire, desperate for it to linger. In my head, I saw the face of the woman I was trying to summon—her wispy gray hair and kind, wrinkled brown eyes. The warm smile she often gave me when I purchased cloth from her and her husband.

Summoning my magic—or rather, *Nix's* magic—I whispered, "I summon you here, Silvia. Your husband calls to you. Return." My voice echoed, and an ethereal murmur hissed from me, making my words sound like they belonged to someone else. I heard Angel's intake of breath and knew she noticed it too.

A faint light shone through my eyelids, and I knew my blue magic surrounded my hands. A tendril of heat tickled my palms as my powers gathered around Silvia's hair. I kept her image in my mind, my face scrunched up in concentration. I didn't know the woman well, so I was afraid I would lose that memory of her. But as I focused, I was able to recall finer details—details I knew I couldn't possibly remember on my own.

It was further proof that Nix was here, helping me.

I remembered the faint freckles on Silvia's nose. The age

spots on her withered hands. The way the top of her hair frizzed with heat and humidity. The way her voice warbled when she laughed. The corners of her lips that wrinkled with her smile.

The more I focused on her, the more I felt like I knew her soul. Her essence burned within me like another presence. I heard her as she called for her husband, her voice broken by sobs.

"Return," I called again, my voice firmer. The fire in my chest strengthened until the heat was so intense I started to sweat again. The glow in my hands brightened, burning against my eyelids. I winced even though my eyes were still closed. Warmth and energy radiated against me like a powerful beam of light.

An echoing voice rang in the room like a song. It grew louder until it blared in my ears. My body started trembling. The flames inside me licked my bones, scorching me. Pain roiled through me in waves, and I hunched over with a groan.

"Brie—" Angel whispered, and I sensed her movement.

"Not yet," I moaned, gritting my teeth. I kept my eyes shut tight against the agony and the blinding light that burned every inch of me.

The voice became clearer—like it had been nothing more than a memory before but now it was coming to life. And then I exhaled, my body sagging. With my breath, power flooded from me like I'd turned on a faucet.

I collapsed, and the magic from my hands vanished. The flames died so suddenly I shivered from the cold, my skin clammy and covered in sweat.

"Brie!" Angel cried out.

A sudden burst of power consumed me, filling me with a foreign energy. My vision cleared and my skin warmed. I stood, feeling as refreshed as if I'd just woken up.

Angel watched me with bewilderment, her face pale as she hovered over me. Beside her was Diego, his withered eyes tight with apprehension.

I glanced around the room, searching. The echoing voice was gone. So was Nix's fire.

But I felt a new presence among us. Something warm and familiar.

A soft white glow emanated from the wall across from me. It intensified until it almost blinded me. A wisp of ethereal smoke poured from the wall, coiling mysteriously in front of us. The smoke collected until it formed the shape of a person.

A woman.

A shiver rippled down my spine as I watched this ghostly figure step through the wall. My blood chilled as I remembered the words of Riker's vision. *Infected mortals will walk through walls.*

Gradually, the figure solidified, taking shape. The smoke faded to reveal solid flesh. It was as if a curtain was parting to reveal a woman who had been here the whole time.

When the smoke fully disappeared, a dusting of ash sprinkled from the ceiling, landing in a small pile at the woman's feet.

The woman gasped, her eyes flying open. She teetered, and in an instant, her husband was by her side to catch her. Silvia touched his face, her eyes swimming with tears. "Diego," she whispered.

Diego nodded, his own eyes watering. "I'm here, my love. I'm here."

I smiled as they kissed each other, weeping and embracing. My smile faltered when Angel touched my shoulder, her eyes wide with fear. "Brie, what the hell happened?" she hissed. "You scared me half to death!"

I shook my head, feeling a mixture of disbelief and gratitude. "I don't fully understand it either. But it was Nix's power that brought them back."

"I thought you weren't connected to Nix anymore."

"So did I. But . . . I think with the gate to the Underworld open, I have some kind of access to the Astral Realm. Access I didn't have before."

"And the Astral Realm is . . . where Nix is?" Angel asked uncertainly.

"Yes."

"Does that mean Lilith has this access too?"

My heart throbbed with fear. "I don't know." I thought of all the other mortals who had gone missing. Diego had mentioned hearing many voices. Were the mortals taken to the Astral Realm? Had Lilith sent them there?

"It's possible she doesn't know Nix is there," I said quietly, rubbing my forehead as I tried to think. "But I have a feeling she's responsible for the mortals trapped there." I hesitated, biting my lip as worry swirled within me until I couldn't breathe. I looked at Angel with fierce determination. "I have to help them."

She pressed her lips together, her eyes uncertain. We both glanced at Diego and Silvia as they continued clinging to each other as if afraid they would be ripped apart again. My heart ached for them. How many others had been torn from their families because of Lilith?

Angel looked at me again, her eyes shining. Slowly, she nodded. "Just tell me how I can help."

33
LEO

A HUSHED SILENCE FILLED THE STREET, BROKEN only by the moans of the wounded still lying on the ground. Izzy and Harrison moved first, crawling forward to the closest injured man and assessing his injuries. Together, they hoisted the man up and dragged him by the arms.

Seeing them spring into action filled my body with purpose. I stood, wavering slightly from my injuries, and pointed over my shoulder. "Take them to my house. I'll see to their wounds."

"You'll do no such thing," growled a voice from behind me.

I turned and found a Madrid warlock I hadn't seen before striding toward me. His gray eyes were cold as they appraised me, and his thick mustache bristled with anger. My eyes roved over his smooth, clean uniform, and I had the sudden desire to punch him in the face. He'd been on the sidelines. The coven leader, no doubt—willing to let his men perish while he stayed behind.

I straightened, ignoring the sting of my wounds and instead taking pride in my appearance compared to this coward's. I lifted my chin. "Who might you be?"

"Lorenzo Valdez," he said in a clipped tone, puffing his chest out as if his name meant something.

I frowned and shrugged, hoping to give him the impression I'd never heard his name before. His lips tightened in response, and a ripple of satisfaction coursed through me.

"Coven leader of Madrid, I presume?" I asked, raising my eyebrows.

Lorenzo nodded stiffly. "Leonardo Serrano, the chaos and devastation this city has endured proves you are no longer fit to lead your coven. Segovia is now under Madrid jurisdiction, and you are stripped of your authority. I place you and your coven under arrest to await trial by the dark coven of Madrid."

I sensed a presence behind me, and though the back of my neck prickled, I didn't turn around. I knew the Madrid warlocks who survived the battle now surrounded me, prepared to imprison me.

But darkness swirled in my chest, familiar and frightening all at once. I knew Lilith's call was near. I didn't have much longer.

"I accept the charges," I said quietly. "But I beg of you, please let me close the gate to the Underworld first. If I don't, Lilith will only gain more power—and it will spread beyond Segovia. Beyond even the entire country."

Fear flickered in Lorenzo's eyes, and I sensed the men behind me stiffen. But Lorenzo quickly composed his features and sneered, "I will not listen to your lies, Serrano. No matter how elaborate they are."

I stepped toward him, shaking off the men behind me as they grabbed at my arms. "You have no idea the power Lilith has," I hissed. "How will you stop her from taking over the city? From taking over *you*?"

Lorenzo sucked in a breath, but his nostrils flared. I read the unease in his face, but there was a stubborn set to his jaw that meant he wouldn't listen to a word I said. He nodded to the men behind me. "Take him."

In a flash, I shifted to my bat form, dodging spells and bursts of black magic as they tried to catch me. My dark figure blended in with the night sky, and I took off toward the rooftops. Using the vibrations and sounds around me, I sensed the shouts and movements of the men below me. But as I concentrated on them, I realized with a bolt of triumph that none of them were shapeshifters.

As long as I could fly, I could evade them.

It took a monumental effort for me to flap my wings and keep flying. Shifting ordinarily took a great amount of energy, but now it cost me nearly everything to stay airborne due to my injuries.

I needed time to heal. Time I did not have.

My wings ached, and a low screech burst from my mouth, but I pressed on, floating over houses until I landed in a dark, narrow alley about a mile from the Madrid warlocks.

I shifted back to my vampire form with a groan, slumping against the concrete wall of the house next to me. Ragged breaths tore through me, and spots danced in front of my eyes.

Just a bit longer, I coaxed myself as red magic crept into the corners of my eyes. *Just a bit longer.*

Following my nose, I edged down the street, staying close to the shadows to avoid being seen. This area was just as empty and lifeless as my own neighborhood. On any normal night, there would be lanterns burning and windows shutting. The signs of life would linger in the city as the civilians readied themselves for bed.

But here, it was like the town had been completely abandoned. No lanterns burned. Not a single noise echoed in the street but my own quiet footsteps.

My ears prickled with suspicion. My instincts knew the silence wasn't right, but I couldn't tell if it was because of the mysteriously absent mortals or because someone was following me.

I don't have the strength to shift again, I thought with a glance over my shoulder. No one was there. I had to be vigilant. If someone approached, I would have to either run or fight them off. And neither seemed like a task I could accomplish. Not while fighting off Lilith's call.

So close now. A familiar flowery scent filled my nose. It once calmed me like a balm, but now it filled me with rage and a thirst for revenge.

I knew precisely who I would sacrifice to close the gate to the Underworld. And she was most likely the only mortal remaining in the city.

Trembling gasps reached my ears. A soft voice muttered incoherently. I made out a few phrases like "promised" and "get out of here" and "where is he."

I rounded the corner and found Estrella pacing the length of a narrow alley between two fruit markets. She froze when she saw me, and the color drained from her face.

"Leo," she breathed in a shaky voice. Her lower lip trembled as she backed away from me. "Leo, I had no choice."

I strode toward her with slow, purposeful steps. My insides quivered with rage, and Lilith's magic prickled to life inside me.

"You were my most trusted Donor," I said in a strained voice.

Estrella's face crumpled, and she backed away from me. "I *had* to do it. Please, you must understand—"

"You betrayed me!" Fury exploded within me, and I couldn't hold back any longer. "I gave you *everything*, and you betrayed me!"

"I know!" Estrella wailed. "I'm s-sorry, Leo. Please."

"I almost died, Estrella. My entire coven would've died because of you."

Estrella shook her head, pressing her lips together. Her dark eyes swam with tears, and my blood cried out to her in defense.

No, I wanted to scream at myself. *She isn't my Donor anymore. I have no bond with her. She is no longer under my protection.*

Estrella read the anger and resolve in my eyes, and a strangled sob burst from her lips. "Leo, please," she wailed. "After everything we've been through—"

"Indeed," I said, my voice soft. "After everything I've done for you, how could you betray me like that?"

"Lilith, she—she offered me my sister back," Estrella sobbed.

"In exchange for what? Sacrificing my entire coven? Is one life truly worth the lives of dozens of innocents who trusted you?"

"To me, it is!" she shouted, pressing a hand to her chest. "I would sacrifice *hundreds* to bring my sister back." Her voice broke as she wept.

A small part of me resonated with that. When Brielle had been kidnapped—when Benito had almost Turned her

—there was nothing I wouldn't have done to save her. No one I wouldn't have killed.

The angry fire within me faded. How could I blame Estrella for her choice when I would've made the same one?

I watched her fearful face for a long moment, remembering the bond we'd shared for years. The companionship. The laughter. The warmth.

I'd pushed her away when I'd fallen in love with Brielle. I hadn't meant to, but it drove a wedge between us. *That* was when our bond had truly been broken. Not when she'd betrayed me.

Even so, I thought. *This doesn't change what has to be done.*

"Estrella," I said, my voice breaking as I finally reached her, backing her into the corner. "Lilith's power is seeping into the city. It'll take over the world if I don't close the gate." I swallowed. "You're the only mortal left. Do you truly want to see your sister again?"

Estrella's eyes went wide as she understood my meaning. Her gaze shifted from left to right as if searching for someone who would save her.

"I will make it painless," I whispered. "I swear it. Regardless of your betrayal, Estrella, I do not wish you harm. But this *must* be done."

Estrella licked her lips, and I felt her heart racing. Her blood called to me, and she leaned in as more tears leaked from her eyes. "Leo—"

"Please, Estrella." I took her hand in mine. "Be brave. One act of bravery, and you'll be reunited with your sister."

"But Benito—"

"He's dead."

Her face slackened in shock and horror. She shook her head again. "No." Her frame sagged as if the news had drawn her energy from her. She raised a trembling hand to her forehead. "No. It can't be."

"Whatever he promised you, he cannot deliver it."

Estrella covered her mouth with both hands and sobbed freely, her moans echoing in the alley. I had to clench my fingers into fists to keep myself from embracing her. The urge to comfort and protect her was so strong that sweat formed on my brow. I clenched my teeth and exhaled slowly. Darkness rose from within me, and I shuddered.

"Estrella," I said again, my voice weak. "There isn't much time. Lilith will take me soon."

Estrella went still and dropped her hands as she stared at me. "Take you?"

I nodded. "I am sacrificing myself as well."

Something unreadable stirred in her eyes. For a moment, our gazes held, and all the secrets, conflict, and emotions circulated between us.

Estrella swallowed and slowly nodded. "I—all right. I will go with you."

I watched her for a long moment, waiting for her to change her mind. But she held my gaze with certainty and determination. Relief and pride swelled within me. Though I still resented what she'd done, I admired her courage.

With a deep breath, Estrella took my arm as if we were on a romantic stroll together. "Lead the way," she whispered.

34
BRIELLE

ANGEL AND I MOVED FROM HOUSE TO HOUSE, working as quickly as we could. The first few spells took me a while to find the connection to the lost mortal, but after I got the hang of it, we were able to summon them back to our realm within minutes.

Each time, I felt Nix's fire consuming me as if burning me alive. And when I pulled the mortal back, I collapsed as if they had taken all my energy from me.

Then, Nix's power filled me again, restoring my strength. I could only assume it was the same power that allowed her to be reborn again and again.

Despite her energy filling me, my body still ached with exhaustion. Each spell wore on me, and my brain throbbed worse and worse as the night wore on. When we left one house and moved to the next, I anxiously searched the streets for any sign of Leo. The battle was over—only a few injured stragglers remained.

Lilith would be calling him soon.

But I was the only one who could bring these mortals back. If the gate to the Underworld closed, would the mortals remain trapped in the Astral Realm?

I couldn't risk it.

Besides, I was bound to Leo. If something was wrong—if Lilith tried to claim him—I'd know.

When we finished summoning the twentieth mortal, Angel touched my shoulder. I was gasping for breath, and my skin felt clammy again.

"Brie, maybe we should stop," she said quietly as we left the house.

I shook my head. "Do you have a better idea of how to bring them back?"

Angel's mouth clamped shut, but her eyes filled with worry. I strode forward, ignoring the exhaustion rolling through me in waves as we moved to the next house.

It took hours before we finally reached a house that wasn't empty. Its occupants bustled about inside, and I heard children laughing as if everything was normal.

I stilled and looked at Angel with wide eyes. This family seemed completely oblivious to what was going on inside their city.

Angel glanced up and down the street with a soft gasp. "We're on the other side of the city now."

I blinked, my gaze roving up and down the street. These

houses were much more magnificent, with pillars and turrets and well-maintained gardens. This was the neighborhood where Izzy lived.

My body sagged with relief. "Did we do it?" I asked in a weak voice. "Is that everyone?" I wanted to call it a day, and every inch of me was begging for sleep. But we had to double check. If even one mortal life was lost, I wouldn't be able to live with myself.

Angel and I traveled up and down the street, pausing by each house to ensure there was someone inside. When we weren't sure, we knocked on the door and waited for a response, then claimed we had the wrong house once the door opened.

At long last, we hit a dead end, and I sank to the ground, propping my arms up on my legs. My heart thundered in my chest, and my head pounded with a crippling migraine.

Angel sat next to me and leaned her head on my shoulder. "I'm proud of you, Brie."

A lump formed in my throat, and I scooted away from her. I couldn't escape the feeling of betrayal, the nauseating *wrongness* between me and Angel.

She wasn't my sister. Not by blood. And she'd kept that lie between us for years.

"Brie," Angel protested, her voice tinged with hurt.

I closed my eyes. "Angel, I can't do this. Not now. Just give me some space."

I couldn't look at her, but I felt her watching me. Regret

and sorrow emanated from her, and my stomach knotted in response.

Suddenly, a bolt of pain shot through me. I flinched, thinking my head was aching again. But then I heard Leo's voice.

A little farther. A little farther.

I felt his agony. His despair. Lilith was calling to him.

I jumped to my feet, and Angel's eyes widened. She stood too.

"Leo," I whispered, looking around as if I would find him ambling down the street. As I glanced around the empty neighborhood, a faint pulse thrummed in the air like a beacon alerting me to Leo's presence.

I surged forward, following the pulse.

"Brie, where are you going?" Angel cried.

"I don't have much time." I strode toward the end of the road, trying to ignore the persistent throbbing of my head. "*Leo* doesn't have much time."

"What exactly do you plan to do?" Angel demanded, hurrying to match my stride. The accusation in her tone reminded me so much of Mom that I ached. *I hope Mom's all right. I hope she hasn't hurt anyone.*

"If I have the power to pull people back from the Astral Realm, maybe I have the power to pull Lilith's influence out of Leo. Maybe I can keep him here."

Angel raised an eyebrow, and I resisted the urge to scowl at her.

"I know it's far-fetched," I said sharply. "But what choice do I have? I have to *try*."

"Brie—"

I stopped short and faced her. My impatience boiled over to full-fledged rage. "Enough! I'm going to him, Angel! You can't stop me. Either you're with me or not."

Angel stared at me for a long moment, her jaw ticking back and forth in contemplation. Finally, she sighed, dropping her hands against her thighs. "Fine, I'll go with you. Lead the way."

35
LEO

IT DIDN'T TAKE ME LONG TO FIND THE GATE. I FELT
Lilith's power pulsing through me like a beacon guiding the
way. Estrella's hand trembled in my own, but I clutched her
fingers firmly, trying to squeeze some comfort into her.

I didn't know why. She didn't deserve my sympathy or
my kindness.

But something in me changed when she spoke of her
sister. And when I imagined myself in her position—if
someone had promised to bring *my* siblings back—I
couldn't say I blamed her.

Besides, a part of me admired her courage for agreeing
to die for a greater cause. Judging by how often she looked
at me, I could tell she felt something similar for me,
knowing I was about to give myself up as well.

"Almost there," I whispered. I didn't know for certain,
but the red magic within me swelled until it seemed to

suffocate me. The feeling intensified, so I knew we had to be close. Each step felt like needles slicing into my skin, but I pushed onward.

A little farther. A little farther.

We walked downhill along a dirt road leading outside the city. My skin prickled as I remembered we weren't too far from Alejandro the necromancer. The thought sent chills rippling down my spine.

The road curved until we reached a church surrounded by a cemetery that looked eerie, bathed in the glow of the moon.

Of course, I thought bitterly. *The gate is in a cemetery.*

At the top of the hill rested a massive crypt that glowed white, its luminescence mingling with that of the moon. The combined glow was so blinding I could almost believe it was daytime.

Estrella sucked in a breath, her eyes wide as she stared at the glowing crypt. "That's it?"

I nodded and looked at her. I almost asked if she was certain about this, but I didn't. Because if she refused, I would simply force her.

There was too much at stake. And though I knew it would torture me to end her life if she fought me, I knew I would do it. I would do anything to send Lilith back to the Underworld.

Estrella met my gaze, her jaw rigid with determination. She nodded, and relief spread through my chest.

Together, we climbed up the hill, weaving through head-stones as we made our way toward the crypt. With each step, the power within me thrummed and pulsed with anticipation. Whispers surrounded me, and my skin prickled with the presence of other spirits. I remembered what Alejandro had said about the spirits responding to the open gate. I felt them here with me, though I couldn't see them.

"We'll do this together, Estrella," I said in a strained voice as we climbed higher and higher. "Thousands of lives will be spared because of our sacrifice."

She nodded. I wasn't sure if I was trying to reassure her or myself, but the words soothed me all the same.

It has to be done, I told myself. *There is no other way.*

In my mind, I saw Brielle's broken expression when she learned of my bargain with Lilith. The way her hopes had shattered, knowing we could never be together. A lump formed in my throat, and I swallowed.

Forgive me, my love, I thought, hoping she could hear me somehow. *I wish with every part of my soul that I'd been able to say goodbye to you.*

We stopped at the entrance to the crypt, and the door swung open of its own accord. White light shone from the other side, stinging my eyes. I squinted, resisting the urge to hide my face.

I'll be good as dead soon anyway. It doesn't matter.

"Leo!" a voice echoed.

Lilith was waiting for me. I shoved down my nausea and revulsion, reminding myself yet again that there was no other way. I turned to face Estrella, who met my gaze with tears in her eyes.

"Quick and painless," I reminded her.

She nodded, pressing her lips together as tears streamed down her face. She closed her eyes.

In a swift movement, I swung her head around until her neck snapped. Then, she collapsed, her body limp in my arms. My eyes warmed, and I closed my eyes, dropping my head to bury my face in her hair.

Forgive me, dear Estrella.

"Leo!" the voice called again. I stilled, straightening. This time the sound was closer. Less of an echo and more of a—

"Leo, *stop!*" the voice screamed.

My blood chilled. I knew that voice. Slowly, I turned and found Brielle racing toward me, her cloak billowing and her sister trailing behind her. Brielle's eyes were fixed on me, and the panic and fear in her face made my heart twist.

She was too far away. Though I fought the power gripping me, I couldn't stop my feet from edging toward the light of the crypt. Estrella's body felt heavy in my arms. Had I more strength, I would've run to Brielle in an instant.

But I was too weak. I could only make it a few more steps before Lilith would take me. And I had to ensure Estrella's sacrifice wasn't in vain.

Brielle stopped at the bottom of the hill, gazing up at me. Her cheeks were stained with tears, and her face crumpled in grief. "Leo!" she sobbed, covering her mouth with both hands and shaking her head.

She knew. She knew I couldn't stop it. I couldn't go to her or kiss her goodbye.

"I love you!" I called to her, my voice breaking with the shattered dreams I once had of living a life with her. Loving her. Devoting myself to making her happy.

Those dreams died with me as I stepped forward into the light, and Lilith's power swallowed me whole.

36

BRIELLE

A WEEK LATER, I SAT ON THE STEPS OF MY PARENT'S porch, gazing vacantly at Leo's house down the road. Through the open window behind me, I heard the faint voices of my parents, Angel, and Riker as they finished dinner. I couldn't bring myself to join them, but the sound of their chatter was a comfort to me. A reminder that things weren't all bad.

When Leo had vanished in the crypt, the possessed casters had awakened from Lilith's influence. Including my mom.

My strange powers had vanished as well. I no longer felt that fire within me. My brief connection to Nix was lost.

At first, I'd busied myself with rebuilding the city—repairing the damage, helping the mortals and the coven, pleading with the officials from Madrid on behalf of Leo and his people. But the warlocks were intent on transporting the entire coven to Madrid for trial. My family was exempt, however, because we practiced light magic.

The thought didn't sit well with me. Leo had always wanted me to be a part of his coven. I should be imprisoned along with them. They were my people too.

Now that Benito's mess had been cleaned up, I had to do something. I couldn't just sit around anymore.

My gaze shifted to the house next to Leo's, which was guarded by half a dozen guards from Madrid. Determination pulsed through me, and I shot to my feet before striding toward the guards. They stiffened at my approach, exchanging wary glances.

I lifted my chin. "I wish to bid the prisoner farewell."

The man looked to his comrades. "Search her."

Like hell. The first guard reached for me, and I twisted his arm until I heard a satisfying crack. He howled in pain as I kicked him to the ground. Two other guards surged toward me, and I swiped my daggers, cutting into both of them at once. Then, I flew up the porch stairs and through the front door, locking it behind me. Fists pounded on the door. I didn't have much time.

A figure appeared in the hall and stepped toward me. He stiffened.

"Brielle?" Jorge asked, cocking his head at me. His gaze shifted to the door behind me. "What're you doing?"

I moved closer to him, breathless with what I was about to say. "I need your help to get Leo back."

Jorge's eyes widened. "Get him *back*? I don't understand. He made a bargain with Lilith. It can't be undone."

"Maybe it can," I said slowly, "with my phoenix's powers."

Jorge stared at me, his gaze hard as if he expected me to say I was kidding. Then, his jaw tightened. "What do you need me to do?"

My lips twitched with a smile. I'd never felt so certain of anything in my life. "First, I need you to help me become a demon."

What happens when Leo enters the Underworld? And to what lengths will Brielle go to get him back? Find out in The Lost Phoenix!

ACKNOWLEDGMENTS

First of all, thank you, reader, for reading my books and getting this far. I am nothing without you!

A special thank you Kaitlin, whose marvelous editing skills helped get my books to be the best they can be.

A huge thank you to my critique partners: Tori, Melanie, Melissa, and Katherine. Thank you so much for your feedback and suggestions that helped to shape the story.

I am super grateful for such a fabulous ARC team! Thank you Janete, Darcy, Erica, Darian, Scarolet, Kristian, Debbie, Rachael, Devika, Jennah, Katherine, and Kirstey! I'm so grateful for your willingness to read my story and give me helpful feedback.

And lastly, thank you to my husband and children for always being a pillar of strength and support during my writing career.

ABOUT THE AUTHOR

R.L. Perez is an author, wife, mother, reader, writer, and artist. She lives in Florida with her husband and three children. On a regular basis, she can usually be found napping, reading, feverishly writing, revising, or watching an abundance of Netflix. More than anything, she loves spending time with her family. Her greatest joys are her kids, nature, literature, and chocolate.

Subscribe to her newsletter for new releases, promotions, giveaways, and book recommendations! Get a FREE eBook when you sign up at subscribe.rlperez.com.